IRONMONGER

Books by Kee Briggs
The Third Removed
The Painted War
Finders-Keepers
Losers-Weepers
The Painted Lady
A Few Good Old Men
The Oregon Vortex

The Usher Orlop Mysteries
The Golden Janus
The Pewter Masks
The Nickel Trophy
The Bronze Bones
The Brass Portraits
The Zinc Ormolu
The Silver Scepter
The Rhodium Dragon
The Copper Shakes
The Stainless Steel Sign

The Asti Fantasies
Charm Catcher/Dream Weaver

The Sage Grayling Mysteries
The Yellow Ochre Stain
The Lamp Black Pit
The Cad Red Dot

Taran Trilogy
Taran
Several title are also on Kindle, Nook and ePub.

IRONMONGER

II in TARAN Trilogy

Kee Briggs

Keescapes Publishing

Satellite Beach, Florida

IRONMONGER

Keescape Publishing books may be ordered through Amazon, booksellers or by contacting:

Keescape Publishing

90 Flamingo Dr.

Satellite Beach, Florida 32937

www.keescapes.com

KeescapesPublishing@gmail.com

This is a work of fiction. All characters, names, incidents, organizations are all figments of the author's imagination and are used fictionally.

ISBN-13: 978-0-9847524-2-3
Published in the United States of America

IRONMONGER

Chapter   1

Andy was stretched out on the dock in the warm, late afternoon sun. He was only faintly aware of the lapping of the water along the shoreline or the occasional thump of the canoe bumping the piling. For the first week of his wilderness adventure, he had luxuriated in those sounds, but his surroundings were becoming less significant during the second week. He was not used to such a prolonged period of inactivity. His mind was beginning to probe the future, where the direction no longer seemed as clear as it once had.

Five years ago, when he was graduating from high school, uncertainty over his future dogged him constantly. Higher education was only for the kids of the wealthy or those fortunate enough to find a sponsorship from a large corporation. Andy had superior grades from a small school, but he didn't know how he stacked up with students of the bigger, more prestigious college prep schools. Fortune smiled. He received a full scholarship to ITI, the top science school, from Galaxy Enterprises, the most prominent aerospace company in the world. His future was laid out before him. Upon graduation, he, along with four other people, was asked to participate in a super-secret project, which turned out to be a six-month, locked-in, simulation of a flight in a new, experimental space craft. Near the end of the stationary shakedown cruise, Centurion, a rival corporation, sent its army to steal the secret craft. To avoid capture, Andy launched "Taran," the short name for Tarantula, the big black, eight-legged spaceship. Even aloft, they were still threatened, so Andy, who was the pilot, headed for Mars. While testing a theoretical method of increasing speed, they added another factor. The unforeseen consequence of that action threw Taran into the Tau Ceti system, eleven and a half light years away.

After alien encounters and slogging through unknown space, the crew brought Taran home. The five enjoyed hero and celebrity status that didn't take long to become more of a burden than a joy. While they were cheered as great explorers by the general population they were hated by the religionists. Finally, the crew was given vacation time. But, where does one go when the whole world instantly recognizes you and wants what you know? Andy and his navigator, Andie, solved that problem by borrowing the CEO's private hideaway.

Around the turn of the last century, logging had flourished in the Cascades of southern Washington State. The terrain stood on end. Instead of roads penetrating the region, the railroads were built into the timberland. Great trestles spanned the ravines. Far into the mountains, a lumber camp was built on the edge of a lake. Then a forest fire swept through the region, burning out the trestles and a lot of the trees. It was no longer economically feasible to reenter the remaining forests, so all was abandoned until the head of Gal X, Artis Malvane, spotted the site on a satellite photo. Malvane turned part of it into a private haunt accessible only by helicopter. He loaned it to the two Andys so they could get away from constant scrutiny. Now Andy was trying to figure out what he could look forward to after having gone on the first intergalactic flight in human history and having had the first face-to-face communication with alien beings. He wasn't even twenty-five yet and he and his four companions had made more history than most people could conceive. What did one do next?

Andy's introspection was interrupted by a shadow falling

across his face. Silhouetted against the sun was Andie. She was as naked as he was, except for the towel hanging around her neck. "I finished my workout and now I have to freshen up," she said as she dropped her towel and wrapped her toes over the end of the dock. "Want to join me? If not, maybe you should check the call that is blinking on your cell phone." Andie executed a perfect dive into the chilly waters of the lake.

Andy had already swum his laps. He shook off Andie's offer and wandered up to the cabin. The call was from Walter Hale, his proctor through the college years and friend and advisor after joining the company. Andy was a little alarmed. He wondered if anything had happened to his mother or Walter or Walt's family. Those were the kinds of things that would warrant a call from his proctor.

It was past working hours further east, so Andy dialed Walter's home number. The answering service picked up the call, but as soon as Andy identified himself, Walter came on the line. He didn't sound particularly stressed, and he engaged in initial small talk until Andy bluntly asked, "Why did you call?"

"The company hates to rain on your vacation, but something has come up. We're recalling TC in case we have a problem. A chopper will pick up you and Candie at 9:00 in the morning. Don't bother to clean up. We'll drop a workman off to take care of loose ends. Just bring yourselves. I'll see you in Houston." Walter rang off without giving Andy a chance to ask any questions.

Andy mentally ruminated on the message for a bit. TC was the Taran Crew....his crew. They were only supposed to be the simulation shakedown crew while the real crew was being trained, but after their flight they had been given the ship. Taran was theirs. Walter had dropped into the flight jargon by calling Andie Carson, Candie. There had been a state of confusion over names. Both he and his navigator had been called Andy. It was Corky Smith, the supply officer and all around handyman, who had solved the problem by calling Andy, Dandy. This was the short form of Andrew and the first letter of the surname, Dawson. The same formula had been applied to the other Andie by adding the C from Carson to the Andie of Andrea. Both despised their new monikers, but the names stuck anyway.

Dandy eased his way back over the bare ground to the dock. He was still a real tenderfoot. Candie was climbing out of the water. As she vigorously toweled herself dry, she gave Dandy that questioning glance that formed part of their unspoken communications in the months aboard Taran.

"TC is being recalled. A chopper will be here in the morning. Walter wouldn't even give a hint of what this is all about."

"Probably some director wants a photo-op for a grandchild," commented Candie.

"When you're dealing with corporations, anything can happen."

"Oh, I rather doubt that. Maybe Hacker is acting up again."

Hacker was the young computer genius who had blasted his way up the ladder to the CEO chair of Centurion. Hacker had been the source of most of TC's problems, both on earth and around the moon.

The recall wasn't bothering either of them too much. Neither was used to total leisure. It was beginning to wear thin. Since their early days with the company, when they both had given body casts for a new generation of space suits, modesty had gone out the window. But during the months aboard Taran, they had strictly avoided any show of intimacy. This vacation had presented them with the unfettered time to engage in sex, which was for mutual pleasure, but also they entered into it with the full knowledge that they were not ready to carry the relationship any further until other horizons had been explored. As the sun went down, the pair adjourned to the cabin for dinner and a final intimate evening.

Precisely on time, the helicopter swooped over the ridge to pick them up for the return to reality. At a company base, they transferred to a small jet for the ride to Houston. The rest of the crew was already there. Tom Rolland and Corky Smith had just moved their gin game down the road to a small town that had a Taco Bell, a Denny's, and a friendly tavern. In jeans and western hats, they had escaped recognition. Beatrice Bell, their resident brain, had gone to her mother's house. Since she never stuck her nose out the door, no one knew she was there. There was nothing in the outside world that could have possibly interested her. Her computer and classical music were all she needed.

For the second time in little over a year, TC and three proctors filed into the huge board room for Galaxy Enterprises. Unconsciously, each drifted back to the seat he or she had occupied on that first day when the CEO, Artis Malvane, had recruited them as the shakedown crew for Taran. Dandy's proctor, Walter Hale, sat beside him. Wayne Percy was next to Candie, and Ms. Bean was with Beatrice.

On the first occasion, there had been almost total silence. This time there was idle chatter and laughter as they waited for the CEO. When Artis Malvane walked in the door, the silence returned. Instead of employing his former formality, Malvane dropped into his chair at the head of the table and started out with an apology.

"That was a terribly short vacation. I'm sorry to call you back. We'll make it up later. But something has come up that may tickle your fancy, as it has mine. The company has been mulling over what to do with Taran now that you have turned the entire aerospace world on its ear. There are suggestions and requests for space time coming in from all over. There are hundreds of worthy projects being proposed. We are making a lot of the data Beatrice recorded available to the scientific community, which is causing arguments that will be going on for centuries. Candie's charting of our part of the galaxy has given astronomers food for a lot of thought. Corky, your "Bip" name has stuck for those aliens."

'Unfortunately, too many of his names stick," growled Candie as she theatrically glowered at Corky. She still didn't like her nickname.

Malvane smiled before resuming. "Of course, you also fuzzed up a bunch of folks. The Catholic Church has started a conclave that will probably last well into the next century. A major bone of contention in the scientific world and with governments is that we have not revealed how you were able to travel such distances. They don't know about Solar Jets and we plan to keep it that way for the time being.

"This has presented another problem. The international astronomy consortium has discovered something that is causing considerable concern in various capitals. Many years ago the Copernicus probe was launched. At that time, several of our planets were lined up, and the vehicle could make close fly-bys. Once its job was done, it was flung out into space to see what it could find. Now it is well above the ecliptic of our solar system in a remote area of the galactic population. There is periodic communication to keep track of it. Recently it abruptly changed course, which attracted a lot of attention, since it should have been going in a straight line. The watchers figured it might have come under the influence of a black hole. Then reports began coming in that Copernicus was not alone. There is what appears to be a large energy field moving in space. It is very compact, but highly visible—so it isn't a black hole. Also it is emitting enormous amounts of various forms of energy. It has quite a unique signature, which has yet to be completely analyzed. We have no idea from whence it came. It is not acting like an astral body. Copernicus headed in the direction of that field—then disappeared. Now that field has changed direction and it is heading toward our solar system. This thing has no precedent in any of our space observations. The worry is that this is not a naturally occurring phenomenon. Since you confirmed we are not alone in this universe, everyone is seeing aliens behind every heavenly body. Taran is the only vehicle capable of space flight, so Gal X is being asked to go investigate.

"We haven't given an answer yet. There is considerable refitting being done on Taran. We are installing all of that diagnostic equipment that was left on the ground, which didn't do you a bit of good when you got out of communication range on the first flight. We expected to be able to train you on the ground, but that would take too long, so we are preparing instructional disks like those you had when you learned how to fly Taran. You can learn in route.

"The reason for this time shortage is that everyone is demanding to put scientists aboard to observe the phenomenon. Those scientists would be more interested in Taran than that energy field. To avoid a lot of problems, we will continue to consider the requests until after you have launched."

Malvane stopped and slowly looked around the table before continuing. "Of course, this is predicated on TC being willing to head back out into space."

The CEO again scanned the table. Dandy raised his hand and got a nod. "Will we have time to pick up our laundry?" As usual the pilot broke the tension and the rest of the crew bobbed their heads in assent—even Beatrice, who stated, "I'd need a lot more memory."

"You will have so much memory you couldn't fill it if you worked constantly for the next 200 years. Also we have devised new, secure download probes, so you can periodically send data back to us." Glancing at both Candie and Corky, he added, "We've also reviewed the suggestion box and we've made several changes in the menu." Candie had visions of more veggies and fruits. Corky hoped for nachos.

Malvane fielded numerous questions before the meeting broke up. TC had two weeks to get their lives in order, while maintaining utmost secrecy. Before their last flight they had lived in the guest accommodations at the home office, but the company figured that might telegraph their intentions, so they scattered the crew around town. Tom and Corky were put up at one motel, Candie and Dandy went to another, and Beatrice stayed with Ms. Bean, her proctor.

The time passed quickly. Before it seemed possible, they were on a jet headed for the New Mexico desert. From the air they could see that much had changed. Taran stood in the middle of a barren plain. As on their first viewing of the ship, the crew was awestruck. This time it wasn't under camouflage netting, which had looked like tailings from a mine, but it stood on the scoured flats like the great, black leaping spider from which it got its nickname. It was enormous. No one had anything to say.

There was ample evidence of the company military in the area, but there were no visible permanent facilities. Everything had gone underground. When Taran launched, the resulting vortex scoured the ground clean, as Centurion forces had found out when they tried to take the ship.

Chapter 2

Launch was at dawn the next day. The world learned of the event when various radar installations picked up Taran hurtling into space. TC knew the routines well. Dandy didn't linger long in earth's influence. He was still edgy about what Centurion's CEO, Hacker, might try. Dandy stayed under power until he was sure he could outrun anything sent to hunt them down.

Once the heavy G-forces slacked off, the crew began settling in for their regular duties. Dandy posted the familiar duty schedule. As soon as everything calmed down, the first item of business was to learn from the instructional disks how to handle all of the new instrumentation as well as the various upgrades to the old equipment. Until they had the entire new material well in mind, they weren't going to enter any Solar Jets.

For two weeks, the crew studied the material at their workstation consoles. During free time, Corky and Tom resumed their gin game. Beatrice was contentedly going through a huge new pile of classic CDs. Candie explored the possibilities of all her new exercise equipment. Dandy kept his nose in the reports concerning the energy event heading their way.

An observation Dandy had made during Taran's return to earth was that as they had moved toward the edge of the galaxy ecliptic, the Solar Jets seemed to be less erratic. The jets seemed to move in straighter lines. He speculated that since there were fewer heavenly bodies there would be fewer attractions on the jets. Dandy hoped that they would be able to go in a much more direct line to the target than when the jets were tugged in various directions by gravitational fields. Water, the source of their fuel, was always a problem. There could be even fewer sources where they were going.

When Dandy noted a slowing of the study routines, he called a meeting in the Fish House, the dining area, so named after Corky's memorable meal of fish that Taran had scooped up while refueling in Lake Baikal. The whole crew was pleased with the changes made in their menu. The main complaint on the first flight had been the selection of foods. At least for the present, everyone seemed contented as they carried their trays away from the food dispensing machines. Corky could eat most anything if he had hot sauce to go along with it. Beatrice was much the same. As long as she had a book or some work to do, she could eat sawdust. Dandy had a larger preference range. He wanted meat and carbs. In a pinch, he could always fall back on beans and franks. It was Candie who had lobbied the loudest for more fruits and vegetables and she had been heard. In addition to the greater selections, more were in the new dry-pack, which were tastier than the frozen dinners.

Under normal circumstances, they seldom ate together. The duty schedules always got in the way. Dandy waited until everyone had finished eating and they were chatting over coffees or teas. He perched on the edge of a table and posed the question, "Is there anyone who hasn't finished with his training tapes?"

The only response came from Corky. "There are a lot of maintenance details for that new equipment that I don't know, but I know where to find it if I ever need it. They're not something one would try committing to memory anyway."

"I found 32 errors in my tapes," said Beatrice. "I've made a memo on them. If you have any errors, I can include them in my report."

Tom shook his head. "I suppose you're also suggesting fixes."

"Naturally," said Beatrice, without recognizing the playful dig until the others started laughing.

Dandy was pleased Bea could smile at fun being poked her way. For most of their first voyage such a jibe would have reduced her to a pathetic lump of quaking flesh.

"The vacation is over," said Dandy. "Now we have to get on with our assigned task. For the rest of the day I want you to ready your work stations and living quarters for flight. Do all your laundry. Secure all loose objects. You know the routine. Then tomorrow, we will begin a full inspection of the ship. Everything that can be tested will be tested. I want any deficiencies noted—even suspected deficiencies. I want to know exactly where we stand. When everything is in order, we'll hop the first Solar Jet the next day.

"Even though the target is nearly half a light year away and at its current speed it doesn't pose any immediate threat to Earth, we have no idea whether it might be capable of much higher speeds. Remember, if we could find a Solar Jet going in the right direction, we could link up with it in a matter of hours. The Bips, with their gravitational strings, could probably do the same. That energy thing, our target, is under some sort of power. However, it might just be on idle. In any case, the boss wants us to make contact as far from Earth as possible."

"Do we have any plan of attack, so to speak?" asked Candie.

"Since we don't know what it is, it's difficult to formulate anything specific," said Dandy. "Those thinkers back at the home office suggest we try to establish communication with it as soon as we are in range. If it turns out to be a manned alien craft, we might have more maneuvering time if necessary. If we get close enough, we are supposed to use all those new instruments to learn all we can about it. The problem is that it might disappear as suddenly as it appeared. You see, the launch team has been keeping contact with Copernicus for years and they should have seen that thing a long time before it could get near the probe. It wasn't there one day and kazam, its there."

Being his usual cautious self, Tom said, "If we try to communicate with the target, that would be advertising our presence and pointing an arrow right back to Earth. Do we really want that?"

"If that's a manned ship, it's from a space faring civilization, a long way from home," said Bea. "It's already heading for Earth, and those flying it certainly know we're coming in their direction."

Corky turned to Beatrice. "When you send in that memo about the training glitches, tell them that my disks didn't have anything about all that new weaponry they installed so we can protect ourselves."

Suddenly TC became quiet. Candie got up to clear her dinner debris. Bea followed suit. The rest policed their areas and headed off to their chores.

The next day was a busy one. In the end, the ship proved to be in good flying order. Their supplies were as specified. There were some things that could not be tested until a real event came along. The techs had improved on Tom's design for an instrument to measure the distance traveled and the various changes in direction they encountered while riding the Solar Jet. They also had automated a directional finder to keep track of Earth during their faster-than-light wanders through space.

The next morning, according to their arbitrary, internal clock, Dandy got everyone buckled in and eased into the most promising jet Candie could find. It was to be only a five minute jump to make sure everything was operating as on their journey home. Dandy eased into the jet and began accelerating. Tom started reading off the elevating positive charge in the hull. At the proper moment, he switched on a negative charge and everyone had that momentary sensation of everything turning to jelly. When the timer threw the five minute switch and substance returned to their surrounding, Dandy eased out of the jet.

"I guess flying this thing is like riding a bicycle," said Candie. "You haven't forgotten. I darn near lost my stomach the first few times you tried that."The rest of the crew gave their murmured their assent.

"Lay off the flattery and tell me where we are," said Dandy.

"We didn't go very far, but we're generally heading in the right direction. There aren't any large jets around here so let's try a longer jump."

"How long?"

"With a half-hour jump we shouldn't overrun anything of importance."

For the better part of the day Dandy moved in and out of the jet until it began to wander too far afield. Candie found another jet heading in the direction they wanted to go, but they were going to have to slog through space for a few hours. Dandy didn't care for that much because they had to expend a lot of hydrogen fuel, but outside of the dish of the galaxy the smaller, commuter jets were fewer.

For the next six days, they zigzagged back and forth toward the target. Candie figured they were about three-quarters of the way there. Dandy was pleased with their progress considering the reduced numbers of jets. He stayed at the controls as long as they were riding a jet, but when they had to move in between them he took his rest periods.

Dandy was in a deep sleep when suddenly he was unceremoniously jerked awake by Beatrice's panic cry over the intercom. "Something's wrong!"

By the time Dandy could respond, he found Tom and Corky already coming out of their rooms. Candie wasn't far behind. Beatrice was standing beside her flight couch with both hands clasped on the top of her head. She was wildly looking all about her, including the ceiling and the floor beneath her feet.

Candie was the closest. She threw her arms around Beatrice to hold her. "What's wrong? What's wrong?"

"Oh, the pain. Someone's here. Pain. Pain. Fear," screamed Beatrice as she grasped her head even tighter.

Dandy yelled, "Tom, scan. Corky check the hull integrity." He dove for his station. The whole board was green. There were no warning lights of anything out of line. He checked all the exterior surfaces of the ship and found nothing.

Quickly, both Tom and Corky reported nothing out of the ordinary. Dandy turned his attention back to Beatrice. Candie had gotten her seated on her couch. Beatrice was crying violently. When Dandy looked at Candie questioningly, all he got was a shrug. Dandy knelt down in front of Beatrice. He took her hands, which were flexing open and closed, slowing her activity before he spoke."Okay, Okay, we're here. You did right by alerting us. Tell me what happened."

"It hurts and it is afraid," sobbed Beatrice.

"What hurts? What is afraid?"

Tom brought a bulb of tea over. Beatrice was shaking so badly she could not have held a cup, so he put it in a weightless package. Dandy put it in her two hands and helped direct it to her mouth to take a drink. Candie continued to hold her shoulders. Little by little Beatrice calmed down. Dandy tried again. "What happened?"

Beatrice collected herself. She looked about at the rest of the concerned crew. Rather shakily she began. "I really don't know. I was just sitting at my station reading when suddenly I had the feeling like you think someone is watching you. At the same time, there was a great burst of pain that filled my mind....just like some part of my body had been pulled off. It filled my skull. Then there was the sense of fear. I don't know of what, but just a panic type of fear. I still feel it, but it is not as intense as it was at first. There is something here."

"Where? Here? In the ship? Outside the ship? In this star system? Where?"

"I don't know, but its close. I can almost seem to reach out and touch it." Beatrice kept looking around like she expected it to be under her couch or in a drawer.

"Does anyone else sense anything?" Dandy looked at each of the crew who all shook their heads. Turning to the two men,

Dandy ordered. "Start in here and work your way down. I want a visual check of everything big enough to house a mouse." To Candie, "Help Bea to her room. Stay with her until we can do some checking." Dandy headed back to his station to start instrument checks to see if there was anything extraordinary happening.

Candie helped Beatrice to her feet. They moved through the door into Bea's quarters. Candie had never been in there. She was rather appalled at how untidy things were, but if she had ever stopped to think about it, that is pretty much what she would have expected. Candie was going to move Bea to the bunk when Bea went rigid. Following her line of sight Candy saw a lump pressed into the corner of bunk alcove. It reminded her of an unbaked dinner roll where the dough had been folded under. But this dinner roll was about two feet across and it vibrated. Candie pushed Beatrice into a chair, backed through the door and hissed at Dandy. She motioned him to the room. "I think you had better see this."

Dandy flipped on the overhead reading lamp to get a better look. The blob was featureless except for the end of the folds that radiated from underneath it.

"The pain is going away. So is the fear. It is getting curious," whispered Beatrice.

Candie looked skeptical. "How do you know all this?"

"I don't know. I just feel it the way I would if something hurt me or fear like when Taran first took off."

Dandy stepped to the intercom to call Tom and Corky. When they stepped into the room Beatrice had a quick intake of breath, "It knows what is happening. Each time someone new turns up, the fear level jumps up a little. But nothing like when I first felt it."

"Anyone has any ideas on what it is or its origin?" inquired Dandy. No one had any suggestions.

"Curiosity is taking over," declared Beatrice. "Look, it has stopped trembling."

"Do you sense any hostility?" asked Candie.

"No. It is just curiosity with a little fear or perhaps apprehension behind it."

Dandy slowly backed away, motioning for Tom and Corky to exit the room. To the girls he said, "Keep an eye on it. Sing out if anything happens."

Out in the Fish House Dandy turned to the guys. "That thing either came in somehow or it has been with us and just now grew. We need some answers. Corky, start trying to find an entry spot. I have no idea what you may be looking for, but try covering all bases. Tom. Apparently that thing is communicating with Bea in some manner, which means it is sentient. There must be some sort of energy output. Use anything we have to see if you can find out what type of energy is coming from it. Also check to see if it may be harmful to us."

Dandy quickly ran another sweep of that region of space to see if anything was playing with them. Nothing was visible other than the energy field, so he returned to Bea's room. Candie motioned for quiet and to go slowly. Bea was perched on the edge of her bunk opposite the thing. She was just watching it. When Dandy advanced further into the room she glanced back. "You are scaring him."

"Him?" inquired Dandy. "Why do you refer to it as a 'him'?"

"It certainly isn't a 'she'. Nor does it really seem to be an 'it'. So it must be a 'him'."

Candie shrugged, "Logic is logic."

Beatrice said, "You guys are upsetting him. Leave us alone. I think I can figure out more about him when he settles down."

"I don't think that is a good idea. We don't know anything about that thing....'him'. Somehow he came aboard a ship in outer space. If he has enough power to do that, then he is a danger to us."

"If anything happens, I'll call you."

"If you're able to call...."

"I don't think he would harm me."

"Right now he might be radiating something that could make your hair fall out or your brain turn to mush. Until we find out we can't take any chances," said Dandy in a very authoritative voice.

"See, the tone of your voice upset him. Not as much as before, but it's not helping things."

"Whether it upsets him or not we have to find out if he is a direct danger to us. Tom is going to run some tests to see if he is radioactive....see if he is emitting any other harmful radiation. He'll just have to put up with it."

Tom was standing just outside the door. Dandy motioned him in. "Take things slow and easy. Bea says our presence upsets him. Use your best bedside manner. Bea, let Tom know if you get any very strong reactions. Candie and I will be outside."

Candie popped into her room long enough to pull on some more clothes. Dandy realized he was just in underwear, so when Candie returned he did the same thing. On the way out, he picked up a coffee and a tea. Handing Candie her drink he said, "Do you have any ideas?"

"Well, I can't see how he could have been with us and now, as you say, he just grew. As sensitive to him as Bea seems to be, she would have picked up something before this. Also apparently he suddenly is overwhelmed with pain and fear. As far as I know, nothing has happened aboard to cause that kind of response."

Dandy thought about that for a moment, then concluded, "If he's not like a toadstool spore that suddenly pops up during an afternoon rain, then we have had some sort of intrusion. None of our warning devices were triggered. Our hull integrity doesn't seem to be compromised. So far Corky hasn't come up with any suggestions as to point of entry. If he did come in, then from where? We're plowing through empty space out there. Could we have picked him up when we were socializing with the Bips? If so, where has he been hiding all this time and how does he move about?"

Candie's eyes seemed to go out of focus as she considered the matter. "Maybe we are looking for an answer based on our own experiences, our own knowledge of our own science or in line with our own belief patterns."

"What do you mean by that?"

"Remember we couldn't pick up any signals from Nacho, the Bip ship. Why? Because our science didn't match their science. Besides, could you have accepted the symbiotic relationship that we observed with the Bips? All I'm saying is that maybe the answer we are looking for doesn't exist in our current framework of knowledge."

Tom came out of Beatrice's room. Dandy jumped up. To Candie he said, "You'd better get back in there."

"Not necessary," injected Tom. He flipped a console switch. There was a view of the blob still in its corner of the bed. Beatrice was scrunched up in the opposing corner of the bed. She had her arms around her knees and was just intently looking at the thing. "I adjusted her personal com unit to pick up the bed. She wants to be alone with it. We can keep tabs of what is going on without interfering."

"What did you find out?"

"As far as I can tell, there's no hazard there. He is not radio-active. He doesn't seem to be putting off any noxious gas. There are no high thermal levels. He isn't going to burst into flame. There is a very high electromagnetic field around him, but nothing to cause a problem with us or our equipment except maybe a little snow on Bea's camera. Of course, I can't tell without affixing electrodes to him, but I would suspect that what we would call brain wave activity is high too or Bea wouldn't be picking it up."

The elevator door slid open. Spotting the little gathering at Candie's station, Corky headed over. Before anyone could ask Corky said, "I didn't find even one dust mote out of place. Nothing came in through any of our accesses. There is no indication of any hull breach of any kind that I can see. Nothing. Any change in Doughboy?"

Corky had done it again. The object in Bea's room was branded with a name, "Doughboy."

Dandy sighed. "It looks as if we have a stowaway. Unless we want to just jettison him out an airlock, I can't think of anything to do with him other than just to watch and wait. Candie pointed out that we may be looking for the answer in the wrong places. There might be some science or natural condition to account for Doughboy's appearance that we have never encountered. Let's just keep a close watch to see what happens. Maybe Bea can shed some light on our little mystery." Everyone glanced at the monitor, but nothing had changed.

"Candie, we'll keep on course for our target. Check to make sure we're still going in the right direction. See if there are any other jets that have moved into the area that might be closer."

"I'll get right on it if you guys would get your butts off my working area," she replied with a shake of the head to set her dangly earrings sparkling in the light.

Chapter 3

Dandy went down for four hours sleep before they were going to grab a Solar Jet. The computer roused him. After getting cleaned up, he went out to meet the world of Taran. Candie was at her station. She motioned him over. She was watching Bea's room monitor. Beatrice was slumped down in the corner of her bed alcove asleep. Doughboy was still in his corner, but something was different. The form was much more elongated than his former round shape. Also there was something more. Protruding out of the form was an appendage of some sort.

"What's that?"

"In a little bit it will move again. But it is an exact duplicate of Bea's hand which is lying across the calf of her leg. It includes part of her coverall cuff."

"You mean, it's trying to replicate Bea? How long has this been going on?"

Candie glanced at the clock. "Oh, Bea dropped off to sleep about two hours ago. That is when Doughboy started to change its shape. It became longer, which narrowed the distance between it and Bea. I have been watching closely and also recording the whole thing on tape. That hand took well over an hour to form. It didn't just appear, but it would appear Doughboy must somehow shape it by trial and error. It changed shape many times. Also you can see that the underside of the hand is not properly formed."

"That would indicate it perceives in much the same manner as we see. We see the surface but not what is inside or on the back side. Have you seen anything that might act as eyes?"

"No, nothing. You'll notice that even though it has elongated itself, it still retains those folds that come from the underside. Maybe there is something different down there. We are getting pretty close to the jet. Shall we hitch a ride?"

Dandy thought about it. "I think we'd better hold off a bit. We're heading in the right direction. Let's let Bea sleep. When she awakens, maybe she will be able to tell us something."

Once that decision was out of the way, he turned to other chores. "I'm going to get Tom up to spell you. You get some rest, but be prepared to get out here in case Bea needs help.

Dandy went back to his station. There wasn't too much to do except minor housekeeping. He turned on his monitor to watch Doughboy. Bea had changed the position of her hand somewhat. Doughboy had added the newly revealed details to his own hand. Also the arm had gotten three or four inches longer.

Dandy was about to go get a cup of coffee when Bea began moving. She was waking up. She stretched out of her cramped position. That movement did not seem to bother Doughboy. He remained immobile. Dandy also figured that Beatrice would react if he became alarmed. She had some strange tie with the object. Gently, she got off the bed and headed out of sight to the hygienic unit. A short time later, she came back into the picture. She had spotted the new appendage. Sitting on the edge of the bed she very tentatively reached out to touch the reproduction of her hand. First, she just touched it with a finger tip. That did not seem to create any problem, so she gently stroked the back of the hand. Her fingers dimpled the surface. It moved gently. It was completely flaccid with no rigid structure either on the exterior or the interior. Beatrice sniffed her fingers. Carefully she got up and headed for the door.

Dandy met her. "How do you feel?"

"Oh, I feel all right except for being as stiff as a board. He has calmed down. He is not crying out. I just feel a slight murmur in the background. I'm hungry."

Dandy immediately stepped out of the way motioning her to the Fish House. "By all means. Get started. I am going to get the rest of the crew. We need your impression of our guest and discuss the situation."

After Candie was awakened, Dandy rounded up Corky from below. Tom had been monitoring everything from his station. He didn't want to use the electronic tone because he didn't want to perhaps frighten Doughboy.

Everyone got something to eat. They settled down around Beatrice at the large round table. Dandy prompted her, "What can you tell us about our guest?"

"I really don't know that much. We aren't in communication other than that I can feel what we call emotions. The moment I sensed it, there was an impact on me of great pain and fear, or perhaps I should say 'panic.' It just burst into my mind full blown. After we found him, the emotions began to ease off. They were replaced by curiosity. Remember, I said your presence caused fear. I think it was just apprehension. It wasn't anything like the panic I felt earlier. Now, it is rather like having a new puppy. I had one once when I was a little girl. I always thought I could tell when it was happy or sad."

Dandy pushed on. "What do you think about that hand?"

"Oh, I think he is just trying to please me."

"Please you?"

Beatrice shrugged. "Well, he doesn't have a tail to wag. Of course, it also lets us know that he is aware of us....that he is just not a blob of something."

Tom spoke up. "To be able to reproduce Bea's hand it has to have some sort of information input. I haven't seen anything that even remotely resembles ocular capabilities. Whatever he uses to gain information is like sight because he can make only that part of the hand that is exposed to him. Furthermore, the hand is limp. There is no rigid structure because he can't penetrate the surface with whatever senses he has, like a dolphin who can look at a swimmer's innards with its sounding ability."

Candie checked in with, "Whatever his sensory perception, he can't make distinctions between flesh and synthetic fabric."

Corky added to the mystery. "If this is a living thing, it needs fuel. How does it eat? Or what does it eat?"

"When you touched him, what did you find out?" inquired Dandy.

"He is soft, very soft. Have you ever touched a mole? He felt like that. He was warm to the touch. If that is his body temperature, then he is a few degrees warmer than we are."

"You smelled your fingers. Did you get any scent?"

Beatrice frowned. "No, not really, but I kept getting the sense of something burning....not like a fireplace. It is more like when my computer shorted out once. It is kind of an electrical thing. I really can't describe it. There was no scent on my fingers. There was no residue that I could see."

Dandy got up to get another cup of coffee. He glanced at the monitor. "Look."

All eyes followed he gaze. Doughboy was changing shape. It was very slowly elongating itself toward the edge of the bed. The lead part flowed like cold honey down toward the floor. Gradually the whole body was on the move. The duplicate of Beatrice's hand was held aloft out of harm's way. Also the folded under section retained its integrity.

Beatrice started to rise to go to him, but Dandy stopped her. "Let's see what he is up to. If he starts to do something that will harm either the ship on one of us, then we will have to take immediate action."

Doughboy started to flow very slowly across the floor to the open door to Beatrice's work station.

"Candie, go to your station," ordered Dandy. "You will be able to see it if it comes out of Bea's room. Tell us what is happening. The rest of us will just continue our discussion."

"Here he comes," whispered Candie. "He is coming out the door and moving in your direction."Candie maneuvered one of the internal cameras around to follow Doughboy's progress. He was having a hard time. It seemed as if he couldn't determine whether he wanted to slip along like a slug or inch along like a caterpillar. He had elongated himself into a much more linear form with four appendages. The hand was on the end of one of those appendages.

"Do you suppose he is trying to assume our general shape?" wondered Candie.

Corky observed, "He's going to have to work on that a bit more."

Doughboy slowly made his way down the hall, around the corner into the Fish House and eventually settled down against Beatrice's foot.

"My puppy analogy is getting stronger," she observed.

Candie rejoined the group.

Dandy brought the conversation back to the problem at hand. "If we, for the moment, eliminate the Earth as the source because it doesn't match any known life forms and it didn't come from the Bips or P-5 because of the existing conditions, we are left with only one other possibility as I see it. We must be dealing with some form of teleportation or whatever the current term may be."

Tom sniffed.

"Well, come up with a better one," challenged Dandy.

No one had anything to say.

After waiting for some response and getting none, Dandy said, "Well, we can't just sit here pondering the problem. There doesn't seem to be anything around here that constitutes a threat. I think we should proceed with our original plans. We'll have to keep track of Doughboy. He seems to be benign, but who knows? Just see he doesn't get into anything that can cause him or us a problem. Bea, go over to your work station. Let's see if he follows you there."

Beatrice slowly moved away from Doughboy. She then walked over to her station. She sat down on her couch. After a moment's delay Doughboy started after her. This time he lifted his middle so he could amble along somewhat like a dog using the four appendages. He settled down alongside the couch pedestal.

Candy observed, "I think we have a fast learner. Any bets on how long it takes him to get up on two legs?"

Chapter 4

Dandy stopped by Beatrice's station. She was busy recording everything about her mental experience with Doughboy as well as all observations she could make about him. He was curled up beside her couch. In the two days since he had appeared, he had changed shape into a caricature of a human in a vague sort of way. There were the four appendages separated by a body. There was still a folded over area in the middle that gave the appearance of a beer belly, as Corky put it. A nubbin for a head had appeared. As yet it contained no features.

"How are things coming?" inquired Dandy.

"Fine. I'm getting it all down and cross referenced. Oh, one bit of new information. Last night I picked him up to put him on the bed. Doughboy is as light as a feather. I had Corky weight him at 2.34 pounds in this artificial gravity. He would be a little heavier on earth."

"Have you come up with any ideas about whether he needs to eat and what?"

"There is nothing to indicate he ingests any food as we know it. Of course, in the middle lump he covers up may be all sorts of things. I don't think we should force the issue. There is still a small residual element of fear coming from him."

"Good work," said Dandy. "Just think of the papers you'll be able to write when we get back."

Dandy returned to his station. Everything was quiet as the crew worked on their various projects. Suddenly the hair on Dandy's arms tingled and stood up as if someone was winding a static electricity generator next to him. He looked over at Candie. She was holding her hands to her hair and looking at him. Dandy switched on Corky's monitor. He was reacting too. The supply officer looked up at the monitor. "What's going on?"

From Dandy's point of view, he could see only the rear of Beatrice's head. She looked rigidly upright, but not moving. He turned on the monitor in front of her. She was looking straight ahead without her eyes appearing to focus on anything. Dandy yelled at her. "Bea, are you all right?"There was no answer.
Dandy jumped up, darted behind Candie to get to Beatrice. Her couch was in the upright position. She was sitting very still. She seemed to be breathing normally. "Bea, are you all right? Bea! Bea!"

Beatrice shuddered a little bit and looked at Dandy. It took a few moments apparently for everything to register, but she said, "Yes, I'm all right, but there is another Doughboy here. We are talking. Give me time." She went back to her vacant stare.

The rest of TC gathered around Beatrice, who continued to stare ahead. Occasionally, she would shake her head like someone just wasn't getting it. Other times, she would toss her head back. If she was in some sort of conversation, it was all mental.

At the foot of her couch was the original Doughboy. He had reverted to his ball shape. He was quivering slightly, but he did not seem to be in any particular anguish.

After a half hour of that, Corky wandered off to talk with Tom who he had been asleep when the incident started. Candie went back to her couch, which she swung around so she could watch Beatrice. Dandy picked up a coffee and a tea and went to perch on Candie's map table.   "What do you think? Is there anything we can do or should do?" Dandy didn't like the whole thing, but he had no idea of what to do. He hated not being in charge of the situation.

Candie just shook her head. "We have no medical facilities available. If we had a doctor we might have something we could do, but I'm afraid we're just going to have to wait this one out."

"What do you suppose she is doing?"

The navigator shrugged. "With Bea, it could be anything. She could be playing mental chess or scrabble in Zulu. When she gets ready she will probably tell us in great detail."

Two hours later, Beatrice sounded the tone that called everyone to attention. She swung around to face the assembled group. "I think we should all take our stations. This is going to take a while. You might as well be comfortable. Candie, would you please get me a tea while I make a trip to my quarters?" Beatrice stood up. She appeared to be having some kind of silent argument with someone. Finally, she wheeled around to head for her room saying, "Privacy isn't in their vocabulary."

Five minutes later, everyone was in his proper place. The monitors were on for a round table meeting.

Beatrice started out. "To begin, let me explain a little of what is happening. Our Doughboy is from another sentient civilization somewhere. He came here under great stress, escaping some situation—ending up in my bed....er....ending up here. A member of his family has come looking for him. Somehow his mind and mine are compatible enough for us to make each other understand. I have been trying to teach him our language because he wants to address us directly. He will have to talk through me, but it will be his thoughts instead of me trying to translate his images. He has assured me he means us no harm. He is delighted to find another sentient life form. I have no way of translating or pronouncing his name. Somehow it reminds me of Tea House. But, I guess he will have to figure that out."

Beatrice's voice continued as before. "Greeting fallow....

fellow....space travailers....travelers. I am a traveler from somewhere else. I can't tell you where, because I no know....don't
know. Yes, don't know. I just followed a trial....trail...."

Corky broke in. "I can see where this is going to get confus-
ing. We cannot tell who is speaking. We can't tell if it is the first
Beatrice or the second Beatrice.....B-1 or B-2." TC snickered.

Beatrice fired Corky an exasperated glance, but said, "Just
give us a moment. We should be able to figure out something."
She went back into her vacant stare.

This time it was only a couple of minutes. "Since the story
is his, he will be talking the most. I will give a little wave of the
hand when I am injecting or correcting something. But I think
we have come to a method where the problem will be negligible.
Let's try it again."

B-2 began. "Greetings fellow space travelers. I am a traveler
from somewhere else. I cannot tell you where, because I do not
know. I followed an energy trail left by our "nibbling," which is
what we call him." Beatrice motioned toward Doughboy. "My people are quite different from you. Many millennia ago we evolved
into a non-corporeal state of existence where we were mostly
thought energy. That was the state we had been aiming at for a
long time. However, when we finally were able to dispense with
corporeal ties, we discovered we had given up too much. We had
no method of experiencing physical phenomena....pleasures or
pain. We couldn't go back, because our world could no longer
handle our numbers. So we devised a method having the best of
both states, corporeal and non-corporeal."

B-2 continued, "Each of us can reproduce by simply snipping
off a small portion of our energy and then feeding it with more
personal or a-personal energy until it grows into adulthood. It
will retain all of the parent's traits. The problem was that the
offspring reflected only an individual, not a matched....mar-
ried....pair. This offspring also had the same limitations we had
placed on ourselves....an entity devoid of sensation. We found
that without sensation, there is little left to talk about.

"So we devised another approach to existence. We developed

the "nibbling." It is a blank, an embryo, a sterile receptacle....I really don't know how to express it. When a pairing is formed.... you would call a marriage....a joining of a male and a female, they then can apply for a nibbling. It is an energized physical entity much like you originally saw in Doughboy, as you call him. When a couple is granted a nibbling, each energizes him with bits of his or her own energy. Through nurturing, guidance, and great care, the nibbling takes physical shape and mental form in the image of its parents. This physical form does not have all the traits of your physical form, but it can savor flavors, smells, touch. It can experience pain. It can know fear. When the nibbling matures, it becomes a full adult member of our society. The mind can leave the physical form at any time. In between times, the body becomes dormant, waiting re-energizing. When we inhabit our physical form we can have a full range of physical experiences. We enjoy the advantage of possessing two forms.

"As a society, we take the proper raising of a nibbling very seriously. It is one of our most serious crimes to violate the protocol. In the case of your Doughboy, a relative of mine attempted to create a pleasure object...what you would call a sex object.... out of the nibbling. There are built-in safety programs in each nibbling to protect it against various problems which might arise. In this case, that program was seriously violated. The nibbling simply fled in a burst of panic energy. Somehow that pulse brought it to you. I have no idea how it got here. Nothing in your space looks familiar to me. I left an energy trail here so that I will be able to follow it home with our nibbling.

"My world wishes to thank you for taking care of our 'child'. He seems to have become quite attached to you."

Beatrice made a motion with her hand. "Our guest realizes you will be curious about this. He will try to answer your questions."

Dandy spoke up. "You undoubtedly know our names. What should we call you?"

"I am fascinated by Beatrice's name of Tea House, because our language is not exclusively verbal. We pass sensations as well.

One sensation of my name is a smell which she equates with a beverage of yours, tea. It was an astute observation. When a few of my people gather in their pure energy state they create a ball so each has a direct line available to any of the gathering. This structure is the second part of my name, which cannot be vocalized either. So Tea House will suit me just fine.

"How come it was you that came after Doughboy?" inquired Candie.

I am the head of my family. Any violation of our ways or laws is a crime against the family. The family must take appropriate action."

"What would you call 'appropriate action' in this case?"

B2 didn't answer for a moment. "The one, who breached the rules, will be placed in a containment field where his energy will be used for the good of the whole until he is used up."

Candie's eyes widened. "You mean it is a death sentence?"

"I suppose you would see it that way. The process may take ages, but the main burden is that he will derive no pleasure or satisfaction out of his life force. It will be a sterile, thoughtless existence. He will welcome the end."

Corky held up his hand. Beatrice nodded at him. "What will happen to our little friend?"

"I will take him back. My family will work to undo the harm done. We have to work to reshape him to eliminate that construction in his middle."

"What's that?"asked Corky.

"It is a hugely overdeveloped erogenous zone. It will take time, but he can be redeveloped into compatible member of our community."

"What would have happened to him if you wouldn't have come?" inquired Tom.

"He possesses some life force, but he would soon have used that up and he would have faded away. A nibbling is constantly being nurtured or supplemented by the parents until he can generate his own eternal supply."

Dandy broke in. "You used the word, "eternal." Are you using that in the same way we use it? Do you exist for eternity?"

"In theory we could live for eternity, but in actuality we have a limited life time since we are subject to various external forces that tend to limit our life expectancy. On the average, we live several hundred of your years. But, that is only if one is very careful around lightning, time anomalies and the sort."

"You mentioned your world. Is it like our world?" inquired Dandy.

There was a period of silence while B1 and B2 conferred.

"Probably, originally it was similar. It sustained a carbon life form, but over time it became nearly uninhabitable. That was when the final breakthrough took place to permit us changing to a non-corporal state. Those that couldn't or wouldn't change died off along with the planet. Gradually it rebuilt itself into a glorious place without us messing it up. When we came up with the nibbling concept, it did not put that much pressure on the environment because the nibblings and then the adults don't use natural resources except in very minor amounts. For example, a single apple could give pleasure to dozens because all we need to luxuriate in the flavor of the fruit is simply to press a small piece against our taste spot.

"We create only a tiny amount of waste. Each adult does have a room, a closet, storage bin....something like that, where we store our nibblings when they are not needed. When we want someplace to entertain or gather physical sensations, we have places like hotels, sports complexes or resorts where we take our corporeal surrogates. Since we can transport instantaneously, going somewhere presents no problems."

"Could we see your physical form if it were here?" asked Candie.

Oh, yes. Just as you see Doughboy."

"Would it look like Doughboy?"

"Oh, no. I'm afraid you would not find us attractive in the

least. It is about time for me to gather up my young charge and return to my world. I must again thank you......"

Dandy jumped back in before the alien could leave. "Will your knowing about us cause us any problems?"

"No, your existence is of no concern to my kind. We have no interest in interfering with your life energy."

"Would your knowing of us generate any fear of us?"

"No. We have had contact with many beings—many of them far more advanced than you. We do not fear them and we give them no reason to fear us."

"You said you did not recognize anything here. Do you think your home is in this galaxy or beyond?"

"I would say that I probably don't belong to this galaxy, but on the other hand it may not be that at all. It may be a different reality or time. I cannot tell. We must go now."

"One more question," said Dandy. "Do you know anything about the energy anomaly we are chasing?"

There was a pause while Tea House and Beatrice conferred. "Our nibbling is aware of the object, but I can't tell how. He might have ridden it through time or space or it might have been dragged through as he passed. He isn't aware of enough to know. Really, we must go before my trail disburses."

Doughboy vanished. Beatrice collapsed.

Chapter   5

Eight hours after Doughboy and his unseen relative had vanished. TC gathered in the Fish House. Beatrice had awakened. Her coming out of her room signaled the meeting. Those who were hungry, got food. The rest sat with their beverages.

Dandy opened. "Bea, can you describe what happened to you?"

"You know about how I sensed Doughboy. When Tea House appeared on the scene I sensed him in the same way, but the feelings were entirely different. It wasn't fear and panic. It was more sympathy and curiosity. Since I had been playing around with trying to contact Doughboy, I did the same thing with the new mind. I didn't get any sense of harm, so I made contact. It was actually rather pleasant. It was like having a conversation with a very knowledgeable person on a mutually understood topic.

"He wanted to communicate with us. The only way to be able to deal with complex topics was to have a common language. His was much too strange for me since it deals directly with all the senses in some sort of mental state. Since all of our sensory perceptions have already been converted into synaptic signals and stored in the brain, no translations were required by him. For example, if I asked you how abalone tastes, since I have never eaten it, you would have to say something like, 'It tastes like chicken.' However, he could send you the taste sensations so you would actually taste abalone. I just let him use my speech center like some sort of mechanical translator."

"At first he was making all sorts of mistakes," pointed out Corky. "How did you fix that?"

"You've heard those radio talk show hosts. They have a five second delay so they can cut out any naughty words. I just installed a delay so I could check the words out before I spoke them."

Dandy was still quite serious. "Are you any worse for wear after this experience?"

"No, not at all. In fact, I have been substantially enhanced by this encounter."

"How so?"

"I am the first person I know of who has ever had the opportunity to wander around in the mind of an alien intelligence. I probably got more out of that exchange than he did. His main focus was to communicate by finding the right words to describe his mental images. I could observe those images. I could see how he thought...maybe not all that he thought, because much of it had no reference with which I was familiar. Even if I don't understand it, I still remember it."

"How come you couldn't do the same thing with Doughboy?"

"There was nothing there yet. It is quite like humans teaching a child. Nothing had been entered other than some sex notions, which I couldn't have understood anyway."Beatrice straightened up. "Do you know what I need?"

Everyone became apprehensive. Dandy said, "What?"

"I need to get back to work so I can record all this while it is fresh and before you get us in some other crazy situation. I never have enough time to complete my work on anything anymore."

Dandy threw up his hands. "I'm taking you on the scenic tour of the galaxy and all you do is bitch, bitch, bitch."

Everyone had a good laugh. Dandy waved Beatrice off. To Candie he said, "Find us another jet so we can get on with our business."

Chapter 6

Everything went smoothly for five days. Beatrice was hard at work on recording her experiences. Candie was charting the system from their new angle. Corky was checking all the little things that could go wrong. The ship had been well used for over six months and it hadn't been back on the ground long enough for a full overhaul. Things needed tightening. For his part Dandy was considering how to approach the energy system that was the subject of their investigation.

Then the routine was shattered.

It was Beatrice. "He's back!"

"Who's back?"demanded Dandy with shaving cream on half his face.

"Doughboy is back."

"What makes you think so?

"I can feel him and recognize his presence."

Dandy ran to Beatrice's quarters. He wrenched the door open and there in the corner of Bea's bunk was a greatly changed Doughboy. Everyone gathered around. Doughboy had taken a much more human form. He was greatly elongated with four limbs and a knob like a head. He still had Bea's hand, but it was where a foot should have been. When confronted by TC, Doughboy tried to move toward Beatrice, but he was having difficulty. Certain portions of his body had become somewhat rigid and they wouldn't bend properly.

One thing that everybody noticed was that he no long had that lump in what had been the midsection. Apparently Tea House had gotten him over that. Also he had altered his color from a pasty white to a shade more approximating human skin and the light blue of their coveralls. As they watched, Doughboy was trying to make changes in his physical form.

"Boy. That is one confused alien," said Corky.

Beatrice jumped to Doughboy's defense. "He's trying. Give him time. Just think of what he is trying to do." She walked over to the bunk and sat down beside him. He snuggled up against her thigh as if his world was right again. She petted him on the portion that she took to be his head.

Candie said, "I wonder how long it will be before Tea House gets here."

Further discussion was interrupted by a blare of sound. "What's that?" demanded Candie as she and the three guys poured out of Beatrice's room.

"It's a radio monitor we have had on since we left on this little vacation. This is the first time we have ever picked up anything but earth signals, which I've filtered out," explained Tom as he dove for his monitoring equipment. "That's a powerful signal."

Dandy headed for his station to check the external sensors. "We've got company. It looks like a little moon, but there can't be any moons out here. It must be some strange meteor. A few minutes ago there was nothing out there."

"It's moving and moving fast," added Candie from her station. "It is on a nearly parallel passing course. If there are no course or speed corrections, we will pass each other in three days at a distance of about two hundred thousand miles."

"That's a really strange meteor," commented Tom. "It is the

source of the radio signal, which is not a naturally occurring phenomenon."

"How do you know?" fired Dandy.

"There appear to be a series of messages in various frequency ranges that I can pick up. There are gaps of about the same time length, which I am assuming are messages that I can't receive. Then the string is being repeated. It's probably some sort of hail that I don't recognize."

"Could it be some sort of distress call?" asked Candie.

"Yes, I suppose it could, but it could just as easily be a quarantine warning, telling all ships to stay away. It could be a penal colony. It could be almost anything except a plain old meteor."

"Can you determine its size? What about composition?" asked Dandy.

"I'm working on it. It is big."

There was a period of silence. Candie was working over her instruments. Tom was fiddling with the transmissions from the thing. Corky had finished his project below. He returned to his station but held his silence while others worked. Beatrice was doing something with Doughboy.

Dandy was running some quick computations for two different scenarios....one to approach the object and the second to get the hell out of there.

Candie broke the silence. "As far as I can determine, the object is pretty much spherical. A rough estimate of size is 400 km in diameter. That would make it about an eighth of the size of our moon. I can't tell its composition from here. One thing I can tell is that it is not ice, if that is what you really want to know. It is heavily metallic, but the readings don't make sense yet."

Beatrice came out of her room followed by Doughboy who was moving in a sort of stiff-legged walk on his two new legs. There were no feet yet, but maybe that would come later. When Beatrice was settled, Dandy inquired, "Bea, did you find out anything about your friend? I was wondering if he was in any way connected with that big metal ball coming toward us."

"No real information. He still doesn't have coherent language. I just get impressions of mostly feelings. He is very happy to be here. Apparently it was not an instantaneous transport from one spot to another. There seems to be some journey involved. He seems relieved to finally be here. There is no fear or panic now. I'm afraid he may have imprinted on us like a gosling does. As far as that ball is concerned I don't pick up anything about it."

"I need a cup of coffee," stated Dandy. "I'm buying. Anyone else want anything?" He spent the next few minutes filling orders. When everyone was served, he returned to his station and opened channels for a conference.

"Candie. Can we outrun that thing if we have to?"

"Really, I have no way of knowing. At the moment, it is traveling at a greater velocity than we are, but we can crank it up enough to more than match that speed. However, it might just be idling now. Another thing is that it would take us a little time to gain the additional speed. The closer we get, the less time we would have to accelerate."

"Tom, can you tell us any more about those radio signals?"

"Nothing other than I think it is the same signal repeated in any number of different methods and in a number of languages. There are multiple transmissions on a similar frequency, but the messages are different.

"Has anyone picked up any energy readings from that thing other than that signal?" Dandy didn't get any answer. He continued on. "I have the notion that the signal is some sort of warning. We don't go through space advertising our impending arrival. I wouldn't think anyone else would either unless he is the ultimate power. Another thing that bothers me is the sudden appearance of that object. Remember, we can do that if we come out of a Solar Jet, and the Bips did it to us by riding that gravitational strand. However, there are no jets in the vicinity of that thing. Maybe it arrived on a strand or something similar. Another possibility is that it has light speed and simply reduced its speed in our vicinity. Any of these situations makes me a little jumpy.

"Of course, that ball could be some unmanned or derelict something or other, which will just pass on by on its way to nowhere. For the time being, I think we should proceed as we are. We are heading toward the closest jet. Maybe we should boost our speed somewhat just to be prepared. Other than that, we just watch and wait. Maybe that thing will just pass by. Does anyone have any other suggestions?"

Candy stepped in. "I'm confused. Do we think we are looking at a huge natural body with something on it, like a crashed ship or colony or are we looking at a huge artificial body, which may be manned or was manned by some intelligent life form?"

"Come to think of it," conceded Dandy. "I haven't any clear picture in mind. What do we know about it?"

Tom added things up. "We know its size, which would make it a monumental construction chore for anyone. You say it is highly metallic, that could mean it's an iron meteor or a constructed ship. It is sending signals, which could be from either source. If it rode a strand or something here, it is probably constructed, but if there was some sort of spacial shift like Doughboy must have ridden, it could be anything. In fact, could it be from that energy field we are going to investigate? We're getting pretty close. How about the speed? Is it natural or propelled?"

"At the moment it is going a little faster than you would normally expect a piece of space debris to be travelling, but it could have just gone through some gravitation slingshot or some other phenomenon," supplied Candie.

There was a lull in the conversation as everyone examined the situation. The silence was finally broken by Candie. "What happens if it doesn't just pass on by?"

"We'll just have to outrun it to the closest jet. So keep track of the nearest alternate jet that is away from that thing," said Dandy. He then turned to Beatrice, who had been silent throughout the whole affair. "Bea, you'll have to take care of Doughboy. See that he doesn't get into anything. Corky, can you rig some sort of sling or restraint for Doughboy in case we have to go into full flight? I don't want him bouncing around, for his sake or ours."

"Sure. Where do you want it?

"It had better be by Bea's couch because that is where she will be, and Doughboy apparently wants to be near her." Turning his attention back to the group as a whole, he ordered, "We will keep our current schedules. Whoever is on duty, constantly monitor that signal and the thing....the ball...whatever it is. If there is any change whatever, let me know."

Dandy didn't even make the door to his room when Candie said, "Oops!"

"Oops. What?"

"The object of our search has disappeared. It couldn't have shifted position very much since the last time I looked."

Everyone crowded around Candie as she searched space. The energy source wasn't where is should have been. Candie adjusted her scanning devices and then leaned back into her couch. "That ball coming at us is the energy source we were going to investigate. It has come to meet us. It has the same background signal, but it is being overridden by that new signal it is putting out."

"How in the devil did it get here,?" said Corky.

"Well, how did it get into our solar system without us seeing it coming?" said Tom.

"Now, what's the plan?" said Candy.

"We're headed for the closest jet right now," said Dandy. "Let's stay on this course and see if we can beat it there. We can put some space between us and then figure out what, if anything, we want to do."

Chapter 7

A change came twenty hours later. Beatrice was on duty again and Dandy was sleeping. His intercom woke him. When Beatrice was sure he was awake, she reported that the signal had just terminated, and immediately the ball started a course change that looked as if it was designed to intercept Taran.

Candie was already at her station. "It has veered off slightly in what likely will become a great arc to meet us. It is too soon to tell."

"Is there a solar jet?" asked Dandy.

"The one we are headed for is still the best. In fact, if we swing more to the starboard we might gain some advantage. We'll hit the jet sooner and it will tighten that thing's arc. Depending on its steering capabilities, it may have to slow to reduce the arc."

Dandy sounded the page. "We'll fire up in ten minutes. Get everything in order. Corky, please help Bea get our stowaway into his sling."

"Sure," said Corky. He also added, "I guess that answers the question of whether or not that thing out there is a natural object."

In ten minutes, Dandy fired the engine. Gradually, he built

up the speed until they had one and a half G force. He also came about to the starboard as Candie had suggested. Actually the two crafts were still a couple of days apart. Taran's speed increased until it exceeded that of the ball. The turn put the ball aft.

Candie's calculations showed that under the present speed Taran would be to the jet before the ball could make its course correction and make up the additional distance.

However, it was Tom who brought them out of their complacency when he inquired,   "What happens if that ball turns out to be a hostile ship and it fires a shot across our bow?"

"Oh, boy," said Candie.

"Why would anyone want to do that?' whispered Beatrice.

"Tom, you really know how to ruin a perfectly good day," replied Dandy. "I don't know. Maybe we should do some thinking on that possibility."

The next day was rather a subdued one. Tom and Corky had their usual gin game, but it didn't have its normal fervor. Candie worked herself into a lather on her exercise machines. The additional half G made for a very heavy workout. Beatrice went back to her computer work, but frequently her hand wandered down to stroke Doughboy.

Dandy tried to listen to music, but he couldn't find any pleasure there. He reverted back to some classic football games that he'd already seen too many times. He watched without seeing. Tom's question had upset him more than he let on. Eventually, he ended up on his couch with his heels crossed on the side of his console.

. Everyone knew that was his thinking position and he was not to be bothered unless there was an emergency.

He pondered what kind of weapons could be employed against them. Earth technology basically threw something at you. It either hit you to do its damage or it exploded near you to accomplish its aim. Then a new item had been added during their first voyage when they got hit by some sort of concentrated beam just before they left for the moon. But, now that they were out in space, it was a new ball game. Dandy had no idea what could be used against them. They had already experienced technology far outside of their realm of experience, such as the gravity propulsion and communications systems of the Bips. This ball was certainly not of Bip origin. And just as obvious, its origin was a space-faring civilization. They could actually possess things that even science fiction writers had not fantasized. His cogitations were getting him nowhere. Their only defense would be speed and evasion. Their anti-grav generators had assisted them before, but that technology may not have any use here. There was no place to hide.

The gin game broke up. Corky went on duty and Tom headed for bed. After Candie cleaned up from her workout she joined Dandy in the Fish House for a meal. Conversation was restrained. Candie didn't even try to bait the pilot with one of her little "gotcha" games. Just as they were finishing their drinks, Corky attracted their attention.

"Would you take a look at this?"

When the pair got to his station, Corky pointed at all the various gauges in front of him. Each one was fluctuating slightly....a tick up and a tick down. It was a regular rhythm. Dandy went to his station. "Mine are doing the same thing."

"Mine too," reported Candie.

Beatrice was alert too. Doughboy was twitching in time to the fluctuations they were seeing on their instruments.

"I feel some sort of pulsing," reported Beatrice.

"Is Tea House coming?"

"Oh, no. It is nothing like that. This is like listening to one's own heart beat."

"I think that thing is slowing down. The arc seems to be getting tighter," reported Candie.

Dandy wanted to see her course projections. He stood up to walk over to her station, but he immediately sat down again. "We're losing G-force," he exclaimed. After a quick check of his instrument he announced. "We're losing speed. The engine output is the same. Corky, get Tom up. Then you two see if anything is wrong down below. My instruments are showing no problems."

Tom was out in a flash. Dandy didn't want to touch anything until they had a chance to look around. "Bea, are you feeling anything different?

"No, nothing has changed. It is just like what you are seeing on your instruments. Doughboy must feel it too, but it is not creating any particular reaction other than apparently keeping time to the beat."

Candie had switched on her navigation instruments....the duplicates of Dandy's. "How did you know we had lost speed?"

"It was easier to stand up. We had been under a force of one and a half Gs. I could feel the difference. It is not much, but enough to make me check. Do you see anything out there that could form any sort of resistance to our passage?"

Candie set about checking all the various sensors she had available. "I can't find anything to account for any sort of drag. The only thing that is different is that pulsing that is screwing up our instruments and that Bea feels."

"In the absence of anything else, it must have something to do with that ball thing. It is pretty big. Do you think that it has enough gravitational attraction to influence us at this distance? Bea, what do you think?"

"I don't see how it could. At this distance, even our moon would not reduce our thrust that much. If we were coasting it might have some minor drag."

Tom came on the intercom. "We've checked everything down here. Nothing is out of line. We have the same fluctuations on our gauges, but the only influence we determine is that there is a minute fluctuation of the hydrogen pressure to the engine. However, it is not causing any reduction in output."

"Okay, come back up and strap in. I am going to run our speed back up to what it was to see what will happen."

Ten minutes later, Dandy moved the throttle up bit by bit. The engine responded as expected. Their speed rose until they were again at one and a half Gs.

Dandy reported what everyone could see on his own instrument array. "We're back up to speed again. However, we are paying quite a price. Our fuel consumption has risen considerably."

Turning to Candie, he said, "Run your figures again to see how long it will take us to get to the jet. And also check our relative speeds to that ball to make sure we will arrive there first." To Tom he said, "Check our fuel consumption figures. Give me an estimate of reserves we will have when we get to the jet."

Dandy swung back to his navigator expecting speed readings, but instead she asked him to check his course headings. His instruments told him the ship had veered off somewhat to port; Dandy compensated. With steering jets he returned to his original course, but the move was costing him velocity. He had to boost power once again to maintain his headway. Of course, that changed all Tom's and Candie's figures.

Corky came up from below, to report that everything was operating perfectly. He could see no reason at all for the drop in speed.

Candie's report was that the time gap had narrowed somewhat but that they should be able to get to the jet ahead of the ball. Apparently the other ship, if that is what it was, had not increased its speed.

It was Tom who had the disturbing news. At the current rate of consumption, they would be down to less than 50% fuel reserve by the time they reached the jet. That meant that they might have to think about finding a filling station to get home.

Dandy found that he was now, periodically having to tweak his course because something was causing Taran to move slightly to the left. Also, it looked like he was continuing to get faint speed reductions. That was making him very uneasy.

Finally, instead of staring at the gauges, he set a timer and recorded speed and direction before getting himself a cup of coffee.

Beatrice had been pretty silent during the whole operation. Dandy stopped by her station. He stooped to pet Doughboy, who was wrapped around Beatrice's feet. "Cold?" he asked nodding toward her nondescript friend.

"He seems to be somewhat distressed, but I can't figure out why. Maybe he is mirroring my feelings."

Dandy came to the point of the visit. "Do you think that thing out there could be exerting a gravitational force strong enough to be affecting our course and speed?"

"I don't see how. It is big, but not big enough to have any particular gravitational strength unless the thing had some enormous density that I can't even start to comprehend."

Dandy hesitated because he was moving onto rather shaky ground. "Do you suppose that could be some sort of singularity or a little black hole or baby universe that is coming our way?"

Beatrice started to snap back a sharp, intellectual reply but caught herself. Instead she just shook her head. "No, from what I know, that thing doesn't fall into any of those hypothetical realms. If it had just been something that was passing....even though it was exerting some force on us as it did, there might be some support for a theory like that, but since it has changed course to catch us I think it is guided by some intelligence."

"I was afraid of that," said Dandy as he gave Doughboy a final pat before returning to his station to check his timer.

The timer and his instruments indicated there was still a decrease in velocity and a deviation to the port. To get some sort of reading on it, he decided to let it ride for an hour before he made corrections. Then he would see what happened in the next hour.

Chapter 8

After an hour, Dandy increased power and adjusted his headings. At the end of the second timed hour, he found even more with which to be concerned. The variations had increased. He gave the new figures to Tom for an amended fuel consumption schedule. He also updated the crew on the situation.

The only one with any comment was Corky. "That ball-thing has a string on us and its reeling us in."

"How do you figure that?" inquired Candie.

"We've eliminated most of the other possibilities. Taran is fine....she has no navigational or power problems, so something has to be working against her. The only thing around is that ball. Our problems started when it appeared. It is getting closer because of that arc and our problems are getting bigger. Besides something is making our instruments go tic, tic, tic."

"What do you mean by 'string'?" asked Dandy. "That thing is too small to have a gravitational force big enough to affect us. Bea doesn't think it's a black hole or anything like that. I suppose it could be some sort of huge magnet."

Corky shrugged. "We're trying to find an answer in things we know. What happens if it is something we don't know? We've already found lots of things we can't explain with our basic Earth knowledge. This is just another of those things. We know what it does, so all we have to do is to figure out a way to undo it."

"Okay," said Dandy. "Let's just call it the string. How do we break the string? It is becoming apparent that even if we reach the jet ahead of the ball, we lose, because we will likely run out of fuel before we could get to someplace with water."

Tom offered, "To break a string you need to put more pressure on it. If we fired up to max for a short time, we might break it or get beyond its reach. On the other hand, we would really suck up the fuel. So, maybe that isn't such a good idea."

"I think we can assume that the ball is not a natural object. Some intelligence created it. The question is, 'Why?' What is its purpose? I don't think it is from around here."

"Why?" asked Candie.

"Well, for one reason it was putting out signals we were able to receive with our equipment. We aren't all that far from Earth. We could have been picking those up on Earth long ago. If this star system is inhabited by a space-going species, we should hear signs of it all over the place. I think we can rule out it being just a meteor or something on which someone crashed and he is sending out an SOS. It wouldn't be chasing us. My best guess would be that it is from somewhere else. Where that someplace else is, is a big question. Nothing there may be familiar to us.... not even basic physics."

The conversation continued for a long time. It seemed that it was more comfortable hashing and rehashing everything with the group than to be alone with one's own thoughts. Dandy wandered away from the discussion. He ended up with his ankles crossed up on the console and his fingers laced behind his head.

Finally, when Dandy sat upright everyone stopped talking. They waited for him to have his say. They needed him to give them a plan of action.

"We're not going to win this battle if we keep doing what we are doing. We are using too much fuel. We might be able to break away, but we will just drift until our supplies run out. I think it might become interesting if we challenge the forces that are apparently aligned against us. I propose we do a flip like we did with the Bip mother ship, using our engines to slow us down and eventually reverse directions. That will make our closing speed with the ball incredibly high. There will be our input, the speed of the ball and the drawing power of the string. At the last moment we sheer off and see if we can break the string. It would be sort of like using a gravitational sling shot. Also we can try using our anti-gravs. They had bad effects on the Bip ship. Maybe they might disrupt the ball, too. We would use only a fraction of the fuel needed to try outrunning it to the jet. If we can break away we can pick up some jet in the other direction. Our escape velocity ought to be really something. Any objections?"

No one offered any comments.

Dandy wanted to make the maneuver as soon as possible so that no one, including himself, had too much time to think about it. "Get ready. We flip in ten minutes."

There was a flurry of activity. Beatrice and Candie got Doughboy installed in his sling. Everything was quickly secured. The crew was at their stations well ahead of time.

Dandy cut the main engine. Using the thrusters, he carefully rotated the ship 180 degrees. He brought the main engine on line again. Gradually, he began increasing power. He had two forces working in his favor, the string and the retrofiring of the engine. Dandy had been prepared for an extended deceleration period. But he found Taran was slowing a lot faster than he had anticipated, which began causing Dandy further concerns. The string must be a lot more powerful than he had expected. Finally, the thrust became positive and the two objects were hurtling toward one another. Dandy set a course that would cause Taran to pass just astern of the ball as it was still in its arc.

Before the G forces started to rise again, Dandy gave everyone a break. They had been strapped in for hours. The Gs began growing into the uncomfortable zone. They had travelled incredibly faster than that, but they had not felt it while being in the Solar Jets. This time they were feeling it all. Their speed passed three Gs and continued to rise. At five Gs Dandy throttled back on the engine.

The ball was becoming larger and larger in their screens. For some reason they didn't seem to be able to properly focus in it. It started to appear fuzzy. Candie kept fussing with the adjustments as much as she could under the strain of their speed. They should have been able to get a much clearer picture of it. It was getting bigger by the moment. It still looked fuzzy.

Beatrice was suffering the most. She had the least physical presence of any of the crew. She couldn't move that much, but she was able to tell Candie to freeze a frame and then have the computer magnify. When the image appeared on the screen it was apparent it was not the image that was fuzzy, but the object. It filled their screen.

As they got closer, Candie froze another picture. It certainly didn't look like a ship of any kind. It was like a big tennis ball that had rolled through the weeds picking up pieces of twigs and leaves.

Dandy was ready to compensate in case the ball changed course or fired at them. He had no intention of exchanging paint as they almost had done with the Bip ship.

Suddenly Corky exclaimed in a strained voice, "It's an Ironmonger."

"A what?" grated Dandy.

"When my great-grandfather came from the old country he became an ironmonger. He collected scrap iron. I've seen pictures of his horse drawn wagon with pieces of scrap metal heaped on it. I'll bet that thing's a garbage scow picking space debris."

"Space debris? There isn't that much junk floating around in space," growled Tom.

"There must be where it came from."

"We're not space debris. Why is it picking on us?"

Dandy broke in. "I'll bet that transmission we received was a hail asking for a response. When we didn't answer it came after us."

Talking was difficult. Besides they were getting very close to whatever it was. Dandy had to concentrate on the controls. No one wanted to distract him at that moment.

The object filled their view screens. They weren't actually getting any closer than about fifty kilometers, but it looked much closer. Besides, at their speeds they could travel that far in less than a blink of an eye. The crew seemed to be holding their collective breath.

Then they were past. Candie was still keeping the cameras on the thing. When they passed, the light of the star illuminated the surface. Candie froze another view on the screen. From that distance and with the magnification she used, the surface was easily observed. Corky had been right. The thing was covered with carcasses of ships of all kinds. It was an incredible jumble of wreckage. It completely covered the surface of the object. There was no telling how deep the debris went.

"Look at all that technology," whispered Tom.

Dandy was busy checking his instrumentation. Now it was time to break the string. Once pasted the object, Taran's speed started to decline, which Dandy expected, so he revved up the engine to try maintaining all the speed he could muster even though the crew was suffering through an awful lot of pressure. The meters weren't giving him any solace. Even with the increase in thrust the speed continued to decrease. It was becoming apparent the attraction of the ball was greater up close. While they were still close to the object, Dandy turned on the anti-gravs. At maximum output, the A/Gs apparently interfered with the force that was pulling on them, but only slightly.

Dandy eased back on the engines until Taran was just holding their position. "We didn't break the string. Right now we can't resist the force without draining all our fuel and then we wouldn't be getting away. About the only thing we can do right now is try for a soft landing and live to fight another day."

Terror was beginning to steal into Beatrice's voice as she asked, "Are we going to crash?"

"Not if I can help it," grated Dandy. He suddenly had his hands full. He didn't want the distraction of having people problems. There was no decision to be made. Ironmonger was making it for them.

Dandy issued a series of quick, terse instructions. "Candie. Start looking for someplace flat to put down. It'd better be close. I don't know how much maneuverability we are going to have. Tom, monitor everything coming from that thing. Look for any signs of life, any EM sources, broadcasts, anything coming from it. Corky, get ready to shift our weight if you can. If we set down on an inclined plane I don't want to tip over. Use the maneuvering jets if necessary and transfer water about to maintain balance. Bea, don't take your eyes off those monitors. I want to know everything we can about that surface. You are our eyes. I want an analysis of everything under us."

Gradually Dandy eased off on the thrust. The string started drawing them back toward the Ironmonger.

Tom's voice was strained when he reported. "Whatever that force is, it is not coming from a single surface point, but it seems to be coming from the center of the ball itself."

"What makes you think so?" asked Candie.

"The debris seems to be uniformly distributed over the entire surface....not at just one or more points."

"You mean no one is pointing a ray gun at us?" queried Corky.

"Right."

"As far as I can see there are no open areas," reported Candie. "The entire surface is just stuff stacked on stuff. And some of that stuff is gigantic. Taran is minuscule compared to some of those ships....or at least what is left of those ships."

Dandy couldn't do much more than grunt. He was fighting the flow of the force. He had to keep the legs of Taran toward the surface. He wanted to ride his tail of flame clear to the surface so he would have the capability at least partially to control the landing. Also he had no idea of what might be waiting. The flame might cleanse an area for them. There could be aliens, creatures, disease, gases......anything.

"How about a lansding site?"

"Nothing looks appealing yet."

"It had better be quick. I'm having to waste a lot of fuel trying to hold her high enough to give us a choice."

Candie started to throw back a sharp response, but her glance at Dandy quenched that. He was bathed in perspiration. His hands were on the controls of both the engine and A/Gs, but his eyes were all over the board trying to keep track of everything. Instead she asked, "Can we sideslip one way or the other to get a look at different terrain?"

There was a lurch as Dandy laid the ship over a little and goosed it with the main engine. That little maneuver moved them several miles off to the side by the time Dandy got Taran vertical again to hold against the string.

"A little further in the same direction. I see something that may work," called the navigator.

Dandy wrestled Taran over, using the maneuvering jets.

"No. I'm sorry it's not what it appeared to be. There is nothing but piles of flimsy debris with canyons in between. Move us again."

Dandy complied, but each time he was dropping closer to the surface. The engine was roaring. It was really sucking the hydrogen and they weren't going anywhere.

The rest of the crew had the good sense not to intervene.

As gently as possible Candie said, "Move again."

As the pilot slipped the ship further along, Candie made an almost instantaneous assessment. "Further yet. Further. A little further. There! A little more and to the left. Look at the enormous ship. If you can get a little higher we should be able to land on it. It has large flat areas.

Dandy spotted what Candie had seen. He slipped Taran in that direction and also engaged the A/Gs and boosted the thrust on the main engine. Gradually they rose up over the lip of the alien structure. Candie was right. There were acres and acres of relatively smooth area. All he had to do is find a flat space so Taran wouldn't tip over.

He eased back on the engine. He didn't want to burn a hole in the structure like they had on the ice planet. There was a pretty level area between what looked like two gigantic platforms of some kind. Dandy inched his way there. Candie had reset all the external cameras so he could see as much as possible.

Taran began to wallow as Dandy eased in. He had the main engine on the closest thing to idle that he could get. The A/Gs poured out their power. Taran slued drunkenly. There was a great grinding sound as one of the legs struck metal. Dandy jabbed the controls. A great circle of the derelict's deck evaporated. Taran side slipped a couple/three hundred yards away.

Tom yelled, "Can it hold our weight?"

Beatrice countered, "We don't weigh as much here."

On the sideslip, Dandy cut the engine and brought the full power of the A/Gs on line. Corky righted the ship with thrusters. Contact was made with the alien ship with a great grinding and gnashing of the two bodies. Actually, the A/Gs were having very little effect, but they did ease Taran at the right moment. Because of its broad stance the ship came to rest without the threat of tipping over. The surfaces weren't perfectly flat, but it was within tolerable limits.

Dandy was saturated with sweat. For that matter, beads of perspiration were sticking out on several foreheads. No one spoke. There was the familiar hum of the machinery for Taran. But it was periodically punctuated with great groans of stressed metals. Occasionally, the vessel would lurch as if punching through the alien deck.

Dandy let out a sigh and then launched into a series of orders. "Candie. Find out what is happening to Ironmonger's direction and speed. Try to figure out where we are headed."

"Tom and Corky. Start determining what is outside. How much gravity, if any, do we have? That force doesn't seem to work on organic matter or we would probably be crushed. Are there any gases out there...oxygen, methane, what? Any radiation? We need to know everything that is out there. There may even be some form of life. We might not be the only ones that were sucked in.

"Beatrice. Check the results as the guys get them. See if you can put them together into some sort of picture to tell us what we are up against."

Everybody....Always keep your eyes open for water, ice or hydrogen. If there is no emergency we will meet in the Fish House in an hour to discuss the situation."

Chapter 9

It was a tense, subdued crew that met in the Fish House an hour later. Everyone got something to drink or eat. Turning to Candie, Dandy started the discussion going. "What is happening to Ironmonger?"

"After it sucked us in, it just flattened out its arc. It is just continuing on the random setting that resulted when it brought its rudder back amidships....so to speak. It doesn't appear to have any particular course in mind. We are headed generally in the direction of Earth. The speed had been constant since we first spotted her. I still think there must be some sort of propulsion involved."

Dandy looked at Tom. "We are sitting on a treasure house of alien technology," said Tom. "From what I can see of that which is around us and what we taped while coming down, there is virtually nothing the same. Everything looks unique. It is obviously junk from space-faring civilizations. This could be the accumulation of millennia. I would imagine it is time-graded, with the oldest on the bottom and each new advance stacked on the top. Also I have noted signs of incredible damage that indicates to me that much of this is the debris left over from wars."

Tom was obviously getting excited, but after a glance around the table he could see that was not the subject of interest at the moment. He gave a little embarrassed shrug and got into the more pressing subject of the moment. "This thing is only about an eighth the size of our moon, but it has nearly the same gravity. I would suspect that is because of density. Whatever that force was that brought us here is not the same as gravity even though it would seem so by the way it pulled Taran. You and I are subject to gravity, but that force did not seem to touch us. It looks like it works on types of metal.

"With our limited testing equipment, I didn't find any noxious gasses present in any great quantities. That is not to say that there is something here that we don't even know about on our world. All of our known metals seem to be represented here, but again I can't test for anything with which we are not familiar.

"There seems to be quite a bit of free oxygen floating around out there....not enough to sustain life, but you wouldn't die immediately from lack of oxygen. Of course, something else might get you. Oh, there is a little background radiation, but nothing serious enough to cause us a problem."

Tom quit speaking and nodded to Corky, who continued. "One of the strange things seems to be the temperatures. Of course, we burned a hole in the surface of this ship under us. We may have filled the thing with heat because our exterior temperature readings don't correspond with what you would expect on a space body. Ordinarily you'd expect temperatures like what we experienced when we were waltzing around on Nacho, but it is only just below freezing. As I said, that could be due to the heat our engine generated when we came in. We can check temperatures periodically to see how fast it is going down. Of course, we are on the lighted side of Ironmonger. Maybe the thing has an internal heat source that would account for readings. Right now I just don't know."

"How's our footing?" inquired Dandy

"We seem to be pretty steady. We burned that hole but it was not as large as the first one. This one we can straddle. We dented in the hull when we came in, but it seems to be holding, We've quit groaning for the most part."

Everyone's eyes swung to Beatrice. Dandy put the question to her. "What can you infer from what we know?"

Most people seem to get nervous when they are called on to perform or speak or put their ego on the line, but when Beatrice was put in a position to use her mind, all of her timidity disappeared. "I think we can be safe in saying that Ironmonger is not from around here. It must have come in with Doughboy. We just assumed that when Doughboy first appeared he had just left his own domain. He may have made the move at the same time our energy target was discovered. It apparently came from nowhere. When Doughboy appeared again, it brought Ironmonger closer. As we speculated before, its mission is probably to pick up space debris that could be a considerable hazard to navigation by advanced spacefarers. When we didn't respond to its hail, it must have figured we're derelict. It changed course and came to collect us. Once that was done, it just continued to plow through space looking for more junk. There must be a computer-like something, somewhere, to guide its operation.

"I would agree it is ages old. However, it is probably not serviced regularly, so it has to have some form of replenishable energy and some sort of auto diagnostic routine and auto repair that keeps it going.

"I would suspect that this was originally a solid metallic meteorite that has been worked over. That would account for the gravity on such a small body. Since the debris appears to be pretty evenly divided on the object, the whole body must radiate the force field that drew us in....not just certain focused points.

"From what we saw coming in, there are a lot of ships that I would judge to be warships. They show signs of damage one would expect from an exchange of fire. The one we're on shows little damage other than the couple of holes we punched in her." Beatrice stopped to smile at Dandy for a moment. She was not above getting in her own little jab once in a while.

"That would tend to indicate that wherever Ironmonger is from, the inhabitants are engaged in some sort of galactic war.

One country doesn't build spaceships to fight with its neighbor. Nor would Earth build a ship as large as the one on which we sit to handle some dispute with Mars.

"Tom is right. This is a real treasure trove.....but it appears it is rather like a Venus Fly Trap. I would say there are all sorts of hazards out there. The temperature is not cold like space, but it is cold enough to freeze anything. That includes alien bodies, animals, insects, spores....you name it. There are probably a multitude of diseases floating around out there to which we have no immunity. In fact, there are probably creatures roaming around out there that can live in that low temperature and low oxygen level. Some may not breathe oxygen at all.

"There is probably little or no deterioration of anything due to the low temps and gas levels. Ancient things would not have rusted away. Certain things may fail due to their own built-in time schedule, like certain plastics, but generally I would not expect that to be the case.

"I would think there are all sorts of supplies out there including water, which of course would be ice now. I would suspect water to be a rather universal item."

Beatrice settled back down and took a drink of her cold tea. She made a face and got up to get a fresh cup.

Now it was Dandy's turn. Everyone was expecting him to get them out of this and back on their way home. He began, "Maybe all this isn't as bad as it seemed at first. We knew we were probably going to have to find more fuel. This may be our refueling station. That is our first priority. We need fuel to keep us alive and fuel to get us back to Earth.

"Then we need to find a way to get off this thing. We now know we can't run against Ironmonger's force field, so we have to find another way. Off the top of my head, two possibilities come to mind. We can try to disable the force field or possibly we can find the answer to the hail so we can lift off without activating the force. There may be other ways to accomplish the same end, so everyone give it some consideration.

"Thirdly, we should take advantage of this opportunity to

collect as much technology as we can get. At the moment, this phase takes a back seat to the first two items, but don't pass up anything that presents itself.

"Now to accomplish our objective of getting home, we need first to secure ourselves. We don't know what is out there. I want to take at least two days just to observe our surroundings. Fortunately, we are on the lighted side, so we can see what is out there. Instead of just one on duty at a time, I want two present at all times. I want to monitor everything that might be going on. At the same time, someone must be watching the monitors for any external activity. As Bea says, we don't know what is out there. I want external microphones activated over the sound system. Any time there is a sound, I want it identified as to location and source if possible. Keep our sensors working to try to ascertain what gases and metals are out there.

"Tom, do you think our shuttles will operate here?"

There was a period of silence before Tom answered. "I would think they would function on a very low level of performance. There is not enough gravity to get much punch out of A/Gs. It may lift the craft slowly. As long as that force field is not active we should be able to use its main engine. The thrusters could probably maneuver it somewhat."

Turning to Candie he said, "Please make a map on a grid system. Place on it the various landmarks we can identify. We will need something for reference so we can find our way around out there. We'll extend the map as more information becomes available.

"Corky, we need some way to decontaminate, so we don't drag in things we don't want. Can you figure out something down on the lower level? We have to be as economical as possible, but not so much we compromise our safety."

To the group generally, "I want everyone to get the rest you need, but when you are not sleeping, be at your stations. There will be a work schedule, but we need a maximum effort from all."

Chapter   10

When Dandy made out the work routine, he scheduled Beatrice for the first rest. Everyone else had immediate projects. Her value would be later, to analyze and then record what the others had discovered. Instead of going to her room, she just snuggled down in her flight couch with her music from home.

Four hours later, when Beatrice roused, she suddenly remembered Doughboy whom they had put in his sling during the wild ride to Ironmonger. She unfastened the sling and stripped it away. When Doughboy unfolded Beatrice keyed the intercom, "Hey, everybody. Look at Doughboy."

He had fashioned himself into a reasonable facsimile of a human form. He had two legs, two arms and a knob for a head. Also he had discovered the bone structure. He was flexible where joints should be and rigid where the bones took over. His feet and hands were still pretty rudimentary, but he gradually got himself in an upright, standing position with a lot of aid from the couch. Although there was still a long ways to go, he was working on it.

Candie gave him a critical look. She asked Beatrice, "Are you sure Doughboy is a male?"

"Oh, yes. He is definitely male."

"Then, Dandy, you had better take him aside and show him what boys look like."

"What do you mean?" inquired Dandy.

"Well, he's trying to develop breasts."

Everyone got a good laugh out of that, which broke much of the tension that had been mounting over their situation.

For the next couple of days, everyone was working furiously trying to find out all they could about their current habitat.

Candie was assembling a map of the immediate surroundings. She was finding artistic talents she never knew she possessed. Instead of using regular cartographic symbols to depict the landscape, she had to rely on her ability to draw superstructures of alien space craft as significant terrain features. Fortunately, recordings had been taken during the descent. She was able to extend the maps far beyond what was visible from Taran as she sat on a gigantic space hulk.

Corky reported he had turned the elevator into a decontamination chamber. It was already sealed to act as an air lock. He had just added a water bath from the reserve tanks. The effluent was piped directly into the conversion chamber. No known contaminants could survive the molecular breakdown into hydrogen and oxygen. Nothing would be wasted.

Of all the crew, Tom was most attuned to the vagaries of noises of Taran. Being an engineer, he was always aware of how things sounded. In many instances, sound was the early warning of an impending problem.

Near the end of the second day, Tom stopped by Dandy's station. He started out by saying, "I can't prove it, but there is something out there."

"What do you mean by 'something'? What makes you think so? We have been watching for any movement, but so far no one has been able to see a thing."

"It's not seeing, but hearing, I know all the sounds of the ship.

I have been able to assimilate the sounds connected with Taran and the alien ship....the creaking and groaning. But there is something else. It is more of a 'swishing sound' than a metallic sound. It doesn't belong here."

"Where is this sound coming from? Do you have any idea?"

"It sounds like it is coming from all around us. It's not from the surface. It is more like coming from the hull itself."

Dandy turned to his console. He sounded the conference chime. To TC he announced, "We are going to do a little self diagnosis. So far we have not wanted to advertise ourselves, so we have been using star light for external illumination. However, that creates a lot of deep shadows which might be hiding a herd of elephants. I am going to activate all external cameras and direct them at the hull. Then I am going to flip on all the external lights. I will watch screen number one. Tom has two...on around the flight deck. Candie, you will have to try watching the last two. Sound off if you see anything. If I don't hear anything immediately, I will go to the next set of cameras."

When TC had settled in, Dandy threw the switch. Intense light blossomed on all screens.

"There," shouted Corky. All eyes darted to their third screen.

"I don't see anything," said Tom.

"Nor I," reported Candie.

"It was more like a shadow than a thing, up against left side of number four leg. It was up on the leg....not the bottom. It was only there for an instant."

Dandy said, "Watch your screens." The pilot changed cameras to other views of the underside of Taran. No one sounded off. He switched to still other cameras high on the exterior of the hull. The surface wasn't lighted, but there was a background of illumination from the underside lights.

"There! On six," hissed Candie, as if she were afraid she would scare it away.

"I didn't see anything. What was it?" asked Bea.

"I don't know. It was long and skinny like a gigantic Praying Mantis...stick-like and as fast as lightning. It looked like it was skittering along the surface of Taran. It disappeared over the curve in the hull."

"Was it an insect?" Bea was in her information gathering mode. Nothing could faze her now.

"I wouldn't say it was an insect. It just is similar to something we all recognize. It's like Bea's abalone and chicken example. It just reminded me of a Praying Mantis because it was long and skinny, but I don't know what it is."

"I don't want to leave the lights on too long," said Dandy. "Now we know there is something out there. It appears that whatever is there may be skittish in light. I'm going to turn the lights off for a while. We'll try again later. We need to get the cameras working because it appears to be too fast to really observe."

Candie noted, "We had two observations. Did we see two or the same one twice?"

Bea was still taking notes, "How long was it?"

"There wasn't anything to give it scale, but if pressed I'd say the impression I had was that it was about four feet long."

Corky broke in, "I think a more pressing question is how does it run across a sloping surface of smooth durathane? If it can climb over the outer surface, then it could get in our engine vents. That could cause havoc with our propulsion system. I don't think we closed the doors after landing."

Dandy snapped to. He started manipulating switches. One of the screens showed images from an articulated camera as Dandy brought it to bear on the snout of the main engine, Things were pretty dark because he was using only the weak star light. There was movement. He started the cameras recording before he flipped on the floods. There was a flurry of activity as a host of creatures fled the lights. They raced along the under surfaces of the ship or launched themselves into space. They were gone on an instant.

Dandy left his station, calling for Tom and Corky. "Candie,

keep an eye on the monitors to see what happens when we get to banging around down there. Bea, look at those tapes. Tell us all you can about our guests." The three men took the elevator down to the engine room. Tom set to work checking all the engine systems. Corky was making sure there was atmosphere and artificial gravity in the fourth level. If anything was not in order, they would have to don their pressure suits.

Everything seemed to be working. Dandy turned on surveillance camera and the lights. Nothing moved. "Everything looks all right," ventured Dandy. "Let's go take a look."

"Let's not get in a hurry," said Corky as he headed for one of his storage areas. Shortly he emerged, toting three shotguns and a box of shells. "I think we should have some way of protecting ourselves. Those things may be pussy cats or they could bite like a cobra. I don't think anyone here is a good enough shot to hit one of those skinny things with a slug, so let's try bird shot. Now don't go shooting at the engine or either of the shuttles. The durathane walls can stand the blast but the machinery can't."

Cautiously, the trio moved out of the elevator into the fourth deck. A careful inspection revealed nothing out of the ordinary. Once satisfied that there was nothing in the bay, they turned their attention to the inspection ports. There were four ports with external covers. On the inside was a thick, heat-proof glass, which permitted viewing of the nozzles of the great engine.

Each guy took a port, which he opened mechanically instead of using the noisy electric motors. It was very dim in the chamber surrounding the rocket nozzles. Dandy couldn't see anything. Corky said he was clear. Tom didn't say anything.

Finally Tom said, "I can't be sure. Come here and take a look at this."When Dandy and Corky joined him he pointed, upward. "There is a little maintenance shelf just above us. I am getting the impression there is something on the platform, which is made of expanded metal. It looks like something is blotting out the light against the walls of the shaft."

Corky volunteered. "I can throw enough light through my port so you can see whether anything is really there. The light might clear out the shaft. They seem to be afraid of bright light."

Shortly Corky was back with a heavy duty work light. Tom and Dandy put their noses to their respective ports. When the light came on Tom yelled, "There they are! They are milling around. It appears they are afraid to go past the light."

"Can you tell what they are?" asked Corky.

"I don't know what they are, but I can tell you they look like incredibly thin monkeys. The bodies are like match sticks and the limbs are like toothpicks. There is a little triangle for a head. They have hair all over them. It looks like they have a mane. No, a mane just moved. It is an offspring. I can see four figures, all with little ones wrapped around their parents' necks. It looks like a nursery."

"We can't afford to have a nursery in our propulsion system. Any ideas on how to get them out?" asked Dandy.

Corky speculated, "If we eliminate the light that seems to frighten them, they may leave. We could pound on the sides of the housing above them. That may drive them out. There is some air out there, so a little sound will travel. Besides, they can probably feel the vibrations in the metal."

Dandy knew that Candie was keeping track of them over the intercom. "Candie. It appears we have at least four adults in residence. Watch to see how many come out when we bang on the housing."

"Okay."

When all was ready Dandy whacked the housing smartly a number of times with a large pipe. Inside, the sound was deafening. Outside, it probably wasn't much, but it seemed to do the job.

"Four, six, eight," counted Candie. "If there are any more they aren't coming out."

The guys spent some more time trying to flood the shaft with as much light as possible. When no more came out, they retracted the thruster nozzles and closed the iris door under the housing.

When the guys got back onto the flight deck they got something to drink before grouping around Beatrice. She showed single frames of various creatures. She started enumerating her thoughts. "It would appear we have a species of what we would term 'rodent'. They look like elongated monkeys. Their extreme length is probably attributable to development in a very low gravity situation....maybe here on this, whatever you call it. They are probably a warm blooded creature...or whatever passes as blood...since they probably could not function in this temperature if they were cold blooded. We are on the sun side of Ironmonger and the temperature is just below freezing. On the shadow side, it would have to be lower. Because Ironmonger is not a natural phenomenon, the sun side can become the shadow side every time Ironmonger chases something. These creatures couldn't migrate to the sun that fast. They have a heavy hair-like covering over their entire bodies probably to conserve heat. I call them rodents because from the size of the knob we would refer to as a head there isn't much brain capacity possible. Of course, the brain might reside elsewhere, but I doubt it.

"What we would call hands and feet appear to be present on them, but the two look almost identical. They can't do too much because they don't have opposing digits like our thumb. The 'fingertips' are huge, which leads me to believe they are used primarily for sticking to surfaces. That would explain their seeming to walk on vertical surfaces. Claws wouldn't work on the hull.

"I would say that the reason we have a nursery in our propulsion system is heat. Mothers with infants would seek warmth. Just from radiated energy, the interior of the tube is several degrees higher than the surface. Ironmonger obviously generates its own heat or the surface temperature would be the same as any celestial body a long way from the sun.

"I haven't yet seen any mouth, nose, or ear formations. There are large eye-like structures, apparently designed for low light situations. That could account for their aversion to bright lights. It probably hurts. They may be like fish with no eyelids. I suspect they have a mouth which is adapted to scraping lichens and various other types of such growth. Ironmonger is probably a virtual forest of such stuff. I would suggest that there are samples of such growth from multitudes of planets from the looks of all the debris we have been able to see. Those life-forms can hitch a ride anywhere."

Dandy cut in. "Do you think it possible that they constitute any hazard to us?"

"I can't see that they would constitute any physical hazard to one of us. In our gravity, one would weigh about the same as a small cat if they are formed like we are. If they had hollow bones like a bird they would be much lighter. However, that doesn't mean they are harmless. Candie guessed they were about four feet long. I would say that is about right if one measures from feet to top of the head. Then there would be the length of the arms. It would appear they can stand upright, but normally they would run on all fours like a lizard. Their rear limbs splay out at the hips so they can get down on their bellies, if that is where the belly is, on the ground.

"Beyond size and weight they still could constitute a hazard. They could bite. They may have retracted claws, which could tear or they may be venomous. They could spit poison like the African rattle snake. Body fluids could be corrosive. Until we find out, we had better be careful.

"Oh, one other thing that may place them somewhere else other than a rodent category is that they appear to have one offspring at a time. Rodents and various other lower species have large litters. Either this thing doesn't have any natural enemies or it can defend itself."

Dandy raised his eyebrows as he looked at the other members. "Well," he said, "I think that about covers it." Everybody laughed. Beatrice was pleased with herself.

Candie said, "Oh, there is one other thing that hasn't been covered. What do we call them?"   Everyone immediate turned to Corky.

"Pretzis, of course. Don't they look like Pretzels?"

That brought more laughs, which Dandy was glad to see.

Chapter 11

Dandy's main concern remained to find water. They needed water to exist whether they got off Ironmonger or not. According to his knowledge of chemistry, water was a pretty universal thing....at least wherever life was found. Taran was sitting on remains of worlds-worth of life. He just had to find what should obviously be there.

Then there came the problem of transporting it. Undoubtedly it would be in the form of ice. They were going to have to rig up conveying devices. Decisions would have to be made to try transferring it either in a solid or liquid form.

Candie had been doing a magnificent job of mapping what they could see from their high vantage point on the hull of their space-giant platform. Suddenly Dandy's mental horizon brightened. A thought was rising: they were already sitting on the largest ship they had been able to find. It also should have the largest supply of stores, which would include water.

Getting into a spaceship could be a problem because spaceships are normally tightly sealed, unless they were blown open by combat or by accident. However, Taran had burned a neat hole in the behemoth beneath them. They had made their own entry port.

Dandy selected the articulated camera closest to the center of the hole. Directing it into the pit, he could see nothing."Corky, do you suppose you can lower a light into that hole from one of the shuttle bays?"

"Sure. We'll have to lower a ramp. We can use the winch on the pickup. But what about our furry friends?"

"We're going to have to learn to deal with those guys one of these days," replied Dandy. "We can try to keep them away with bright light. Maybe we can keep them at bay with some of Bea's music."

That brought an ugly face from Beatrice, which brought more chuckles.

Dandy continued, "We can monitor the area with the camera. One of us can stand guard with a shotgun if nothing else works. This will have to be done ¹in pressure suits. We'll start as soon as Corky can rig up a lamp. Make it bright and shielded on the top so it doesn't blind us or the cameras."

"I'll anchor the pickup to the ramp so it can't be pulled off. I can make an arm with a pulley to run the line over the edge. Also, we had better make provisions to cut that line in case it gets fouled or something falls on it," said Tom.

A couple of hours later, Tom was at the head of the ramp with a shotgun. Corky was in the pickup operating the winch while Dandy, who was tethered to pickup, guided the lamp into the abyss. Candie was monitoring other cameras for movement, while Beatrice was giving a running account of what the camera was seeing in the hole, which was virtually nothing,

"All I can see is melted metal and charred whatever. We are not getting anything useful," declared Beatrice. "We have to be able to see laterally."

"Okay," said Dandy, who from his perch could see nothing of value. "Candie, send one of the remote cameras down in the elevator. Don't forget there is a vacuum in that elevator."
When Dandy told Corky to pull in the light, Corky advised him,

for information's sake, that there was 300 feet of line out.

It took a little doing, but finally they attached the camera just above the light. Again, they slowly lowered the apparatus into the hole. It kept rotating back and forth. Finally Dandy figured out a way to swing it slowly one way and then reverse the strain on the cord to make it track the other way. Beatrice was always yelling at them to go slower. Dandy couldn't really see much. From the way he was tied off, he could only see about half of the hole. He was looking down on melted or burned material. All he could see was devastation.

Finally, Beatrice announced that it looked as if they had reached the bottom of the hole. She wanted Dandy to very slowly rotate the camera in a complete circle. Once that was done, she had the camera slowly lifted. On several occasions, she wanted the camera rotated as it had been at the bottom.

When the line was retrieved, Dandy had Candie scan the area for Pretzis. Neither she nor Tom saw anything, so the bay was closed. They gave everything a thorough inspection just the same.

"You know we had over 850 feet of line out and we weren't even close to the middle," said Corky. "What do you suppose they used a ship of that size for?"

All Dandy could think of to say was, "Mind boggling isn't it?" Besides he didn't really want to get involved in a conversation at the moment. Working in a pressure suit was a draining experience. He just wanted to get out of that stinky thing and relax for a bit.

Later, TC sat at their stations as Beatrice started the images from the pit. "One thing we neglected to do was to use some sort of scale so we could have a better estimate of relative sizes. I will tell you one thing. Everything is huge. I would guess that the occupants of this ship could have been as much as 12 feet tall. They must have been broad too, judging by the size of the passageways and the doors.

"There isn't too much detail left. Everything that could burn, did. In certain areas there are frames that look like they came from furniture. They are big. Instrumentation is high on the walls."

Not too much was distinguishable in the burned out mess. The images were somewhat blurry because of the movement of the camera, which had used a set focus.

Beatrice continued, "About midway down there is a gigantic room. I would suspect it is a dining room. It is full of what appear to be tables bolted in place and a lot of small debris, which could be eating utensils. The light didn't penetrate to the end of the room." Beatrice just let the rest of the crew view the camera's findings.

"Another guess is that it will be difficult to move around in that ship. The doors appear to open in the middle, by sliding into the walls. They probably were powered. Most of the doors are closed. I would doubt if you could open one by hand due to the size and probably weight. Also they are at awkward angles. There should be access tunnels between floors for pipes, lines, etc. It may be easier to travel through them."

"Oh, yes. One other thing. Everything looks so badly melted or burned. But think of how hot our exhaust was. Any of our materials would have vaporized. I doubt if we can burn through with any of our torches."

Dandy was beginning to squirm. He didn't like anything that he was hearing. He had assumed they could wander around in the ship, scrounging whatever they needed or found of interest.

As Beatrice wound down, the crew turned to Dandy for direction. His first question was for Candie, "From your observations in making the map of the area surrounding Taran have you come up with any indication of which is fore and which is aft on this ship?"

"From what we can see from here, I would guess the front is toward the Sun. I'm confused about which way is up. I had thought it was that way." She nodded her head off to the left. "But, from the looks of the floor in the burned out section we are sitting on the top."

Dandy cut in. "Good, now we've got a general idea of what is out there. We need to start some positive action directed to getting us off of this thing. I see two obvious avenues of attack. If that is a mess hall down there, there should be a kitchen or bathroom in the near vicinity. If water is a necessity of life wherever this thing came from, then it should be piped to that vicinity. Tracing the plumbing back may get us to some storage tanks we can raid."

"The second item is locating the bridge. Getting there on the inside may be impossible, according to what Bea figures. So we will try some exterior recon using the pickup. Tom feels it will function minimally, but function. We will see how much capability it has and then try to record the exterior surface and surrounding debris as we look for the control room from the outside. I would think there is some visual, exterior indication that will pinpoint it. Remember, we spotted the control room on Bip ship. Then we might have a time trying to get in, but let's find it first. We need an answer to that message Ironmonger kept sending us. If we can't find that, then we will have to try figuring out a way of disabling this scow."

Corky was waving a finger in the air. "We ought to use the sport car for the survey. We don't know for sure that the shuttles will fly here. The pickup has the winch. We can tether the pickup and send the other out for a trial run. If something happens, the pickup can reel it back in. Besides, I can rig up a cage for the pickup winch to lower someone down to the mess hall."

"Now we're getting somewhere," said Dandy as he rubbed his hands together. For the next couple of hours, plans were considered. The TC broke for a meal. Afterward everyone got busy on assigned projects.

Chapter   12

On the exterior exploration, Corky would fly the shuttle and Candie would do the survey. When they found the bridge they would map its location and also try to confirm that it was indeed the bridge.

However, it was finally decided that finding water took preference. The chances of locating water in the vicinity of the bridge did not seem likely. Tom and Dandy were to be the ones to scout the interior of the ship. Corky would operate the winch. Candie was to handle the shotgun in case any Pretzis got curious. As usual Beatrice would be in the control room recording everything.

Everyone was very jumpy when they were putting on their pressure suits. It had been a grand adventure to land on Nacho, the Bips ship, when they thought it was a derelict. When they discovered it was occupied, they didn't have time to get scared. Things just happened. But this was different. There was what amounted to a small, alien world out there. They couldn't even begin to understand what hazards they might encounter. They probably wouldn't even recognize the really dangerous ones. There was a real possibility they might never be able to break away to resume their journey home to let Earth know what was coming their direction.

When they got onto the elevator, the die was cast. The pressure in the elevator was reduced to match the exterior air pressure. They were on their individual breathing system, which had three hours of life in each. Everything was ready. The pickup ramp was lowered. Dandy and Tom climbed into the cage. Corky picked up the weight on the boom he had fashioned. The cage swung out over the abyss. On Dandy's signal, the winch began to play out line. Descent was purposely rapid to conserve air. They stopped at the mess hall level. Being lowered off the end of the ramp put them much closer to one edge of the hole, but there was still probably thirty feet out into space. They were prepared for that. On the third try, Tom's grappling hook attached to a substantial support. Corky let out line so they could pull themselves to the edge, where they tied off the cage.

The light attached to the cage illuminated everything. But the ship's interior still looked gloomy, because everything was charred or, at least singed. Both men moved very carefully. They weren't used to low gravity. Both had experienced no gravity, but this was different. They would have to learn how much energy to expend to accomplish a task.

They found themselves about a third of the way down a gigantic room. Away from the hole that Taran had burned, there were rows upon rows of built-in tables and stools. It looked like old-fashioned picnic tables with attached stools instead of benches. Since there were stools on both sides of each table it was probably as Beatrice had speculated, a mess hall as opposed to some sort of lecture hall.

As they moved out of the devastated area Dandy hopped up on one of the stools. He felt as if he was sitting on a high-chair as he had done as a tiny child. Twelve feet seemed to be a reasonable estimate of the aliens' height.

Each of them kept flicking his light around to make sure nothing was lurking nearby. They would have liked to have brought pistols, but in a pressure suit they couldn't handle them. The best thing Corky had come up with was some high powered flares that could easily be struck. The flares would seriously intimidate anything but an asbestos-plated armadillo. They also would provide some sort of defense against Pretzis, should the stick figures turn out to be a danger.   About   midway   down the cavernous room, they found a series of large openings in the wall. For the record, Dandy slowly panned the area with his helmet camera. "This reminds me of the handout window in the cafeteria back in college."

They really couldn't tell what was in there, because the counter was about six feet high. Further on down the wall they found an opening that had a partial door. There was a space at both the top and the bottom. Dandy dropped to his knees so he could see under the door. "Yeah, this looks like a kitchen or at least a food dispensing location. It is in much better shape than out here. Let's have a look."

Both men ducked under the door. The huge room was littered with what could have been beverage and food containers. Tom picked one up. "These are a lot lighter than they look like they should be....some kind of alloy. "On the way back, I'm going to pick one up for testing."He tossed it back to the floor.

Dandy stopped. He flipped a switch on his control pad. Then he kicked some of the floor litter . "Hey, turn on your exterior audio. There is enough atmosphere out there so sound travels. Before, we've always used these suits in a total vacuum."

After the two got their volumes adjusted, they started in search of water pipes. Everything was so high that seeing on top of counters was difficult. They found that in the light gravity they could hop up for a quick look, provided they kicked a clear area so they wouldn't twist an ankle when they came down.

Finally, Tom sounded off. "Look at this machine. It looks like a huge, old world cappuccino machine. It appears to be plumbed in."

To get a closer look, they piled debris high enough to clamber onto the counter top. Approximately a four-inch pipe came from the ceiling to a valve on the side of the machine. It looked like a filling mechanism. Of course, the valve wouldn't turn. They opened side access doors.

Tom studied the mechanism for some time. "I'm sure this is

some type of beverage machine. The liquid comes down this pipe into a tank. I presume it is heated before it flows across a black substance which is about the same size and looks like a concrete block. There is about half a block still there. Then it flows into the holding tank at the bottom. That must hold well over two hundred gallons. From the wiring it appears to be a heated container."

"How can we tell if it's water?" asked Dandy

"We can't be sure until we take a sample back for testing."

"Then we need a sample from above that black block."

"If there is anything there, it'll be frozen."

Dandy motioned Tom aside. "Get a sample container ready to hand me." Dandy unfastened a flare from his belt. When he struck it there was a burst of light. Clearly audible sounds of flight came pounding through their external pickups. Both Dandy and Tom flashed their lights about, but there was nothing to be seen.

He thrust the flare under a spigot. He moved the heat around the bottom and the spout. Finally a wisp of steam appeared. Then a drop formed. Shortly there was a slight trickle. Dandy quickly filled his sample vile, which he handed back to Tom to seal. Dandy had gotten some of the liquid on his glove. He watched very closely to see if there was any reaction. He was relieved to see no obvious hazard, such as acid eating its way through.

After the pair had gotten back to the floor, Dandy called Beatrice, who was recording everything. "Bea, did you pick up the sound of thrashing about when I lighted the flare?"

"Yes."

"Could you tell how many sources or anything about them?"

"No, but there were several distinct patterns of activity."

"Well, I hope they were Pretzis and nothing new."

To Tom, "Let's see if we can trace that line." The pipe went along the ceiling where it tied into another pipe. They followed the plumbing along without much difficulty because it was on the surface. They passed into two other rooms. One had all the looks of a food preparation area. Tom poked his light into another room.

"It looks like they have KP even on alien ships." He was looking at what appeared to be a dish washing facility, except the dishes looked like over-grown frisbees....more like garbage can lids. In the corner of that room the pipe connected to a much larger vertical one that went through the ceiling and the floor.

"This is about as far as we can trace it without going back to the hole and either going up or down," said Tom.

Bea cut into their conversation. "It's time for you to come back. Your air supply is at 50%. So far we don't have any reading as to the safety of Ironmonger's air."

As Dandy and Tom made their way back through the cavernous hulk, there wasn't much conversation. Dandy was trying to reconcile what he was seeing with the various possible scenarios that could put such a great ship in a scrap heap. One thing that was bothering him was that there were few useable items. There were huge quantities of broken objects scattered about but the interior he'd seen showed no signs of suffering any structural damage.

Tom picked up the container he'd spotted on the way in. "I'll bet this is some sort of disposable beverage container like we use to bottle milk or soda. There could be tons of these stored away somewhere. No matter what they contain, we could probably recycle them into usable form. I rather doubt that we will find one big reservoir of water. It is probably scattered in smaller tanks throughout the ship because of weight distribution and use requirements. There should be a lot of it unless the ship was just returning from a long voyage."

"If we can raise the temperature a few degrees, we can pump water instead of handling ice as we did on that comet," said Dandy just as he stopped abruptly, nearly causing Tom to run over him. They had just entered the room where the cage was tied off to the edge of the burned hole. The cage was gently swinging in the center of the hole. The rope and grapple were gone.

"Bea," called Dandy. "Have you noticed any activity down here? We're not alone."

"No. Outside of those sounds you asked about earlier, I've noted nothing."

Both Dandy and Tom started swinging their light beams about, but nothing was visible.

"Mr. Engineer, do you have any idea how we're going to get that cage back over here?"

"I'll have to take that question under advisement," said Tom.

"Don't take too long, you don't have much air left," said Bea.

Tom shook his head inside his helmet. "I can't recall anything long enough to reach it,"

"Nor I."

"There's probably some sort of electrical or optic wiring in those conduits, but I don't think we can get into the pipes to see."

"Corky," called Dandy. "The cage is hanging straight down in the tube. It's about 30 feet away. Something took the grapple and rope."

"I can pull the cage up and send Candie down with ...."

Corky's comments were interrupted by a blast from the 12 gauge shotgun. The sound reverberated around in the hole through the alien ship with echoes returning from all directions.

A series of events happened in quick succession. "Damn," yelled Candie. "I hit it. A Pretzi just tried to come up the ramp."

Both Dandy and Tom were attracted by the sound coming down the tube. They turned just in time to see a stick-figure drop down the tube. And across the gaping hole there was some screeching and thrashing around. At the far end of the enormous room was an open door. A shape dodged across the doorway. "That's not Pretzi," said Tom.

"And there's more than just one," said Dandy. "Did you get

enough of a look to see what we're dealing with?"

"No, it was just a shape, but it wasn't a twig-figure. It was more on the proportions of a teddy bear. It wasn't tall enough to be one of the crew on this ship if the size of those tables and stools are any indication."

"Bea, did either of our cameras pick up enough to give us an image of our new visitor?"

Wham. "We've got Pretzis all over the place," yelled Candie.

"Keep'em out," said Dandy. "Corky, can you close the ramp enough that they can't come in?"

"Not until you get back in. The arm is in the way."

Bea injected herself. "You only have about 15 minutes of air left. Candy, you too."

"I've got more air left because I haven't been exerting myself. I've got enough to go down and throw a rope to the guys."

"What about the Pretzis?" said Beatrice.

Wham, Wham. "Damn I hate shooting those little things."

"Heads up," said Tom. "We've got company." Across the hole, a solo figure slowing moved out into full view.

Dandy hit it with the beam of his light. The creature jumped either in fright or because of a defensive instinct. But, apparently it decided the light wouldn't hurt it. Dandy centered the beam on the figure and held still so his camera could get a sharp image.

The figure took a couple of slow steps forward. It was hard to distinguish any features or even the body shape because it appeared to be covered with layer upon layer of clothing.

"Bea, can you see any weapons?"

"Nothing I can recognize, but there are a lot of things dangling from its clothes."

"Is it wearing any type of breathing device?"

"I really can't tell what I'm seeing. There is a smooth, glossy protruding surface over the front of the face. It could be a mask of some sort. The eyes are side mounted, but the rotate forward. They aren't covered. There is also a dome shape over the eyes, but it is covered with a piece of fabric...a hood of sorts."

The alien took a couple of steps forward. It was still too far away to get a good look. There was the sixty-foot-wide burn hole and the alien was probably another hundred feet beyond. Even Bea's enhanced computer images weren't furnishing much useful information.

Again the alien moved, bringing it closer to one of the six-foot-high tables. Bea came on the radio. "It looks like your friend is about eight or nine feet tall. It is not wearing a mask. It just opened its mouth. It has a smooth-skinned muzzle. And it is no herbivore with all those long, sharp teeth."

"Come on, you guys." said Candie. "Quit the anthropological discussion and figure out how to get back up here. You don't have much air left."

The alien was on the move again. It advanced down the center isle of the room to a point about half way to the hole. It stopped again. Dandy and Tom still didn't react other than to follow its progress with the beams of light. From under the pile of clothes, the alien raised an incredibly thin, long arm straight over its head.

An irritable Bea snapped, "Hold still. How can I get a clear picture? That's better. That arm must be twelve feet long. It won't have much strength, but watch out for the claws. There are more of them coming."

Filing through the doorway were eight more. They split, with four going down each side of the room.

"Tom, turn your light and camera on the ones on the right. I'll watch the left. Bea, do you see any weapons?"

"No. Still don't see any."

Dandy began to cough.

"What's going on?" yelled Candie.

"He just opened his face plate, "said Tom.

Wham. Another Pretzi fell down the hole. The aliens stopped their advance.

"Boy, this place stinks," said Dandy in a breathless wheeze. I can't even begin to describe the smells, but I think it a livable atmosphere, for at least a short period of time."

"Yeah, you'll probably get lung rot tomorrow," said Candie.

"Tom, see if you can tolerate the air."

Tom snapped back his visor and went through the same spasms as Dandy.

"Ugh. Don't ask me to run the 440 down here."

The aliens were beginning to advance again. There was a narrow rim between the burn hole and the walls. One side was about six feet wide and the other slightly narrower.

"Okay, gang. Here's the plan. Corky, reel in the cage as quickly as possible. Close the ramp. Candy, replenish your air supply and get two extra bottles for us. Rig all the halogen lights you can along the ramp. Maybe that much light will keep the Pretzis out. Corky, when I give the word, turn on the anti-gravs and run up to 15% capacity. When you hear things hitting the underside of Taran, shut them down. Candy, you be in the cage. You'll need a hundred feet of soft rope with a light weight tied to the end so you can swing it over to us. Oh, bring your shotgun too.

"Corky, as soon as the debris falls away, open the ramp and drop the cage to us."

Dandy snapped his face mask shut to replenish his air following the first part of his instructions.

"Tom, slowly move to the wall on your side and I'll go to the other. Get there before the aliens. It those things make any hostile move, strike a flare. I'll bet those rags they're wearing aren't fire retardant. In any case, when I give the word, put a lighted flare in the middle of the space and join me at the last bench in the corner. With our harnesses, we'll strap ourselves to the legs to keep from getting sucked up in the vortex. Then I'll give the word for the A/G. Save your air until we make the move into the corner.

"Corky, tell me when you're buttoned up."

"Roger."

The cage disappeared up the hole.

Dandy and Tom, still coughing, headed for their respective stations along the wall. The aliens paused when the two humans began to move. But, as soon as it became evident where they were going, the aliens became very vocal and started for the same ledge around the hole. They moved in a strange loping motion while waving their arms as if they were trying to take flight.

Grabbing one of the flares hanging from his belt, Dandy yelled to Tom to also strike one. The brilliant light pierced the near darkness. Obviously, the aliens weren't sensitive to light as were the Pretzis. They only hesitated a few beats before charging again.

As the aliens started around the edge of the hole they had to come single file, meaning Dandy only had to face one at a time. Tom's side was even narrower. The lead alien hissed at Dandy. Under the bright light Dandy could see all the features plainly, but he didn't have time to study them. A long arm whipped out. Dandy ducked just in time to get a sharp rap on the side of his helmet. In a reflex reaction, Dandy whipped the flare up, painting the retracting arm with the igniting chemicals. The alien shrieked and jerked back its arm. Dandy took advantage of the moment and advanced, waving the flare ahead of him. The creature recoiled against his companions. The group moved back.

Tom's adversaries learned from their companions, and they didn't try to advance against the flare.

The alien with the singed arm seemed to be the leader. He started yelling at the rest. When Dandy started to say something to Tom, Beatrice cut him off. "Be quiet. I'm recording their language."

Four of the aliens detached themselves from the group and quickly retreated out of the long room.

"I'll bet they'll try to come in behind us," said Dandy. "Corky, are you ready yet?"

"I'll be able to close up in another three minutes."

"We've only got a couple more minutes of these flares. I only have one more since I used one to melt that water. Tom, as soon as yours goes out, watch those guys with your lamp. If they start to advance strike another flare. I hope they will be content to stay there until the other ones can get around behind us.

Dandy's flare sputtered and began to go out. While there was still light, in a theatrical move, he pulled the other flare from his belt. Then he threw the burned-out one at the aliens, who recoiled. Dandy lighted the scene with his lamp. As soon as the spent flare came to rest, the two remaining alien squatted down practically over the top of it.

"What do you make of that?" said Dandy.

"They are sapping all the heat out of it," said Beatrice. "I think heat is a premium commodity on Ironmonger."

"Tom, throw your flare over there."

The same thing happened. The two aliens on his side hovered over the hot stub.

Dandy still had has helmet open listening for any sounds from the other four aliens. Corky reported that everything was ready in Taran.

"Tom, strike your flare and put it in the middle of the narrow section pointing away from you, and meet me at the last table in the corner. We can't wait until those others cut us off."

Two more flares were struck. Both the humans moved as quickly as pressure suits would permit into the corner. The flares gave sufficient light so they could weave their ways through the tables to the corner furthest from the door. They had covered about half the distance when the other four aliens burst through the door on the humans' side of the hole. The two groups of aliens started yelling back and forth.

"Use your air and run for it," said Dandy. He snapped his face plate shut turning on the air flow. He gratefully gulped sweet air as he lumber toward the corner. The aliens moved to surround them in the corner. They formed a 90 degree arc around the humans, who had taken cover under a six-foot-high table that protected them from above.

"Use your flare to keep them back while I hook us to the table."

Tom faced the advancing aliens, who began flicking out their long arms. Tom swung the flare around in random patterns so no opening could be timed. Occasionally, he got a squawk, indicating he'd singed one.

"Oh, one got me in the leg," groaned Tom.

"Get ready, Corky."

Dandy got Tom hooked to the table. Then he had to manipulate his own belt around the pole.

"Got me again."

"Hit it, Corky!"

In the distance the whine of a generator changed tone as it came under a load. Metal started screeching as the anti-gravity forces shifted Taran's weight. A sucking sound began to rise as a vortex developed. Air was being pulled through the carcass ship they were occupying and expelled up the burn hole to the underside of Taran. Loose items began to fly toward the hole. The aliens were screaming. The flares were the first items to disappear up the hole, plunging the hull into total darkness. The aliens joined the vortex. Objects from other parts of the ship clattered through the doorway at the end of the room. Dandy and Tom were out of their line of trajectory.

Since Tom had been fighting the aliens, Dandy had hooked him up with his back to the pole. Just the belt might not been enough to hold him, so Dandy wrapped his arms around the pole and Tom, just below the helmet. The helmet ring kept Tom from being strangled. The forces built rapidly. Dandy locked his fingers together and tried not to think of the strain.

The vortex began to diminish. Dandy vaguely figured some sort of venturi effect had sucked much of the air from the ship. As soon as the A/Gs went off, air came rushing back into the voided areas. That was followed by a great clamor of objects falling back into the hole. He wondered how many aliens and

Pretzis were included in the mess. As Taran settled back onto the hulk, the sound of metal stress became dominant.

"Corky, send down the cage. Tom, are you still with us?"

"They poked a couple of holes in me, but I don't feel any toxins. They hurt like hell, but not like a sting or a poisonous bite."

"Where did they get you?"

"In the left thigh and the left pectoral area. Don't worry. I'm not going to think about it until we get back up."

Dandy shined his lamp around. There was a lot of dust in the air. He could hear Tom breathing heavily. Dandy unhooked their belts so he could get around in front to see Tom. There was a hole punched through the pressure suit in the left chest. He couldn't tell much about it because the material had closed back. The same was true of the leg, except there was a blood smear on the damaged plasticized fabric. Since they were not operating in a vacuum, not much air was being lost through the punctures.

"I'm out of air," said Tom through clenched teeth.

"The air is cleaner by the hole. You'll have to put up with the smell of the local stuff."

"I'm clear. Lower away," said Candie over the radio. "I don't see any Pretzis hanging around. I'm coming guys."

Tom was having trouble putting weight on his left leg, so Dandy got under his arm to help cover the distance to the hole.

"This stuff still stinks, but it's not as bad as it was," said Tom.

"I'll be breathing the same stuff in a few moments."

Dandy and Tom arrived at the edge of the hole as Candie dropped into sight. Just as she passed through the hole in the ceiling, Dandy had Corky stop the descent.

"Tie one end of the rope to the rail and throw the other end to me," said Dandy. On the second try Dandy was able to step on the rope before it fell back into the hole. He ran the line around a solid fixture on the wall. Then he had Corky slowly lower the cage as he pulled it over to the edge. It took a lot of energy, and he had used up the remainder of his air. By the time the cage was on the dock and tied off, he was gasping for breath. Tom was propped up against a piece of debris, trying to draw in enough oxygen too.

Candie hopped out of the cage with two air bottles, which she quickly snapped into the back packs of the two. When Dandy's breathing became more regular, he and Candie helped Tom into the cage. Tom was obviously in pain, but he was trying not to show it. With the lower gravity, the job was easier than Dandy had expected.

Once the three were squeezed into the cage, Dandy had Corky gently pick it up. With the rope looped around the stationary object, Dandy played out the rope until they were in the center of the hole instead of swinging like a pendulum.

Corky lifted the cage up to the ramp. Once it was swung aboard, they closed the ramp and pressurized the area. The stink of Ironmonger was still evident.

As soon as Corky could leave the shuttle controls, he took over the care of his card partner. He put Tom on a work dolly and pushed him into the changing room to remove the spacesuit.

Before abandoning the shuttle bay, Dandy and Candie make a quick check to make sure no Pretzis had sneaked aboard. To be sure, they turned on the sound system and a camera so they could keep an eye on things from the flight deck.

Corky was examining Tom's wounds when the pilot and navigator got to the changing room.

Chapter   13

After getting the ship buttoned up and Tom to the control area, Candie took over the medical aspects of the program. In a short time the wounds were washed, closed with little suture devices, and covered with a transparent film. Tom also got an antibiotic and pain shot. He elected to take up residency on his station couch instead of being dumped in his room away from the functions of the ship.

Beatrice had pulled up all appropriate medical information in case Candie would need refresher material. Then she returned to handling the mass of information gleaned from the journey into the interior of the alien ship.

Dandy activated all the remote alarms and piped the video into the Fish House monitors before calling a meeting. Tom limped in to join the group. Dandy kept the conversation light until everyone had eaten.

Over beverages, Dandy turned to Beatrice. "Can you give us a summary of what happened down there?"

"From the beginning?"

"No....start with the aliens. They were a strange looking

bunch. What did you learn?"

"Of course, we have no direct references on Earth that would apply to alien life-forms but I think that Pterosaurs come the closest to what you met."

"The what?" said Corky.

"The Pterosaurs, more popularly known as Pterodactyls, were Mesozoic flying reptiles that lived during the age of the dinosaurs," said Beatrice. "They preceded the dinosaur that evolved into birds and bats."

Corky made a little sound that Beatrice took as a sign of disbelief. Instead of expressing irritation at being challenged, as she once would have done, she reloaded and launched herself into a bonehead discourse on winged lizards.

Throwing up his hands, Corky said, "If they're bird-kin, that's fine with me."

That was close enough for Beatrice. She reverted back to plan number one. "Those creatures have certain reptilian features, such as the sharp teeth. However, I suspect your bird-kin are not cold-blooded or they wouldn't be able to function in the sub-freezing temperatures outside. Their physiques suggest they came from a warm climate.

"Of particular interest are those long arms. They are probably vestiges of wings that have lost their membrane. The long fourth finger that used to form the lead part of the wing tip is now the sword that poked holes in Tom.

"I suspect they have all those layers of fabric draped all over them to protect them from the cold. The arms disappear into the folds when they are not needed. That keeps them warm.

"Their faces are very reptilian. The Pterosaurs had long, toothed bills. The Bird-kins have either lost their bills or didn't have one. They have a very smooth facial skin." Beatrice called up on the screen an enhanced mug-shot of the creature. It had a round muzzle with a broad, lipless slash for a mouth.

"It looks like it's smiling," said Tom.

"It was anticipating you for dinner," quipped Corky. Apparently that shot was a little too close to home to get the laugh it ordinarily would have garnered.

Beatrice forged ahead. "You couldn't have seen it, but there is another similarity. Your Bird-kin's knees fold backward as a chicken's. When they squatted by the flare, I could analyze the motion."

"What more can you postulate about them?" said Dandy. "We'll probably run into them again."

"I would say that they don't weight very much. Their bones are probably hollow. They shouldn't have much arm strength. That's on the negative side. The other side is that they are much faster than we are. They have about a nine-foot longer reach than we have and they are armed with a very quick claw-weapon. You've already seen what they can do to a space suit. I'll bet there is quite a nick in Dandy's helmet."

Beatrice stopped, looked at each before saying, "This time we were lucky. We had some technology available. Without weapons you'll lose the next time you meet."

There was a prolonged silence before Candie said, "We've run into two alien life-forms, the Pretzis and the Bird-kins. I wonder how many more are running around out there."

"There may be hundreds or maybe thousands," said Beatrice. "We have no way of knowing how long Ironmonger has been collecting space junk. It could have been doing this for eons. The debris is probably miles deep."

Doughboy had been curled at Beatrice's feet. When he moved a little, she leaned over to pat him as she would have a puppy. Doughboy wiggled with delight, the same as a puppy.

"What do you think the Bird-kins were doing up here?" said Dandy.

"Probably scrounging for food," said Beatrice. "I doubt if this metal ball grows any food other than lichen, mold and meat. So any new catch may have supplies, food stuffs, frozen corpses and game."

"We're the game," said Corky.

"Yep," said Dandy. "That's us."

A psychic shudder seemed to pass through the group. They all looked at Dandy.

"I've been trying to figure out the cycle of life on Ironmonger," began Dandy. "Somewhere down below us is the original machine that was sent out. From what it has accumulated, it would appear to be ancient, as Bea pointed out. Based on my technological teachings, no machine can operate that long without some sort of refueling. I would theorize that somehow it converted things like us into energy. It needs a lot. Remember how fast it is going? We were leaving a long tail of flame, but it didn't have a tail, which means it has some other system of propulsion. But, whatever system it has, it needs fuel.

"If fuel is consumed, it follows that it would radiate energy to produce heat. There must be heat generated somewhere or the temperatures outside would be the same as open space. I would think the routine is that Ironmonger scoops up anything that does not answer its signal. Most of it is probably dead junk. But, occasionally a manned ship is pulled in. If the ship cannot break away, the crew would remain with it as long as the necessities of life are available. Those necessities would include food, water, air and energy. If they can breathe Ironmonger's air they could stay after their air supply failed. Once their energy supply fails, they would have to leave due to the cold. They could probably live in this temperature, but their water and maybe food would freeze. They would have to move to either another hull where they can find what they are missing or migrate downward to the heat.

"There are probably foraging parties out all the time looking for equipment, food, water, whatever they can use to survive. Included in the survival equipment are probably weapons. So I would suspect we'll run into aliens who are armed."

"How come the Bird-kins weren't armed?"said Candie.

"They have natural weapons of their own. But, if Bea is correct on their weight and strength, they may not have anything they can safely handle. Think what a blast from your double barrel would do to their spaghetti arms.

"Any time we go outside Taran, we run the chance of encountering some alien. I doubt if we can count on any of them being friendly."

"I might point out," said Beatrice, "that anyone on this thing is from a space-faring race. So we can expect to run into all levels of sophistication."

"Our first consideration," said Dandy, "is to provide for our safety. If we're going to get off Ironmonger, we're going to have to move around outside."

Corky raised a finger to get attention. "We should be able to remove the gloves from our pressure suits. I can seal off the wrists so air can't get out. It's not so cold that we can't just wear gloves and if necessary, we can carry hand warmers. That way we can use the firearms we have on hand. I don't know how primitive they are compared to what our neighbors may be packing, but something is better than nothing."

"That will help," said Dandy. "At least we can get our fingers in the trigger guards of the rifles and pistols. Now, if we can hit anything...... Corky, in the pouch of my suit is a vile. Please check to see if it is water and if there is any strange substance in it.

"Candie. How's the map of our immediate environs coming?"

"It's about as complete as it can be with the information we have available."

"What can you tell us about the neighborhood?"

"We're sitting on the largest ship, by far....at least, within sight but it is not the newest. When this thing was pulled down, it must have loomed way above everything else. Its weight may have caused it to sink into the pile somewhat, but it didn't get buried. It appears that later arrivals filled in around it, leveling the field. I have no idea of the time frame. But I would suspect it didn't happen overnight. In our terms, this ship we're sitting on could be incredibly old."

"You're saying, the newer, more technical equipment would be on those other, smaller ships?" said Tom.

"Not necessarily," said Beatrice. "It depends on the relative stages of development. The most advanced civilization may be buried under a lot of lesser ones."

Eyeing Dandy, Tom asked," What are you planning?"

"Our next forays will have two goals. We need to search for weapons and water. It appears we need the weapons to protect ourselves while we do all the rest. Once we replenish our water, then we'll turn our attention to getting off this thing. Right now, we could lift off, but as soon as Ironmonger activates its magic attractor ray, we'd be right back here. So we'll either have to find the code so Ironmonger won't chase us or disable the force that reels us in."

"The Pretzis are back," said Candie. One of the monitors showed movement in the shadow of a leg. "I wonder if they constitute any real hazard to us. When I had to shoot those little guys, I felt as if I was blasting my little old neighbor lady's cat."

"We can't afford to take the chance they have a poisonous bite and toxic dandruff." said Dandy. "I need to see your map to see where we want to go next."

The group broke up. Tom limped back to his couch. Beatrice clamped her earphone on her head and went back to her computer. Doughboy crawled along behind. Corky headed below to check the water sample. Dandy got refills and joined Candie at her map table.

On the big table was a sheet of velum full of lines and symbols. "Everything is laid out in relationship to the actual longitudinal axis of the ship under us. I can only guess at its length. We have some recorded images Beatrice made while you were trying to land. We approached from what appears to be the stern of the ship. I'd guess the bridge is somewhere in the opposite direction. We can't see anything from here."

The map showed the locations of numerous smaller ships and indefinable pieces of debris scattered on both sides of their hulk.

They were easier to see because they still were lower than the top hulk. In addition, Taran's camera mounts were positioned another couple of hundred feet above the surface on which they sat.

"The force that reeled us in is no longer active," said Dandy. "But it could come on again at any moment. We can only guess at what it would do to one of our shuttles. That much energy would likely crush it like stepping on a bug. We don't dare take one out until we know more about Ironmonger.

"It looks like the first expeditions will be confined to this big ship. Getting to those surrounding vessels will be a real chore. We'll probably have to descend through this one and either find a hole or make an opening to get down to the level of the other ships."

"Are you planning on going through the ship or along the surface?"

"We'll probably not find anything useful to us along the outer hull, but from what I saw of the inside, it would be slow going. Moving through that will be like finding one's way through a labyrinth. We'd have to mark our way or in some way map our progress."

"Look at this," said Candie. She flipped on one of the cameras. "This is view toward what we think is the bow. In the distance, the ship seems to disappear as if it curved out of sight. There are all sorts of irregularities that could be damaged areas, or they could be sensors, utility hookups, entry bays or whatever. I think we need to know. Let Corky and me take a look."

Dandy began to object. "Someone has to be here......."

"You be that someone. If anything would happen to you and Corky, what would two women and a wounded man do?" Candie's dangly earrings were flashing as she punctuated her argument.

Dandy recognized the worth of her point, but he still was uncomfortable with sending people into potentially dangerous situations. He could lead a hazardous mission but to hang behind was much more difficult.

Since Taran was on the lighted side of Ironmonger, there was no day or night. Dandy continued on the same cycles they had used on earth. He, Beatrice, and Tom took watch shifts while Corky and Candie rested.

In the scheduled morning, the explorers suited up and took the elevator down to the hulk's surface. In the perpetual twilight, they headed toward what they thought was the bow of the ship. Corky had modified the suits to remove the bulky gloves. They wore conventional gloves and kept their hands warm in a chemically heated pouch strapped around their waists much as quarterback does in the snow-belt. Each had a .45 automatic strapped on the hip. Corky had an M-1 rifle and Candie carried her 12 gauge shotgun. Both long guns were equipped with shoulder slings so they could free their hands.

Candie tested radio communications after they emerged from Taran.

"How's your footing?" said Dandy.

"Fine. I can get good traction. Walking is easy with the light gravity. As soon as we get away from the hole, I'll test the air. Maybe it won't stink as much as it does below.

They skirted around the hole burned in the hulk to head in the desired direction.

Tom was following the progress. "Corky, if you can find a little piece of the hull material, bring it back so we can test it. It would be a great benefit if we could cut through that stuff."

The pair made good time toward the horizon line. Occasionally, they stopped to inspect features on the surface.

"There are doors of various sizes all over the place." said Candie.

Corky added, "There are holes near each one that look like a place for a key to open them manually. If we could make a key, we might have access through the hull."

Candie set up a routine of ten minutes on Ironmonger air and ten on bottled air. The local air still stunk. It was tolerable, but thin. The ten-on, ten-off plan could double their extra-vehicular activities.

Finally, Candie reported, "We're coming to an edge."Ten minutes later she said, "The ship is segmented. There are four huge tubes connecting this section with another that looks just as big as this one. It is at least a couple of football field lengths down to the tubes."

"Come back once you give Bea a good view of everything," said Dandy. "We'll go the other way next."

When the pair got back to Taran, Corky asked Dandy to bring down a welding rod, a sticky strip used to hold items in a weightless environment, and a durathane welding kit.

With the requested items, Corky found that the holes next to the access doors were eight inches deep. They were square—approximately one inch on a side. He made a pattern using the thick adhesive side of the sticky tape. Then he squeezed a bead of the durathane welding paste along the hull of the hulk and fired it with the igniter. It didn't burn through the skin. Corky doubled the bead size and ignited the strip. There was no penetration.

Later, in the Fish House, everyone was pretty glum. Dandy asked Beatrice if she had found anything of interest in the images from the helmet-cams.

"There was lot of interesting things, but nothing that will help us find water. We can't go over the side of the hull. It is too far to climb down. Getting down to the tubes still won't necessarily put us inside and the tubes would be an unlikely place to store water. Pipes may run through there, but they'd be frozen too."

"If the stern is in the other direction," said Candie, "there will probably be another drop-off."

"We can't afford to guess," said Dandy. "Tomorrow you two will have to go in the other direction to see what is there."

Corky shuffled around a bit before saying, "Maybe I can make a key to open those hatches. I suspect the key is a mechanical override to a power mechanism. I poked around with the rod long enough to get an idea of what is down there. I'll make a prototype and see what happens.

"The hull of the green hulk is much stronger than the durathane hull of Taran. A double bead of welding paste would have cut a line through our hull. I'll see if I can concoct something else."

The following day produced no encouraging discoveries. Candie and Corky found they were not on the stern section but on a segment connected to the engine by the same four tubes as on the other end. It was like being on an island.

In summation, Candy added, "When we walked over the top onto the other side we could see that there was substantial damage to the engine section. It looks like there is a great hole toward the rear. It would have to be something to be seen in this dim light and at that distance.

Chapter 14

Dandy spent a good portion of the night tilted up on his couch so he could cross his ankles and lace his fingers behind his head. It was incumbent on Dandy to come up with a plan. He was the pilot. The crew's spirits were going down with every day devoid of positive results. Also, Tom wasn't getting better. Candie kept him loaded with antibiotics to guard against infection, but there didn't seem to be any healing. The wounds weren't bleeding, but they weren't scabbing over either. Even though Tom maintained a stalwart front, it was obvious his pain still had to be masked with heavy analgesics. His lack of progress was dragging the group's spirits down.

As the next work day began, Dandy brought everyone together in the Fish House. Tom limped over to join group even though he could have participated from his station. Dandy got right down to work, without reference to notes, which always amazed everyone except Beatrice.

"We're dealing with a whole bunch of question marks. We need some answers. First, the Green Hulk, as Corky calls it, holds the means for our return home. Corky's report on the vial Tom and I brought back from down below is water with a few additives that don't appear to create any problem. I wouldn't want to drink it, but we can recycle it into useable form.

"My theory is that a ship as large as the Green Hulk should contain more than enough water for our purposes. It should still be there somewhere because when the ship came down, the water would have frozen before any denizens of the lower reaches could get here to drain it. Oh, I know there are hundreds of various scenarios that could have taken place, but our working theory is going to be that there are tons of water down there with our name on it. If that proves not to be true, then we'll move to another hypothesis.

"Another working hypothesis is that this section of the Green Hulk was the housekeeping section. Aft was the engine and forward appears to be the control area. With the huge dining facilities I'd guess this is where the troops and/or crew stayed. I think this section is relatively undamaged. When we had the A/Gs on, there was only a subdued vortex as if we were just sucking air out of the interior. It there had been large damaged areas such as Candie and Corky found on the aft section, there would have been a much more robust vortex. Oh, there have to be entries, or the Pretzis and the Bird-kins wouldn't be in there, but I think those opening are insignificant.

"One thing that we haven't found out yet is how the interior is arranged. We have punched through several layers of ship, which would indicate that we are sitting on the top and the floors are stacked from bottom to top. However, this ship might have been using spin gravity which would give us layers like an onion, so no matter where we punched in we would find what we have already seen."

"I don't think they were using spin gravity," said Tom. "If those were tables we were seeing down in the hole, they should have been mounted on the ceiling. With spin gravity, your feet are toward the outside."

"Come to think of it, you're right. Artificial gravity can be configured in a number of ways. We'll just have to check," conceded Dandy, before he got back on track. "Another matter we need to investigate is if there is a dead space or utility space between the skin of the ship and the actual room. The way the blast from our engines turned the metal inward, there could be a huge space outside of that first room we found. Water lines may run through there.

"Corky, have you come up with something to burn through the skin?"

"I've formulated a couple of compounds that might work, but I've got to get outside to try them. We never found a piece of hull metal small enough to bring in."

"I want you to test the durathane material on the interior floors and wall. I suspect they are not as durable as the outer hull. We need to be able to go where we want. How about the key?"

"I've designed one, but I haven't had time to make it."

"Keep working," said Dandy. "Tom, can you work with Bea to get some sort of dimensional diagram of this hulk, so we have an idea of the distances involved? Bea, do you have any ideas concerning the age of the Green Hulk?"

"Not really. I suspect it is a lot older than it looks. I have the impression from what I've been able to see that it was probably a dead ship when it was picked up by Ironmonger. It could have been adrift for a long time. It's been on Ironmonger a long time too.

"Do you think there are any of those twelve foot figures walking around out there?" said Candie.

"Some may have survived."Beatrice left her comment dangling.

Dandy resumed, "We're still looking for weapons and water. One operating procedure we will follow is that before we open up the bays of the ship or go into the Green Hulk, we will suck everything out with the A/Gs. That doesn't mean we'll be safe from all dangers, but I hope it will reduce our exposures. Yes, I know some Pretzis and Bird-kins may be in the way, but I want to reduce our exposure to them."Dandy looked around the room. Most of TC was not too happy about the precaution, but no objections were raised.

"There is one other thing I want to toss out for consideration. Remember when we first approached Ironmonger, it started sending out that signal that meant nothing to us. When we didn't respond, it turned off the signal and altered course to intercept. That recognition signal persisted for twenty hours. If we put a shuttle in the air, would Ironmonger give us warning with the signal before it turned on its attraction beams?"

"Are we going to do any flying soon?" asked Corky.

"Getting water is just the first phase. Then we have to get off this thing, which may mean we have to get down to the core. I'd rather not try climbing down all those miles. Maybe there's a route where we can take the shuttle."

Dandy kept the crew engaged in a flurry of activity as if they were working against a short time schedule. It took Corky several trips on the Green Hulk to get a working key to the access panels. He also found the durathane welding kit could cut through interior partitions. He was still trying to find something that would cut through the hull material.

Candy and Beatrice established the dimensions of much of their surroundings. Everyone was astonished at the enormity of the Green Hulk. Their segment was nearly a mile long. The width was that of three football fields.

They found that there was a space between the hull and the first interior room. By human dimensions it was spacious, but Beatrice pointed out that the normal occupants would have found the space rather tight. TC still didn't have a way of getting into it. They couldn't cut through the outer plating. The fused edges of the hole folded down over the space. The two access panels Corky opened with his key were self-contained utility boxes. Unless Corky could come up with a hotter compound, they'd have to punch through the ceiling of the uppermost room.

They dropped a line to the bottom of the hole with lights and cameras showing side-shots as well as what was below. On the lowest level there was a heap of debris dropped by the A/Gs. One notable absence was the remains of any Pretzis or Bird-kins. Beatrice pointed out that the bodies may have been buried, but

Dandy suspected, although he didn't vocalize his thoughts, that the bodies had been recycled.

During the latest flurry of activity there was one disturbing aspect. Tom was not getting better. He continued to hurt and he was getting weaker. Candie spent much of her own time going through the medical databases looking for anything that might help. She could find nothing that shed any light on his condition. Finally, they had to move Tom to his room where he'd be closer to the sanitary facilities.

Corky was taking the situation harder than the rest. Since Tom was no longer interested in playing cards, Corky spent his free time trying to make Tom more comfortable. He moved monitors and a keyboard into Tom's room so the Tom could keep abreast of everything happening in Taran. Although Tom wasn't feeling badly, he had trouble sleeping, so Dandy had him pull his duty shift watching for external threats.

One result of the minute inspection of their surroundings was the discovery of an anomalous flat area. The whole segment of the hull on which Taran sat rounded off slightly toward the sides. Three or four hundred yards forward of their position, the curve was broken. That was the only variance that could be detected in the uniformity of the hull.

Dandy and Candie suited up to investigate. Dandy still wasn't taking any chances. He retracted the line with the lights and cameras before clearing the hull with the A/Gs. He still insisted Candie carry her shotgun. He slung a rifle strap over his shoulder.

In the half-light of Ironmonger, it turned out to be a spectacular walk. Candie opened up her visor to better see the brilliance of the stars.

"I've never seen a sight like this," said Candie. 'We've walked in space many times before, but I've always had to look through my tinted face-plate. There is so little atmosphere on Ironmonger, there is virtually no distortion.

Dandy opened his helmet and sniffed the evil smelling air. However, his nose was forgotten when he looked up to view the points of light. "Wow, this really is spectacular. How could one ever describe this?"

"There is no way to do it in our language."

A rather grouchy reminder from Beatrice concerning their limited air supply returned their attention to their mission. Moving on Ironmonger was easy. They had a level, unobstructed path with good traction in light gravity. They covered the distance quickly.

"This is a larger area than I thought." said Candie. "Look at the seams in the hull. This is some sort of work area."

"I've been wondering how a ship this large was supplied. It certainly can't land. I'll bet this is where they do a ship-to-ship resupply in space."

In the center, there was a featureless rectangular area. Candie paced it off. "It's about eighty by a hundred."

Dandy began walking around the edge of the platform. Finally, he bent over to insert Corky's key into a square hole. "Stand away from the platform. Let's see what happens."

When Dandy turned the key, there was a faint vibration under foot. To his left, a section of the hull, approximately eight feet square, depressed a few inches and then slide to the side revealing a hole about 25 feet deep. Along two sides were pipes that looked like handrails that lead to the bottom.

Both Dandy and Candie stood with their toes at the edge of the opening, looking down in wonder.

"Wow, the old girl still has a little pop left," said Candie.

"Anyone got any explanations?" said Dandy.

Tom responded. "Any ship of this size has dozens of power systems and backup systems. It looks like one or more is still active."

"After all those years? How can it hold energy that long?"

"Dandy, just because our technology can't do it, doesn't mean aliens can't do it," said Beatrice. There was a slight sneer in her voice.

Under the subdued light not much could be seen of the bottom. "Bea, can you make out what's down there?"

"It would be easier if you held still," came a terse reply.

Beatrice had to wait while Dandy and Candie glanced at each other.

After a pause, Beatrice said, "I can't see any detail but it looks like there is a door on the forward side. There is, what appears to be, a key pad on the wall. There is another door that should go into the service area under the hull that you've been trying to enter. I can see more of the key pad for that one. Of course, I have no idea of what the symbols mean but from all appearances, this is an air lock. Since there is only a hand rail, this area must be outside of any artificial gravity area."

"We've found our entry," said Dandy. "Now we have to figure out how to use it. Since Ironmonger has gravity, we can't just float down."

"I'd be hesitant about going in until we know if we can get out. If the power is still on to those other doors and if this is an air lock, this door would have to close before anything else would open."

"Yeah, you're right. We could have access to the entire ship, but it won't do us much good if we get locked inside."

Tom's voice came faintly over the radio. "Take measurements. We can build a prop to hold the door open. From the prop we can suspend a work platform. We can burn through the interior walls to the utility area or the rest of the ship."

With Candie holding the end, Dandy measured the opening with a utility cord he carried in his emergency pack. A reverse twist of the key shut the door. By the time the pair got out of their suits and back to the crew area, Tom had sketches of the entry mechanism. The exertion had taken all his energy. He dozed off while trying to explain his drawings to Corky.

After Dandy cleaned up and drew a cup of coffee, he stopped at Beatrice's station. He leaned against her console, but she had her earphones on and she was staring at her computer screen.

Doughboy was moving restlessly at her feet. Dandy slid sideways until he moved into her peripheral vision. She looked up with a start.

"Hi. I just stopped by to fix whatever is wrong."

"Wrong? Nothing's wrong."

"Sure, nothing's wrong. Just look at Doughboy fidget. I don't even have to look at you to know something is wrong. Doughboy is so attuned to you, that he mirrors your every thought. And if that wasn't enough, when emotion shows up in a common routine response while we're working, there has to be something wrong. We need you focused on the matter at hand, not stewing over something else."

Beatrice stroked the uneasy Doughboy. She took a deep breath before speaking. "Before Taran, I used to be perfectly happy soaking up the knowledge gained by others. It never occurred to me to take any action on my own. Then when we started doing things no one on earth had ever done before, I became a participant...making history. I was directly adding to our store of knowledge and therefore to history, and I still am. That was a great feeling. But when Candie raised her face plate and looked directly into the universe, I realized I'm still recording the experiences of others. You two are the only ones of our kind who have ever done that. I guess I'm jealous, but the thought of doing what the four of you do just petrifies me. I'm sorry. I won't let that happen again." She let out a long sigh and stroked a much more contented Doughboy.

Candie translated the string measurements into useable form. Corky went below to fabricate Tom's plans. Dandy called the shop to tell Corky to put wheels under the door prop so they could pull all of that weight instead of carrying it.

The next morning, TC gathered in the Fish House. Corky had rigged what amounted to a wheelchair so Tom could get around. Corky pushed Tom out to the meeting so he wouldn't have to expend too much energy.

Dandy started out by saying, "We're changing the routine a little today. As soon as we turn off the A/Gs, I want the cameras lowered into the hole. Corky, you're on the winch. Candie will run shotgun. Try to get shots of the interiors off all the exposed rooms. What we are looking for is some sort of pattern to the interior layout of this crate. Instead of looking for rooms, we are looking for passageways to take us from one area to another."

"Tom, you watch the monitors for any problems both in the hole and outside on the hull. Bea and I will drag Corky's new gear to the airlock and set it up."

Doughboy started to fidget all over the place. Beatrice was sitting as rigid as a rock, staring at Dandy with huge eyes.

Dandy forged on ahead. "Candie, please help Bea get into her suit. Oh, yes, Bea. We want to take a light with us so we can see better what's down the shaft. We'll set up the equipment, but going down will come later."

"Tom, be sure to record our camera views of the airlock so Bea can make enhanced views later."

Dandy stood up to indicate it was time to work. Everyone was surreptitiously watching Beatrice to see her reactions. Beatrice was absently stroking Doughboy without uttering so much as a sound. She followed Candie, like a mechanical toy, to the elevator.

Dandy and Corky got Tom setup on his couch so he could reach the various controls. Then the two men followed the women down to the changing room on the next level. When they walked in, they gave Beatrice something else to think about. She was standing naked in front of her locker as Candie was trying to get her into a body sock.

All the rest of the crew was used to being seen without clothes, but this was a new experience for Beatrice. Dandy fought to suppress a snicker because Beatrice was as pasty white as Doughboy.

Beatrice was just barely functioning. She responded to each of Candie's commands, but she wasn't functioning on her own brain power. Dandy was beginning to have second thoughts about giving the librarian a more active stake in the operation.

Finally, Candie got their suits checked and pointed Beatrice toward the elevator. Dandy took over to guide her into the conveyance. When the outer door in the Taran's leg opened, Dandy led Beatrice out into the Ironmonger day.

After Dandy pulled the equipment out onto the hull, he closed the door. Now both of them stood on the hull of an alien ship far from Earth with a clear view of the galaxy overhead. Dandy turned to Beatrice and took her by the shoulders. He bent forward until he tapped her face plate with his. "Bea, it's time to turn on your brain. You're right where you want to be, doing what you want to do. Don't waste the opportunity."

Beatrice's eyes lost their vague, faraway look and eventually focused on Dandy's face.

"That's better," said Dandy, to lend encouragement, although he could see panic was not far away. "Wiggle your toes. Move your fingers. Breathe in and out. Count backwards from ten. See, everything works just like it did before, right?" Dandy waited for a few beats before saying "Right?"

This time he got a slight bob of the head. She shuffled her feet and flexed her gloved hands.

"That's better."Dandy handed her a large spotlight. "Carry this and follow me." Dandy picked up the tow rope for the equipment cart and started off toward the platform. Beatrice remained immobile until she must have thought she was being left alone standing on an alien ship's hull. She scampered to catch up.

By the time they had covered half the distance, Beatrice was walking much more naturally. She was starting to take in her surroundings. Dandy stopped, dropped the tow rope and asked Beatrice for the lamp. He put the lamp on top of the cart and snapped open his face plate.

"It doesn't smell very nice out here, but it won't hurt you."He hit the release on Beatrice's face plate. It snapped back into her helmet.

Beatrice's eyes got round, with lots of white showing. She was holding her breath.

Dandy waited until the explosion came and she had to exhale and then suck in Ironmonger air. That set off a spasm of coughing. Finally, the distress subsided and Beatrice declared, "It stinks out here."

"I agree, but I think it is worth it." He pointed up.

Beatrice had to flex her knees to get a better look upward, because of her helmet.

Dandy could see tears trickling down Beatrice's cheeks. He didn't know if they were caused by the coughing or the emotions of the moment. Dandy took his companion by the shoulders, turning her around so she could take in the majesty of Taran standing on the Green Hulk against the star-studded blackness of space.

After the sightseeing interlude, Dandy returned to the task at hand. He moved off to the airlock. Before opening it, he tack-welded two durathane rails over the hold from which Tom's ingenious electrically controlled working platform would be suspended.

When Dandy opened the airlock, he tested the platform to be certain everything was working properly. Then he had Beatrice stand on the edge and shined the spotlight on the interior features of the airlock while Tom recorded the images from her helmet camera.

Tom's voice came over the radio. "Bea, slow down. How am I supposed to see anything with you jumping around?" The radio also picked up Corky's snicker.

Dandy closed the airlock before they headed back to Taran. Candie came down to help Beatrice out of her space suit. Beatrice was effervescent, rambling on like no one had ever heard her before. She wasn't even aware of being naked in front of Dandy and Candie. The rest of the crew was enjoying the change. Back up in the control center Beatrice even gave Dandy a thumbs-up sign as she disappeared into her room with Doughboy in tow.

The rest of the afternoon was consumed by trying to figure out the interior layout of the Green Hulk from the images captured from the hole. Nothing conclusive could be ascertained.

Dandy decided to punch through the airlock walls into the service area if they were not able to activate the door with the outer hull door open. Tom's design prohibited the closure of the airlock in case it was automated.

Dandy and Corky made the attempt. Although there was power to the system, the service area door would not open. On the hinge side, which they hoped was away from any wiring, they started cutting. When the metal cooled, Dandy stepped onto the edge of the cut to kick a hole in the wall. His light picked up a mass of pipes and conduits running in all directions. There was a central handrail running off into the darkness beyond the reach of the lamps. It was designed as a weightless area. Under gravity it would be a monumental obstacle course. The area was about twenty feet high but much space was occupied with terminal boxes and modules of varying size and configuration.

Dandy hadn't known what to expect, but he certainly wasn't prepared to undertake such a trek without more supplies and equipment than he had on hand at the moment. He changed his plans to try entering the ship itself.

They lowered themselves to the bottom of the airlock and cut another hole through the wall. Corky kicked the severed plate, which fell with a muted clatter. The opening entered into a hallway, but they couldn't see too much until the melted edges cooled. While they waited, Dandy stood on one side of the opening and Corky on the other, both with drawn revolvers in case something popped through the hole. In the freezing air, the metal cooled rapidly. Corky tested the cut and nodded to Dandy, who shoved his light into the hall and quickly checked both directions for Bird-kins or any other threat. Finding none, he stepped into the alien ship.

"I can see to the end of the hall to my right but not to my left. One thing I do see is a line of periodic, faint spots of light along the wall. There is still some power to this part of the ship. I wonder if the lights are for key pads."

Corky joined Dandy in the hall. "They may be sensors or

warning devices."

The hall was a featureless, rectangular tube, colored in a light gray. It was about eight feet wide and twice as high. As the pair moved into the ship, they were interrupted by a faint call from Beatrice. "You guys are beginning to fade out. I can't pick up any camera images. Do you have it on?"

Dandy returned to the hole they had cut. "Can you hear me now?"

"It's better, but not clear. The camera is only giving fuzzy images."

"The hull is blocking our signals," said Corky. "If we want to continue to communicate with Taran, we'll have to set up a relay.

"I don't want to be out of communication. You stay here in case we need to talk to the ship. I want to go far enough down there to see what those lights are about."

Dandy moved to the closest light. "It looks like a door control. There is a panel that will slide into the wall. It's just like those we saw in the mess hall."

When Dandy pressed the lighted button, there was a groan of protest as the panel split in the center and jerkily retracted into the wall.

"Yipes," said Dandy.

"What's wrong?" demanded Corky.

"Now we're about to see what the crew looked like. There are bodies all over the place. Something killed them in place. It must have been quick. This is a control room. There are consoles filled with instrumentation. Some of the lights are still on. There is a window beyond the control panels. I can't see anything out there."

Dandy backed out of the control room and returned to the airlock. "Go take a look, then we'll return to Taran. We need more equipment and more time to really do anything."

"Boy, are they big. They're all wearing uniforms, so they must be some sort of military. I count twenty bodies from here," said Corky.

Chapter   15

It took an extra day to put the proper relay equipment for both audio and visual together and get it installed at the air lock. Then Beatrice tossed out another problem that took some consideration. They had not communicated with Gal-X since they had confirmed their successful launch. Because the whole world would be eavesdropping, TC was not expected to maintain any reporting routine. But Beatrice had pointed out they had been on Ironmonger for some time, and the home office would be getting pretty anxious by now.

Dandy argued that, by the time any communication got back home, they should be off Ironmonger. That didn't fly well with Beatrice, who responded that so far nothing had happened to even give them hopes of getting off any time soon. Everyone seemed shocked when she pointed out they had already been sitting there three weeks.

It wasn't that Dandy didn't want to send the information, but he was reluctant to share any information with Centurion and any of the other entities that would gladly slit all of TC's throats to get Taran. Finally, he agreed to forward sufficient information concerning Ironmonger to alert Earth in case they were not successful. He certainly didn't want the world to find out there was a treasure trove of alien technology on this flying garbage heap.

Once the information relay question was settled they returned to the search for water. The next time Dandy stepped into the control room of Green Hulk, he was much better prepared. Relay devices had been set up to maintain both audio and video links to Taran. Both he and Corky were carrying bags of supplies and equipment, which included extra air, food and water. There had been a long discussion concerning the advisability of opening their face plates to take on sustenance while inside Green Hulk. Something had killed the crew in situ. It may have been a poisonous gas or some completely unknown, fast-moving agent. The plan was not to spend enough time down there to have to open the suits, but in case they got lost, locked in or detained in some other manner, they might have to risk exposure.

Beatrice had been insistent on getting a complete description of the aliens. Her scholar's button had been pushed. Dandy's initial time was spent trying to describe the alien corpora.

"I really don't understand what I'm seeing. These things aren't as big as I had visualized them when I was looking at their mess hall. They're probably ten or eleven feet tall. Their two legs are enormously long, but skinny. That accounts for the high stools. There are stools instead of chairs here in the control room, because it appears these things are carrying a large sack on their backs. The legs seem to be attached to a rigid form in the front. Four arms are attached to the same area. The lower two arms are short and they look to be powerful. The upper two arms are thinner, but much longer and they have more dexterous-looking digits. There are three opposing digits. The head is on a long slender neck that comes up out of the same form as the arms and legs. That sack I mentioned is attached right below where the neck juts out. That's about all I can tell without stripping the clothes off. I don't want to take that much time right now."

"Can you at least give me a good look at each one?" said Beatrice.

Dandy made his way down the line centering his camera and light on each body in turn. The corpses were in all differing positions. Some were draped over their work area. Others had slipped off their stools and were in a heap on the floor. Others seemed to have gotten on their feet before falling down. It was difficult telling much about their skin. Only hands and heads were visible, and it looked as if flesh had been subject to freezer burn. It was modeled in various colors. From the temperature in the ship, Dandy figured they were frozen and perhaps they had been frozen even harder if they had been exposed to the temperatures of space.

"Bea, file this info away. Now, I'm going to give you views of the various work station on the console. We need to know more about the controls."

While Dandy was giving Bea the views of the bodies, Corky had been conducting his own inspection of the control panels. He'd also been trying to ascertain what was beyond the window by shining his light around. "Whatever is on the other side is big. This flashlight doesn't reveal anything beyond a few feet. Look at the thickness of this glass or whatever it is. It could face out into space except we're down inside the ship."

"There still seems to power to certain systems on the control panel. Since there are no lights on in here or on the other side of the glass, I wonder if there is emergency power going only to critical functions. We've assumed the ship was damaged in battle, but so far we haven't come across any catastrophic damage to explain the crew deaths or the reason for the ship being down."

Candie had been listening to the conversation. She tossed out the question, "Do you suppose that something could have killed the crew and the ship was just drifting in space and there was no one to answer the warning put out by Ironmonger? When it was pulled down to the surface, there probably was some damage in parts of the hull, which would have been entry points for the various aliens."

"That sounds like a better hypothesis than the battle sequence. That large damaged area you saw on the engine section could have been caused by something other than battle. This part of the ship must be sealed because the carnivores didn't get in here, and we haven't seen any signs of Pretzis."

"If there is no power to open the door, it would be hard to get around. There is probably some mechanical way of getting through, providing one knows how and has the strength to do so."

"Corky, can you make any sense out of this control panel?" said Dandy.

"There seems to be certain logic on it. The main functions are right in front of the operator. To the side are peripheral functions." Without waiting for any discussion, Corky flipped the end switch on a long line of identical toggles. A row of dim lights glowed on the far side of a big vacant area beyond the window. Corky chuckled. "That's what I thought. Under full power there should be a whole battery of lights over there, but under emergency power there are only enough lights to make your way around. When the main power is off line, its common sense to have auxiliary power to keep vital operations going like the support systems, power to open and close doors so you can move around....that kind of thing."

"This is some sort of control room, but what does it control?"

Corky snorted, "That's one humongous elevator out there. It runs up and down those rails on the four corners. The actual platform is down below somewhere. I think this is where they provision the ship. The supply ship attaches itself to the hull and the platform opens, exposing the freight elevator. Apparently, part of the time, the area out there is exposed to space because of the window, but it must be able to be closed up so that the work area can be pressurized. I wonder how many decks are served by that thing?"

"If that is a resupply facility, then water would be pumped through there. Maybe we can trace the pipes to the storage tanks." Dandy began scrutinizing the panel in front of him. There were tags on each control but the alien printing was of no help. "I'll bet this is the main elevator control," said Dandy, indicating a couple of buttons with up and down arrows and an unlit window next to it. "If there was power to the elevator, that window would probably indicate which floor it was on."

While Dandy was giving Beatrice views of the control board, Corky was rummaging through drawers, coming up with what looked like training manuals. He put a couple of small ones in his pack as samples of the writing.

"We need to find an entrance to the elevator shaft," said Dandy. "It will probably be an airlock."

"It has to be further along the hall," said Corky, as he moved out of the control room.

They were fortunate—the emergency power still activated the locks. Before long they were walking around a deep, dark pit. The guard rail was at head level for the humans.

"I wonder how far down it is," said Dandy when his light revealed nothing.

Corky stepped to the side and fumbled around in a cabinet, coming up with a strange looking metal tool. He dropped it into the void. It took a long time before they were rewarded with a metallic crash. "The first step would do ya in, even with the light gravity." said Corky.

"We need to find the water hookup. You go to the right and I'll go the other way."

As Dandy ranged along the forward end of the room, he found a parking lot for cargo- handling machines. Each was locked into its own little stall. Dandy climbed onto one. Again there was a stool for seating, bracketed by two bars that appeared to be positioned as hand holds for the two lower arms. Above were delicate controls for the upper hands.

"I think I found it," called Corky. "Both wet and dry goods are moved through pipes."

When Dandy joined Corky, he was inspecting four large valves. There were labels which, of course, meant nothing to the humans. On each side of the bank of valves were bins holding sections of semi-flexible, eight-or-so-inch pipes with quick connectors.

"The two on the left move dry goods....flour, grain, I'd say. There is dusty residue in the tubes. The two on the right look like liquid conveyers, but I can't tell what."

"I'd guess they are food stuffs," said Dandy. "There shouldn't be need for motor oil or diesel in this section of the ship. This looks like a housekeeping unit. Let's see where they lead."

The pipes passed through the wall. Dandy found an airlock and they cycled through into a vast hallway. The first room on the left was full of bodies. "This was probably a staging area," said Dandy. "It's not a living area."

Beatrice came on the radio. "There is a rack on the wall that looks as if it has reading material. Bring back a piece."

Not wanting to take too much time, Dandy quickly grabbed one that had a lot of pictures, similar to an American magazine.

Corky pushed the control for a door across the hall. The door slowly recessed into the wall revealing a utility area full of wiring and plumbing. The pipes in question came through the wall and promptly elbowed down through the deck.

Again Beatrice came over the radio. "The pipes and wiring are all color coded. The blue one is probably water."

"What makes you think that?" asked Dandy

"On earth, blue pretty universally designates water. Light refraction could be the same on other worlds. Besides there is another blue pipe going up into the service area. They might pump water to other parts of the ship but probably not maple syrup or whatever other liquids are pumped in."

"Thanks, Bea. Corky, that storage tank must be below us because the large pipe goes down. There's got to be a way to get personnel up and down. Let's try to get down as far as the freight elevator to see if that big blue pipe is still there."

Corky came back with, "Let's also keep an eye open for the source of the emergency power. I'd like to see what runs this thing."

When they found the elevator, they decided not to chance

getting caught in it with too little power to get out again. A staircase led them deep into the ship. Bodies were everywhere. Dandy marked every turn with chalk.

After descending thirty decks, Corky made the observation that it was going to take much more energy and breathing air to climb back out than going down. They had already decided they didn't want to chance breathing local air until they were certain the air hadn't killed the crew of the Green Hulk. The big blue pipe was still going down. Fortunately, there was an identical utility room in the same location on each deck. Periodically, they had been checking to see if the elevator was still below them. At the thirtieth level Dandy checked the air supply. Based on Corky's warning, he decided that they would risk running out of air on the return trip if they delayed any longer. It was a long climb back up to the outer hull.

By the time Dandy and Corky got back to Taran, they were exhausted. In a pressure suit, each movement took considerably more energy. Also thirty floors was a misnomer. Due to the height of the rooms, it was like sixty floors on earth. Also the steps were twice as high. Low gravity helped.

After Dandy woke up, Candie joined him in the Fish House as he ate. Corky was still asleep. Tom was in his bed. Beatrice was going over the printed material that had been brought back.... trying to translate it and the signs and tags she'd recorded. Her bare foot was absently rubbing Doughboy, who had settled on four short limbs like a dachshund as his means of locomotion.

Dandy wasn't feeling all that energetic, but he looked to be in better shape than Candie. She had been trying to exercise herself back into psychological health but it hadn't worked. Now she was physically exhausted as well as depressed.

"Tom's on a straight downhill slide," said Candie, in a low voice designed not to carry. Nothing in our files is of any help. I've performed all the tests we have aboard, and they are all within normal parameters. I've tried various pharmaceutics, which do nothing but disrupt his system. Dandy, we're losing Tom."Candie's eyes were moist.

The whole crew knew there were multitudes of unknown dangers swirling about them, but this was the first time a member had been struck. Candie was a doer, but no matter what she did, nothing improved the situation.

Candie continued, as she batted tears away. "We've got to get off Ironmonger soon or Tom will never make it back home."

"Today's foray added a little bit to our store of knowledge, but it didn't find the water supply. Once we find it, we have to figure out how to get it up here. Youre right, we need to speed this operation up."Dandy refilled his coffee cup before heading to his station where he leaned back to think.

Candie's small smile indicated her faith in Dandy as he settled into his thinking position. Beatrice also took note.

Chapter   16

Hours later, when Dandy rejoined the rest of the crew, he singled out Beatrice. "Have you come up with their numbering system yet?"

"Oh, yes. From that printed material you brought back, all one has to do is decided on which is page one and then go from there. It's based on a base nine system rather like the triangular base of the Bips in the Tau Ceti system. This is probably because they have three appendages."

"Please write their system down on a card I can take with me. Have you come to any conclusion concerning the control console?"

"The big control in the middle of the board is probably the big elevator. There is a window that shows which floor it would be on. The up/down arrows are the same as for us. The switch to the right may be the outer door. There are several reading windows, which probably give various statuses before opening the door to space. There is nothing to indicate what the lesser controls operate."

"Good," said Dandy rather absently as he changed mental gears and subjects. "We have to pick up our pace and try some new things. Remember when we first approached Ironmonger, we received a signal that was repeated for twenty hours. I'm banking on Ironmonger working on a default system where it will issue the same length warning before it takes any action.

"What we have seen of the inside of Green Hulk would indicate that the entire crew was killed at one time. No one would have had time or reason for diddling around with the controls, so it might be possible that there are a lot of systems still functioning. It may be that when there is a power drain, the generators might kick in to provide the necessary power.

"There is one thing that we must seriously consider. I would suspect that, by normal standards, when there is a new arrival on Ironmonger, there is one hell of a crash. The vibrations of such a collision probably are felt down to the core, alerting the various denizens of this lump of metal that there is new salvage available. Our landing was probably too mild to attract very much attention. However, when we start thrashing about, we may attract a lot of attention, especially if they think there is a flyable ship available to get them off this scrap yard. A ship the size of the Green Hulk has to have weaponry. We need to find it."

Tom was following the meeting from his bed. In a weak voice he added, "There are no turrets visible from what we can see. They must be recessed and opened when needed. You'll have to find them from the inside, and probably fire control will be in the command section."

"If that's the case, then the ship wasn't brought down during a battle," said Candy.

"Then what's that big hole we can see in the engine section?" said Beatrice.

"Another chunk of incoming space junk may have bashed into it," said Candy.

"Anyway," continued Dandy, "we need to find those weapons while we are finding that water. I've laid out a new approach. To accelerate our pace, I've cut out a few of the security procedures we've been using. On some things, we're going to have to work solo instead of using the buddy system. Our first priority is to find water and this is what we are going to do. Our future action depends on what we find out in the next few hours."

After Dandy laid out his plan of action, there was a flurry of activity. Dandy, Candie and Corky suited up. Dandy left Taran to trek to the elevator assembly, where he opened the access hatch and lowered himself into the ship.

He made his way into the control room. He didn't let himself think too much about all the bodies strewn around. After a momentary hesitation, he heaved the body slumped over the main console off to the side. He had to climb up on the stool to get close to the console.

Dandy started flipping switches on the bank where Corky had found the elevator lights until he found some illumination for the control room. He didn't want to have to devote one hand to operating his flashlight. He turned his attention to the large up/down lever in the center of the console. He had to practically crawl onto the work-surface to reach the switch. Since he had visualized his approach to the problem, Dandy continued as if he knew what he was doing. He pushed the lever up. In the adjacent gauge window a number appeared in a red glow. However, there was no accompanying sound of movement. The number, according to the list Beatrice had given him was down 45 floors....providing they counted the floors from the top down.

Since the elevator wouldn't move, Dandy turned his attention to the other complex of controls. The main element was a horizontal slider. He moved it to the left a fraction of an inch. Nothing happened. A little more movement set up a host of flashing lights all over the control board. Lights started blinking in the elevator shaft, apparently warning the crew they were about to be exposed to space. When the board activities ceased, Dandy advanced the slide. More warnings went off. He couldn't move the mechanism until certain functions had been completed. When the board turned yellow the slide was free again. The third notch produced a groan of protest. A shaft of light cut through the darkness in the elevator bay. The great door dropped a few inches and then began to retract toward the front of the ship. Movement was slow. It reminded Dandy of the roofs of domed stadiums.

While Dandy waited for the retraction of the door, he called

Candie. "The door's opening slowly. It will probably take another fifteen minutes....providing it opens all the way. Go ahead and clear the hole so you can open the ramp."

"We sucked up something more than Pretzis and Bird-kins,"said Candie. "I just got a glimpse of a different figure on the monitor. Bea, did you see anything?"

"I wasn't looking. Maybe there's something on the tape."

Dandy broke in. "Don't worry about that now. Get ready to launch."

"We're ready as soon as you give the word," said Corky.

Dandy slid down off his stool to close the control room door. He did so with the thought he'd have to burn his way out of the room if the power failed or the door jammed but he didn't want to get sucked out by the A/Gs.

Now that there was daylight in the elevator shaft, Dandy could see much more equipment than was evident when he and Corky had investigated the area with flashlights.

The door stopped moving and the control panel lights changed to blue. "Launch," said Dandy.

A couple of minutes later Candie announced, "Bay open and locked. It's all yours Corky."

"Here goes," said Corky in his usual casual manner, but this time there was a tinge of tension in his voice as he tipped the shuttle out of Taran. The instant the shuttle dropped below the ramp, Corky brought the anti-gravity generator on line. The shuttle dropped into the hole in the Green Hulk before the A/Gs were able to arrest the free-fall. Slowly Corky was able to elevate the shuttle back up to surface level.

"Don't try this at home. Under earth's gravity you'll be splattered all over the landscape. Here there's just barely enough gravity to fly."

"Take it for a spin before you pick me up," said Dandy.

As Corky moved out over the hull to practice his driving techniques, Beatrice asked him to activate his cameras so she could get more information on Ironmonger.

"This thing is slow and sluggish," said Corky as he moved it around using maneuvering jets. It wants to side slip. This is not what I call precise driving."

"Get some elevation and then try to bring it straight down."

"It wants to wallow quite a bit, but I think it'll work."

"Okay, sit down here and turn off the A/Gs so I can get to you."

Once the shuttle was grounded, Dandy made his way to the surface. He closed the entry hatch before getting into the shuttle. "Let's see what's down below."

Corky lifted the shuttle off the deck and crept over the elevator opening.

"Turn around so we face the airlocks."

Corky swung the craft around before beginning the unsteady descent. Dust and minor debris rattled on the bottom of the shuttle. As the air was sucked out of the elevator shaft, the vortex diminished until weightless objects floated by. Slowly the shuttle settled down into the bowels of the great spaceship. Floor-by-floor the scenery changed. It appeared that different materials were unloaded on specific levels.

Occasionally Corky banged into the edges of the floors, but there didn't seem to be any damage. Candie was the designated driver of that unit. Corky was actually the operator of the pick-up. On this occasion, Candie had bowed to Corky's superior driving experience.

As the shuttle sank deeper into the hulk, tensions mounted. The radio finally went silent because the signal couldn't get out. Dandy offered no advice to the driver. Finally, the elevator platform came into the view of the bottom-mounted camera. The landing site was clear of any cargo. Corky set the shuttle down with a thump.

Dandy unbuckled his harness. "Open the hatch as soon as all the debris falls back down." The external lights from the shuttle gave sufficient illumination. Dandy quickly made his way to the airlock, which was closed. He started to play with the buttons besides the opening, but nothing altered the blue light that glowed above the door.

"I was afraid of that. There is no override on this side of the door when the shaft is exposed to the void. Corky, bring the cutting compound."

To avoid going through the door retraction mechanism, they burned through the wall into the adjacent room. It proved to be a staging area similar to the one they had seen on the upper floors. A few bodies were strewn about the area.

In the utility room, where they had originally found the pipes, there was the same setup. Both pipes penetrated the floor.

The tanks can't be much further," declared Dandy. "We must be near the center shaft that connects all three segments of the ship together. Let's see what's underneath us."

There were many more steps going down to the next level. They entered a huge corridor which ran far beyond their flashlight beams. There was what looked like a subway train track. Rails showed behind sliding doors. The pipes didn't reach that level.

"We're into the core," said Corky. "Those pipes must go to the rear between floors."

The pair retreated to the next level up. Further down the central corridor toward the rear, they found access into the utility area between decks. Stretching off into the distance was an enormous tank.

"If they use water, I'd guess this was where they stored it," said Dandy. There was a ramp that led along the top of the tank. "Let's see how big this tank is."

"This tank must be twenty feet thick," said Corky. "It disappears into the distance, both to the sides and aft. If there's any reasonable percentage of water in this thing, what we can see from here is more than enough to replenish Taran."

"Yeah," said Dandy. "But if it is water, it's frozen. We have to figure a way to get it to Taran quickly. Tom is running out of time. Let's follow this tank and see if we can figure out how to get the water to the surface."

The pair moved out smartly because their air wouldn't last forever. Every hundred feet or so there was a low, rectangular structure. Corky stopped to examine one. "I think these things are hatches into the tank. I'll bet these are clean-outs."

There was a control pad mounted on one end, but it was not lighted and Dandy got no response punching buttons. He could see no device, such as a wheel or dogs, to mechanically open the cover.

Corky knelt down to closely examine two handles that ex-tended downward on either side of the box near the key pad. He tried to draw the handles toward himself, but he couldn't move them. "You pull on one and I'll work the other."

When both men brought pressure to bear, there was a click and the top snapped up on one end. It was hinged on the far side. It took their combined strength to raise the lid.

The lip was so high they couldn't see over it. Corky lowered himself to his knees so Dandy could stand on his back.

"Oh, boy, it looks like water to me. It's one big ice cube. I'd guess the tank's about half full. This is a pressure seal around the edge. They must have used an air-pressure system in a non-gravitational environment. Let's seal this thing up and see how far this tank goes."

Dandy paced the distances between the access hatches and calculated the distance they had traveled. "We should be getting close to where Taran burned its hole. The ship will be off to the right fifty yards or so. We're about there. The heat has discolored the ceiling."

Dandy marked the closest clean-out and made a right turn to see how close to the hole they could get.

"We've got a wall ahead of us. I'd guess that is the edge of the tank, but we're not to the hole yet."

"The hole doesn't come this deep," said Corky. "We're a

hundred feet or so below the bottom of the hole. And it's still off to the side. We're far enough away we didn't melt anything."

"Let's get back before our air becomes a problem."Dandy started toward the center of the tank and then he stopped so suddenly Corky walked right into him. "Turn up your gain and listen. Can you hear anything?"

Corky listened intently for a long time before returning to the wall that had blocked their way. He pulled off his glove and placed his palm against the flat metal. "It feels like someone is trying to bash his way through doors or walls.

"There has to be some passageway from the bottom contact area of the Green Hulk to the hole to let in the Bird-kins and the Pretzis. Apparently, they're trying to get into other sections of the ship. We probably burned through the electrical circuitry when we landed, cutting off the power to the doors. Now they have to bash their way through. It sounds as if we have attracted the attention of the denizens of Ironmonger. Let's get back before we have to fight our way through aliens."

Dandy and Corky broke into a ground-covering shuffle on the way back to the shuttle. Without delay Corky slid into the pilot's seat and lifted off. Dandy was thankful he didn't have much in his stomach. Occasionally, something ripped loose and crashed into the bottom of the shuttle.

When they cleared the hull, Dandy called Taran. Beatrice came back immediately. "You better get back. The hole is full of new creatures and we can see movement on the derelict ships below us."

When Dandy got out to close the elevator door, Corky made a brief reconnaissance run along their section of the Green Hulk. "Dandy, I see something I want to look at. Can you hike back to the ship? I'll be back as soon as I can."

"Watch yourself. We've got company. Don't stay too long. I'm going to need your help on a project."

Candie broke into the conversation. "Before you get here I'm going to have to clean out the hole. There's lots of activity and the new ones are armed. They just shot down our camera."

"Do it now. Corky's out of range and I'll be in the control room for awhile."

By the time the Hulk was sealed, Candie had sucked everything clean with the A/Gs. Dandy made his way back to Taran. Candie met him in the changing room.

"Damn. I hate turning on those A/Gs. I have no idea how many creatures I killed this time but there was a bunch."

"We can't take the risk of losing Taran. You can bet none of the Ironmonger inhabitants would let us stand between them and escape from this pile of junk. They probably aren't aware they are in a strange galaxy."

"Beatrice has some pictures of the new aliens that were taken before they blasted the camera. This is another strange looking bunch."

"Let's wait until Corky gets here so we can all see them at one time. Right now our immediate concern is getting through the hull. We've found water. Getting it out will be our next chore. We can't burn through the outer skin of the Green Hulk with our regular incendiary material."

"How about that first concoction Corky made to mine water from the Comet? That was pretty potent."

When Corky joined them in the control room, he asked Beatrice to turn a camera on the shuttle, which he had parked by the elevator. "I'd hate to have someone or something steal or damage my cute little sports car."He smiled at Candie as he said it. "We can defend it from the ramp if we have to."

When everyone was settled at his console Beatrice started playing the tape showing the new arrivals. "I heard them on the audio system. I raised the video unit four levels before I found them. After the camera was in place, I turned on the lights. The brightness surprised them and I had seven seconds before one of them blasted the unit. I've made stills of the best views."

The first shot showed three figures at various angles to the camera so a good impression could be gained of their general physique.

Beatrice continued. "I compute their height to be around ten feet. On earth, they'd weigh four to five hundred pounds."

"I'm beginning to get an inferiority complex." said Corky. "Everything's bigger than we are."

"It gets worse," said Candie. "These guys are armor-plated."

"At least on their backs," said Beatrice. "Their fronts seem to be of a softer material, so they wear elaborate light-reflecting plates over their soft tissue, which leads one to speculate that their weaponry involves energy rather than projectiles. We are either dealing with one sex or there is no discernable difference while they are dressed. Their backs are covered with what looks like a rigid shell such as on a turtle, but it is articulated in four places similar to an armadillo's. The tail, upper arms, back of the neck and head have what I'd call fish scales. They have virtually smooth heads....no protruding ear or nose forms. Their mouths are lipless gashes with lots of pointed teeth....another carnivore. These guys are heavily burdened with weapons."

Beatrice shifted to another image showing a close-up. "The main item of interest is the gun he's carrying. It certainly doesn't shoot a projectile. I was watching this one when the flood lights came on. He shot from the hip in a sweep at the lights. The screen went black. When Candie pulled in the lines, the nylon was melted. So was the electrical wiring. I have no way of knowing the range of these weapons. I didn't see any large power source but that may not mean anything.

"Just a few other observations: This batch will probably be very strong, but slow. Watch out for their tails. They appear to be constructed to be used as a weapon. They also have claws."

"And ray guns," said Tom in a weak voice from his bed. "You need weapons."

"Yes," agreed Dandy. "Something is trying to batter its way into other regions of the ship. That could interfere with our water collecting job."Dandy gave the rest of the crew a brief résumé of his and Corky's trip into the Green Hulk.

Corky was doing his nervous little shuffle, indicating that he had something important to add. Dandy finished his report and nodded to Corky.

"I'm not sure, but I think I found the ship's armament. Scattered along the top are several doors like elevator bays, but smaller. I went far enough over the side to see similar structures all along the flanks. I'm guessing they are gun ports. Maybe they will have access bays like the one at the elevator. I'd like to take my key out to one to see if I can get in."

"Right now I need your expertise down in the shop," said Dandy. We need to cut through the hull to find that water pipe."

"How far away is the closest gun port?" said Candie.

"There is one just beyond the hole we burned and another about a hundred yards beyond the elevator. The closest one may be damaged by the heat. And those aliens may be wandering around that part of the ship. The best bet would be the forward port."

Candie stood up. "Let me take a look while you guys breech the hull."

Dandy nodded. Turning to Corky, he continued. "Check with Tom for any ideas he may have for getting through that outer shell."He walked over to Beatrice's station. "Keep an eye on Candie. We don't want any aliens getting between her and Taran."

"You'd better turn on the A/Gs, but you'll have to move the shuttle first," said Beatrice.

"Good thinking."

Dandy headed down to the changing room to help Candie suit-up. "When you're ready to leave the elevator, wait until Bea says it's clear. Then make for the shuttle. When you've moved it out of harm's way, we'll clear out the hole. It's time you did some practicing with the shuttle. Corky says it's really slow and sluggish. Don't get out of sight."

"Aye, aye, Captain," said Candie as she gave him an impish little smile.

Dandy was glad to see the smile. It was a flashback to earlier days. Lately, she had been so depressed over Tom's condition, her smile was on hiatus.

Corky was busy in his workshop when Dandy arrived. "Tom seems to think that first formula we used on the comet might be hot enough."

"Candie is of the same opinion. Let's give it a try."

Half an hour later the pair was in the changing room again. This time they weren't getting into their bulky suits, but pulling on additional overalls. Since they weren't entering the Green Hulk and they planned on only being outside a few minutes they decided to brave the Ironmonger elements and air. Both were carrying side arms.

The two men waited in the elevator until Candie landed the shuttle a safe distance away. When the vortex subsided, they stepped out of Taran. Candie had to raise her face mask to talk. After her initial coughing fit, she said, "You were right, Corky. They are firing ports. Those guns are massive, ugly things that work on some sort of energy. I'll tell you about them when you get back."

Dandy led the way to where he calculated the four-inch water pipe ran fore and aft. Corky inscribed a four-foot square. He stuck in an igniter into the gel before they retreated to the protection of one of Taran's legs. Corky set off the charge remotely.

There was a brilliant flash and the sound of hissing in the air. The light persisted until the entire gel line had been consumed. The heat had been so intense, they couldn't approach within ten feet. The green hull had changed to a charcoal color, but the square was still in place. Under the subfreezing conditions it soon cooled enough to examine the results.

Corky still couldn't touch the cut marks. "I think the material has crystallized enough that a good rap with a hammer will break through. I know how to concentrated more heat in a narrower strip."

"Let's head back to hear what Candie found out. Then makeup

enough material to burn four holes. We should be able to locate that pipe in that many tries.

Chapter 17

Beatrice, Dandy and Candie met in the Fish House to eat a meal. Corky took his food into Tom's room to keep the ailing engineer company. They could follow Candie's report concerning the gun ports over the intercom.

"Next to the gun ports are airlock access doors similar to the one by the elevator. However, there are glass or plastic....clear walls into the gun. There are no visible controls. It looks as if all activity in there is for repairs. There are all sorts of storage cupboards facing onto the corridor that circles the gun. My guess is that it is fired from some other location."

"If the forward unit is the command center, fire control is probably up there," said Tom. Even though Tom could hardly stand, he still could think clearly.

"Do you think there would be any value in burning our way into those guns?" said Dandy.

"No," said Candie. We would have to find the control center to fire them and they are of no use against our local problem. I imagine they are ship to ship weapons."

"Okay," said Dandy. "Let's put that aside for the moment. We have several other pressing matters. Candie, do you think you can drop a small mike on a thin line down the hole so we can keep track of the Pretzis, Bird-ins, and now those new things."

"The Hornitoads?" said Corky,

"Hornitoads?" asked Beatrice.

"Yeah. They sure look like the horn toads we used to find under most every rock in the deserts out west. These guys don't have horns on their heads but they sure have scales, claws and tails like those little critters."

"Okay, Hornitoads," said Dandy. He continued on. "Get those charges ready and also be thinking of the best way to get the water from the pipe into Taran. I plan to put fire in the hole, flooding this section with heat to melt the ice in the tank. I'm banking on a pressure feed so if we can generated enough steam, maybe we can push it up this high. Even at this low gravity, I doubt if we can lift a column of water that many feet. Work out with Tom how to get the water, no matter what form it's in, into the ship."

Dandy was interrupted by a sound out of their past. Ironmonger's original hail came blasting over the speakers.

"Candie. Check the sensors. See if we have company. Has Ironmonger changed directions or speed?"

"Bea. Have you noted any change on Ironmonger? Any changes in conditions—temperature, gravity, light—anything?"

"No." There was a pause. "Except that the radio frequency you guys use where you're outside has developed periodic static."

"What do you mean?"

"In the last two days there have been irregular periods of light static. I'm not familiar enough with radios to know whether that's abnormal."

"Tom. Please check our transmission records to see if there is any cause for concern."

Dandy went to stand behind Candie as she searched what space was visible from their vantage point. She kept shaking her head as she went from sector to sector.

"Everything that I can see is clear. Of course that isn't saying much. There could be a whole fleet on the other side of this garbage scow."

The only revelation coming from all the activities initiated by Ironmonger's warning was that Tom found that radios were being used inside the hull. The alien frequency bled through to the one Taran was using.

Chapter 18

The primary result of the Ironmonger warning was to drive TC into a much more intensive round of activity. They didn't want to be carried even further from Earth should Ironmonger start chasing another piece of space junk going in the opposite direction.

Dandy and Corky found the water pipe, tapped into the line, and connected it to the pipe segments they had brought up from the elevator shaft. That got the water line to about 200 feet from Taran. The remaining sections would have to be elevated off the deck to keep them out of the heat that would be generated by the main engine burn. Dandy was going to heat the interior of the Green Hulk.

Corky ended up dangling high on Taran's side attaching hoses into the fuel intakes. Everybody, except Tom, got into the labor routine. Even Beatrice put in shifts working outside.

The warning had sounded for only two hours instead of the twenty hours of their first encounter. There was no change in velocity or direction. TC doubted that Ironmonger had received any recognition signal from anything in their galaxy. Corky speculated that maybe the Bips had appeared and then grabbed another gravitation strand and disappeared again. The question was left hanging, but the accelerated work schedule continued.

Dandy called TC together in the Fish House for a final session before they started their water recovery effort. Corky wheeled Tom in to give him a break from his room.

The first question Dandy threw out was, "Candie, what are we pulling out of the hole now?"

"It's pretty much the same old debris but I don't see any more Pretzis or Bird-kins. They must have learned that the hole is dangerous."

"There's a lot of noise coming out of the ship," said Beatrice. "I think it's the Hornitoads and they are very active. Until they showed up, the other aliens were almost silent."

"The aliens may have abandoned the hole so the A/Gs don't get them, but when we put fire in the hole, everything in the vicinity will be fried. I'd like to avoid killing very many. I'm going to fire up the engine for just a moment. Maybe they'll get the idea and evacuate this section. I'm going to get the whole place hot enough to make steam."

"What happens if there are closed valves somewhere in the system?" asked Tom.

"Then I'll send you inside to open them."

That comment produced an excessive amount of laughter, which embarrassed the crew.

Lamely, Dandy continued. "At least it shouldn't be clogged with ice."

"How hot do you think it will get in there?" said Beatrice.

"It'll be red hot in the hole. The rest of the ship will also be hot, but the space suits will be able to handle the heat for enough time to make a quick trip. I hope it doesn't come to that"

After all the work assignments had been made, Dandy settled into his station. It seemed like an eternity since he had flown the ship. Normally Tom went through the preliminary checks with him, but that function had been transferred to Candie.

When all sections were ready, Dandy started the main engine, keeping it at the lowest idle level. He didn't want to generate any thrust that could shift Taran's weight. As a safety factor he powered up the A/Gs so they could be engaged should the ship become unbalanced. As soon as the engine fully fired, he shut them down.

There was no telling how far into the pit the tail of flame had penetrated. As the flame winked out, Dandy said, "I hope those aliens get the message and evacuate. I'll give them another blast in two hours. In four hours we'll start heating the whole thing. It should be pretty uncomfortable down there."

Dandy got himself a cup of coffee and a tea for Candie. He leaned against an empty map table. "There isn't much to chart above the ecliptic."

"Oh, there are things of interest out there, but from this vantage point, I can't see enough. The Solar Jets are really weird. It looks like they're lonely and intertwine. Out here they don't have as many nearby forces working on them."

Candie dropped the volume of her voice so it wouldn't carry. "If we could get off this garbage scow tomorrow, I doubt if we could get back home before life just drains out of Tom. He's trying to put on a resolute face, but it is changing into a fatalistic waiting game."

"If we can get Taran refueled, we still have the problem of getting off Ironmonger. We're either going to have to deactivate that towing force or find the recognition code."

"The ships that are here probably didn't have the code."

"Not necessarily," said Dandy. "I suspect the crew of the Green Hulk was dead long before Ironmonger showed up."

"Did you ever find out what killed the crew?"

Dandy shook his head. "Best bet is a poisonous gas that caught everyone so fast they couldn't move"

"I don't see how a gas could pass through the entire ship without someone sounding the alarm. We're looking at everything from our experience. The Bib ship we encountered on the first trip had a propulsion system beyond our knowledge. I think the Green Hulk has an entirely different system....some energy force. I'll bet they were zapped with something like that."

"If they were, it didn't interfere with the electrical system. It's too bad Tom can't investigate all those ships. Everything here is far ahead of us."

Two hours after the second start-up, Dandy inched the throttle up. He hoped he could burn down a little closer to the water tank without rupturing it. Corky was on the surface near the elevator, monitoring the hull temperature under Taran's legs. They couldn't afford to melt the metal holding them up.

In three minutes Corky sounded the warning to shut down. "We've got to move the shuttle further away. The hull is getting too hot. Any more heat and I won't be able to walk on the surface."

"Go ahead and park it far enough away to be safe and then check the water line to see if we're getting any activity."

"Don't be so impatient," said Beatrice. "It will probably take three or four days to thaw out everything. Maybe you've got a column of ice several hundred feet high. There are going to have to be a lot of calories exchanged."

"You're right Bea. Corky, just move the shuttle and come back. I'll heat things up again."

Beatrice was correct in her estimate. Three days later, a wisp of steam came out of a coupling. The deck was so hot Corky had to make special foot gear to get himself elevated off the surface. They had to move the shuttle even further away. The monotony of waiting was interrupted once when Ironmonger's warning sounded again. Still there was no visible reason, and no action was initiated. The warning sounded for only three hours.

Corky was monitoring the inlet. "We're getting steam and it's condensing in the tanks. There doesn't seem to be very much pressure. We may be using more fuel than we're generating."

"That's not what we wanted to hear," said Candy.

"Another thing. Heat is building up in Taran's feet. We'll have to watch that we don't start boiling our own water. Then we'd have to shut down until we cool of."

"I was afraid of developing too much pressure," said Dandy. "Maybe we have a leak or a blow out." Dandy shut down the power. The ship became silent, except for the groaning and popping of the heated metal underfoot.

"Take a look at this," said Beatrice. One of the screens showed a camera view across the top of the Green Hulk. In the distance, the perpetual dim light of the sun reflected off a cloud rising above the hull. "Since there doesn't seem to be much climate on Ironmonger and hot air rises, I'd say you're losing pressure through the bottom."

"Of course," said Dandy. "We're using the water supply to what we consider to be the upper part of the ship. There must be a like supply to the lower half. When this thing fell onto Ironmonger, the opposite side water line could have been crushed. Under gravity, that side would get more water than this side. We've got to close off that other side."

"How?" asked Candie, with a hint of sarcasm.

"We'll have to let things cool down a bit, then we'll have to go down the elevator shaft again."

Beatrice pointed out, "There are several hundred feet of red hot metal down there."

"I'll open the elevator door to let the place air out. Our space suits have a high temperature coefficient," said Dandy.

"At least we don't have to worry about aliens coming up through the hull," said Candie.

Two days later, the Green Hulk had cooled enough for Dandy to get into the control room. The emergency power was still operating in that part of the ship. There was a great groaning as the elevator door opened ever so slowly. Corky speculated the hull had warped somewhat.

Great billows of hot air rushed out into the sub-freezing air of Ironmonger. The following day, Corky and Dandy took the shuttle into the depths of the Green Hulk. Temperatures were still high. Corky remained in the air conditioned shuttle while Dandy searched for the other pipe. Corky was the safety backup. He could dash out to help Dandy in case an emergency developed. The two would have radio communication inside the hull.

There was no trace of a second line in the room where they had found the first blue pipe. Dandy had to go down below the central tubes that connected the three segments of the ship.

"Corky, the artificial gravity must be right down the middle of the ship. I'm walking on the ceilings down here. There's a duplicate room to the one on the upper side. I've found the other water line. It comes directly out of the other side of the tank. The problem is that the mechanical valve is about six feet over my head."

"How are you feeling? You don't have too much air left."

"It's getting damned hot in this suit. I can't stay down here much longer. My air is getting hot too. Bring me a new tank and a rope. Hurry."

Following Dandy's direction, Corky hurried to the site. After changing the gas tank. Corky threw the rope over a pipe to steady himself while he clambered onto Dandy's shoulders. He was able to grasp the two pinch levers similar to the ones they had encountered on the entrance to the water tank. Corky's weight drew the handles together, shutting the valve.

Dandy was exhausted by the time he got back to the ship, but he fired the engine again to regenerate the hull heat. It didn't take long for a wisp of steam to seep from a hose coupling. Beatrice could find no trace of the cloud rising from the bottom. Corky reported the pressure was building in the system. Dandy collapsed into his bed.

Slowly, Taran took on water. It became a waiting game with occasional snippets of activity. During a lull, Candie brought Dandy a cup of coffee. She settled down on the floor next to his couch out of view of the rest of the crew. She took a sip of her tea. "Tom is slipping deeper into whatever malady he has. Corky has to tend to almost all his needs. He's still mentally alert but the ability of his body to consciously function is fading away. Involuntary actions still seem to be on line. He can't last much longer."Distress was written across Candie's face.

"Yeah, I know. I hate to have to work Corky so much. He never complains and never misses a beat. As soon as he finishes his job, he's back with Tom. Beatrice spells him so he can get some rest. At least, now, things aren't as strenuous."

"Beatrice is having her own concern. Something is wrong with Doughboy. He's reverting more to his original lump. He still maintains Bea's hand, but he's losing the rest of his humanoid forms."

"Remember, Tea House said a nibbling was infused with energy that had to be replenished periodically. Do you think he is running out of energy?"

Dandy shrugged. "I have no way of knowing. I wonder if we have any energy source around here that would help him if that is his problem."

 I'll ask Corky to ask if Tom has any thoughts along those lines. Tom needs to feel he can contribute."

Ironmonger's warning sounded again. Dandy switched on the scanners, which showed nothing more than on the several other times the warning had gone off. "I wonder if there is a rat in Ironmonger's wiring."

The sound was muffled but the impact was sharp. It rattled Taran and brought TC to an instant alert. The main engine had not been firing at the time, so Dandy started looking elsewhere for the cause. He didn't get far before a second jolt rocked the ship. The sound of metal protesting assaulted their ears. Taran began to tilt.

Dandy yelled, "Strap in."

He didn't have time to wait for compliance. Balance had to be regained. The A/Gs came on line. He rammed the throttle up to rectify the tilt before any added power would help push Taran on its side.

Taran wallowed sluggishly. The A/Gs were not strong enough in Ironmonger's light gravity and rarified atmosphere to lift the ship's great weight. The best he could do was sideslip to a more stable location on the hull. When Dandy could see fresh metal beneath him, he eased off the power, permitting Taran to settle again.

"Does anyone know what happened?"demanded Dandy over the intercom.

"The shuttle is gone," said Beatrice.

"We're under attack." shouted Candie. "There's an alien ship rising over the far side of the third section of the Green Hulk. Look at the size of that sucker."

Corky, who had been on a lower level, came out of the elevator on the run. "They blasted the shuttle to pieces. They can do the same to us."

"They won't," said Dandy. "They want this ship."

On one of the screens, TC could see a gigantic ship rising into view. It was obviously not designed for landing. Bits and pieces and antennas stuck out in all directions.

"That thing is so badly damaged it can hardly fly," said Tom in his weak voice.

When the full extent of the attacking ship could be seen, it proved to be a fraction of the size of the Green Hulk but it also dwarfed Taran. There were several damage sites visible. Slowly it moved along the top of the third section.

TC sat watching the monitor. They had no defense against an armed aggressor. Their only alternative would be to attempt flight, but with the demonstration against the shuttle, Dandy held little hope of lifting off before they would be shot down. Then, where would they go? They didn't have enough fuel to get home and they still hadn't solved Ironmonger's attractor ray problem.

"What are they going to do?"Beatrice's panicky voice had returned.

"Nothing at the moment," snapped Dandy. "Come on Bea, get with it. We need your input. Candie, look around and find out where we are now. Corky, get up to the intake valve and secure everything."

"Bea, keep up a running commentary on what the aliens are doing."There was a long pause. "Bea, I don't hear anything"

There was another silence before a shaky voice said, "They're coming toward us.........."

"How high, how fast, right at us?"

"The ship is just barely off the surface. It's coming very slowly. It's moving back and forth."

"Back and forth?"asked Dandy, who was going through pre-flight checks.

"They're wallowing around just like we did."

"They can hardly keep it in the air," whispered Tom.

Candy had been searching with a couple of the cameras. "We are almost over the elevator. The shuttle debris had disappeared as well as all the water connections. I can see a plume of steam coming out of the hull where we cut through to get to the pipe."

In the background, Beatrice droned on. "The front part of the ship is over this section."

Corky reported that the water intake was secure.

"They've stopped," said Beatrice in a much more forceful voice. Candie flashed Dandy a smile. She was wearing her dangly earrings, which flashed too.

"The ship is settling down, spanning the gap between the sections," continued Beatrice.

"They're making a bridge," said Corky, who had just reentered the control room.

"Can we hop over to the front section?" asked Candie.

"We can, but I'd rather not. We still need water and there may not be any great quantity there or at least where we can get at it. Also those guys can probably pass to that front section through the connecting tubes that don't seem to be damaged."

Something is happening but I don't know what," said Beatrice. "It's too far away."

Dandy turned to Candie. "Can you depress one of your scanners far enough to watch the aliens?"

"Sure, but it will just show blips on the screen."

"It'll show movement, right?"

"Yeah."

"Set it so, if there is any movement, the alarm will go off. Corky, dig up a set of design specs for Taran and put them through on Candie's screen."

The affair turned into a waiting game. Suddenly Tom became aware that the Ironmonger warning was no longer being sounded. No one recognized when it had gone off. Tom postulated the warning they had been hearing over the past days came on every time the Hornitoads tried to get their ship to fly.

Two hours went by without any movement. Dandy had Candie and Corky take a rest. Dandy left Beatrice watching while he checked in on Tom.

Tom hated his situation. He refused any offer of aid by Dandy, choosing to limit the demonstration of his almost total incapacity to Corky's eyes. He still was mentally alert.

"This is going to throw your schedule off again," said Tom with a wan smile.

"Yes. I can afford the delay, but how about you? Are you going to be able to hang in there?"

Tom weakly shook his head. "Don't know. There isn't much left. I'm on a strange road. I don't know where it's going or how long it is. I feel like I can get there mentally, but I don't know if I can drag this body that far."

"You keep dragging and I'll try to hurry things along."

Dandy went to sit at Candie's station, where he studied Taran's specs. Two hours later, when the scanner alarm went off, he was still sitting with his fingers laced behind his head and his heels on the map table.

The alarm brought Candie and Corky out of their rooms. Beatrice reported she could not see anything different optically even though the scanner registered movement.

Finally, Beatrice was able to separate movement from the jumbled background of the alien ship. She let out a sarcastic snort. "It looks like an ancient roman phalanx advancing behind shields reaching to the ground."She switched the enhanced scene to the other monitors.

Corky's voice came over the intercom. "Tom says they think we have impulse weapons. Those shields are designed to deflect the energy." There was a pause before Corky continued. "We'll have to guard against that kind of weapon. They're not prepared for projectile weapons. Bullets will go right through those flimsy shields."

As the group advanced, more details became visible. There were about thirty Hornitoads in full body armor. Each carried a curved shield with the concavity directed toward Taran. "It looks like the shields are designed to redirect the energy back in the direction of its source," relayed Corky. "The reflected energy must still be hazardous."

"Do we have anything that could deflect their weapons?" said Dandy.

Corky answered, "We have those emergency thermal blankets, which are highly reflective, but I'd hate to rely on one of those to repulse whatever artillery they're carrying without a little prior testing. That would be a big leap of faith."

"We're not quite that desperate," said Dandy. "I'm pretty certain they don't want to damage Taran. We'll let them get closer and then try to disrupt their plans with an A/G vortex."

Dandy was ready to lift off if the situation deteriorated to the point where there were no other alternatives. Beyond that, there was little left to do except watch the advance of the Hornitoads. The cluster was still a speck when they began to disburse into a staggered skirmish line.

"They're trying to determine what kind of weapons we have." said Tom, who was the only one with military training.

Slowly the advancing troops formed a half circle around Taran far enough away to prevent scorching their feet. The Hornitoads took up stationary positions behind their shields. After a five minute wait, one attacker left its shield standing and stepped into the open. It was still carrying a large, lethal-looking weapon. After another five minutes, the alien unplugged a cable from a connection near his waist and set the gun on the deck.

"That must be a high powered weapon," said Beatrice. "The one that was used to shoot down our camera was much smaller and it didn't have a backpack battery."

The alien slowly advanced until he reached one of Taran's legs. Beatrice was keeping him under constant surveillance with the various cameras. The troops edged a little closer. The lead alien minutely surveyed the underside of Taran.

I think he's spotted the cameras and he knows we're watching him," said Beatrice.

Eventually the alien found the elevator door as he made the rounds of the legs. With a claw-like fingernail, he circumscribed the split in the durathane. He stepped into view of the troops and signaled one, who advanced with his shield and armament.

After a consultation, the pair stepped back and the trooper started to raise his weapon to take a shot at the door. It hesitated as the big generator kicked in when Dandy brought the A/Gs on line. As the vortex developed, the aliens tried to brace themselves against in incoming rush of air. They were snatched off the surface before the rest of the troops came tumbling in. The impacts of the bodies on the underside reverberated through the ship.

"Yuk," said Candie.

Dandy quickly shut down the A/Gs. "I want to see if we can salvage any of those weapons. Come on Corky. Let's make a dash outside to see what we can find."

Dandy and Corky paused long enough in the changing room to pull on jackets and gloves and strap on 45 automatics. When the elevator door opened to Ironmonger atmosphere, the pair remained inside long enough for the coughing fit to pass. When they cautiously stepped outside, there wasn't much to see. There hadn't been any debris lying around to pull into the vortex. There were only three Hornitoad bodies left under Taran. The rest had passed into the air column over the A/Gs and they had been carried much higher and disbursed more widely or had fallen into the pit.

"There's not much to look at," said Corky, as he stood over one crumpled heap.

"The ones out there will probably be in worse shape. That one over there looks like he was carrying the backpacks."

As Dandy was trying to disengage the battery pack and drag the gun from under the heavy corpse, Corky went for a shield that was lying out beyond Taran. There was no other equipment in sight.

Dandy and Corky managed to move the heavy artillery into the elevator. They had gotten liberally smeared with alien blood. Corky quipped, "They can't be all bad. They have red blood just like us."

Candie's voice came over the intercom. "Decontaminate yourselves and that equipment before bringing it aboard."

Two naked, shivering men finally made it back to the changing room. When Candie asked about their cleanliness, Dandy grumbled that the alien blood had all the characteristics of aniline dye.

Corky was particularly elated over the recovery of the gun. "Although, it has been knocked about a bit, it's all here, so it can be replicated. We've got the world's first impulse weapon."

"Something new that'll kill people, huh?" said Candie with a trace of disdain in her voice.

"No," said Corky immediately. "We'll now have a way to defend ourselves against aliens with impulse weapons."

"I think you'd better look at this," said Beatrice. She started to rerun one of the taped records taken just before Dandy had engaged the A/Gs. The view was of the alien ship bridging the two sections of the Green Hulk. Suddenly there was a little camera movement and then objects began passing upward in front of the lens. When the air cleared, Beatrice turned off the tape.

TC sat for a bit before Dandy asked, "What were we supposed to see?"

"Watch the alien ship."She reran the tape. Just before the end, the alien ship began to wobble ever so slightly. "I think that when the A/Gs were sucking air there was enough turbulence clear over there to upset the balance of that ship. Give it another jolt and it may fall into the void."

"Let's give it a try." Dandy started the A/G generators. Gradually he increased the power to a level where Taran was just barely touching the surface. No visible change was seen since there was little debris to be sucked up. Under extreme magnification, it could be seen that bits and pieces of the alien ship that had broken off the ship when it landed were beginning to tumble across the deck toward Taran. Then the ship began to tremble slightly. More pieces began to break off. The wobbling became more pronounced. The ship lurched and then became airborne rising only a few feet above the Green Hulk. It slowly turned away but it didn't appear that the ship could gain head-way. After a prolonged struggle, the vessel came about, heading toward Taran.

"They're going to ram us," cried Beatrice.

"No," said Dandy. "They're doing as we did trying to break Ironmonger's attraction."

The ship was baring down on them at an ever-accelerating rate. However, it was gaining elevation, but not fast enough for TC to keep from holding their collective breathes. When it disappeared from the cameras as it passed overhead, everyone ducked.

"I was hoping that ship would tumble into the split between the sections, but it looks as if we'll be seeing it another day." said Dandy as he shut down the A/Gs.

"What's the new plan?" asked Candie. "All our equipment is gone and we're losing steam through that open pipe."

"According to my calculations," said Dandy, "Taran can straddle the elevator opening. There are still several lengths of the 12-inch pipe used to download water. We're going to hook that pipe to the clean-out door in the leg that got shot-up when we were avoiding Colonel Tokla. We're going to suck up the water with the A/Gs.

"Corky, you'll have to make a fitting to hook the pipe to the leg hatch. I'm going to open the elevator door and suck out any loose stuff. Then we'll hook up the pipes. The value to that big intake pipe is at this end. I didn't see any other valves below."

TC worked furiously on the new hookup because they needed to complete the operation before the heat Taran had pumped into the Green Hulk dissipated. Dandy would have to reposition Taran over the burn hole to heat things up again.

The most difficult operation was getting air into the water tank. When they were depending on steam, they needed a closed system to develop pressure. Now they needed air entering the tank to create the vortex to carry the water up to Taran.

That meant Dandy had to go back down to the water tank to open one of the clean-outs at the far end of the system. Before they could make the other connections, they had to get the other shuttle out of the bay. Dandy didn't want to expose it to danger, but even his soccer-player legs wouldn't carry him down and up in the heat that still remained in the hull. With both men suited, Dandy and Corky lowered the smaller shuttle out of the bay and maneuvered it down the elevator shaft. As before, Corky remained as backup while Dandy hustled to the tank and down its length toward the end, close to the burn hole.

Dandy came prepared. He carried a small block and tackle that Corky had made for him so he could compress the handles of the valve alone. When he got the door open, he reset the tackle to hold the door open when the vortex formed.

This time Dandy didn't have to call for back-up. Corky had considerable trouble getting the shuttle back into the bay. It was not made to perform such a feat under a gravity situation.

When Dandy was back at his station, he remarked, "We don't

need to worry about things freezing up down there anytime soon. The Pretzis should really like the new climate."

The crew turned its attention to making the water hookup. Dandy and Candie took care of the outside work, while Corky managed the leg that Dandy had left dangling in space over the elevator shaft.

After the attachment had been made, Dandy ordered a rest period, saying, "If this goes as I visualize, it could get quite busy around here for an extended period of time."

When the time came to try taking on water, Dandy was at his station. Candie and Corky were in the lower level. Beatrice was monitoring all the other ship's functions. Even Tom had his duties of scanning for alien activity.

Dandy started applying power to the A/Gs. Other than an occasional loose object striking Taran's underside, little happened. The seconds piled up but there were still no signs of success. Dandy raised the power slightly. He could not get too reckless, for fear of sucking up the water pipes. Nor could he afford to produce enough lift to raise them off the hull.

More time passes without any results. Beatrice reported steam was still coming from the old blue pipe hookup. Dandy was stretching his brain trying to figure out what might have gone wrong when a gusher came in. Corky and Candie became very busy venting air and transferring water to other tanks to maintain their balance.

The system was filling fast. To get as much capacity as possible, Dandy cracked enough water to fill the hydrogen and oxygen tanks. "Shut down. We're full."

All TC cheered. Even Tom made his exuberance know by tapping a fingernail on his mike. Doughboy picked up on the exuberance. He came out of his recent lethargy to wiggle like a happy puppy.

Before Dandy would let the crew celebrate, he had them tear down the hookup and store the equipment away in the utility entrance. He moved Taran a few feet so he could close the elevator door. After the hull was sealed, the crew met in the Fish House for a little celebration over a joint meal. Tom had eaten earlier because he wouldn't let Corky feed him in front of the others. He still could handle a vacuum container for coffee.

As the meal wound down, everyone became more somber. Their refueling success would be hollow if they couldn't get off Ironmonger. Gradually conversation halted and everyone waited for Dandy to bring up the topic, that was foremost in everyone's minds....escape from Ironmonger."

Dandy started out with a question. "What do you think our chances are of finding the recognition signal that would satisfy Ironmonger?

"Not good," replied Candie immediately, indicating she had given the question considerable thought. "If any of the ships here had the proper response they would have had to be derelict. Besides, even if we could find a ship that had the response, how would we recognize it?"

"There's a possibility that none of the upper layer of derelicts ever could have had it," said Beatrice. "Ironmonger probably isn't from this part of the galaxy. It might not have been in its own system for a long time before arriving on our doorstep."

Dandy waited to see if there were any more comments before continuing. "Let me throw out a few things for consideration. I need your input. First, an observation....The shuttle doesn't activate the alarm but the Hornitoad ship set it off. Why? Was it size, height, location, construction, materials or what? I suspect those alarms we've been hearing were caused by the Hornitoad ship. From the looks of it, there were a number of trial runs before coming against us."

"It may have been brought in from another location, or there may be more ships," said Beatrice.

"If there are more ships," said Corky, "they must be in lousy shape. The one we saw could hardly fly."

"Whichever is the case," continued Dandy, "it or they set off the alarm. The shuttle doesn't. Also it would appear the warning has to run its course before Ironmonger is activated to either give chase or turn on its attractors. If we do set off something, we should have the twenty hours before action is taken."

"I'd rather not have to test your theory," whispered Tom. "There might not be as convenient a spot to land as here."

"In any case, I think we'd be wasting our time trying to find the recognition response. Our time and effort might bring better results in trying to disable the warning mechanism or the attraction force, or both, if necessary.

"We're going to have to do some reconnoitering to get answers. Some of the questions are: How big is Ironmonger? What is its fuel supply? How does it get its signal out and from where? How does that attractor beam work? Where is it? What powers it? There are dozens more questions, but it all boils down to disabling the damn thing.

"Beatrice, apply yourself to these types of questions. Tom, we need your expertise on the technical aspects, such as how those signals come through all those miles of metallic debris.

"Our first concern is getting Taran over to the front section. I'm pretty sure the A/Gs won't do it alone. I'll move back over the original hole. Before we take off.. Then I'll park Taran on the other side. I wish we could figure out how to block the connecting tubes between the sections. I hope that when I heat up this section, it will give us a little time before any of the aliens can make it through to bother us."

Chapter   19

Moving Taran across to the other Green Hulk section turned out to be a white knuckle event. The ship was heavy with water, even in the light gravity of Ironmonger. Dandy had to use much more lift with the main engines, which started to melt the metal under Taran's feet. As soon as Taran got some elevation, the warning started.

Dandy set the ship down about midway down the length of the front section. He burned a small hole in the Green Hulk. Corky had moved the shuttle out of harm's way during the relocation. Then he found he couldn't immediately get back into Taran because the derelict's hull was too hot to cross.

While waiting for the metal to cool down, Dandy sent Corky on a surveillance mission. Beatrice recorded all that showed on the shuttle cameras. Corky found what he believed to be the control center or bridge. It was located in the upper, front edge, just as in olden airplanes. There even seemed to be windows in areas for direct observation instead of remote viewing. He also spotted several possible weapon turrets.

After Corky flew over all three of the segments, he called Dandy. "When I cross from one section to another I experience a little loss of lift. I think I now know how to compensate. I'd like to take the shuttle out over the edge to see what's down below."

Dandy glanced at Candie, who was frowning at the suggestion. Beatrice was giving him a scared look.

"Go to the side away from where the Hornitoads disappeared. Elevate to 200 feet above our current level and then pass beyond the edge so the cameras can scan the sides of the Green Hulk. I would hope you'd be too high for ground fire to reach you and out of sight of the gun that blasted our other shuttle. In case something goes wrong, you'll have a little elevation so you can get back on top. It would be a long hike from the surface."

TC watched the monitors as Corky elevated over the middle section, then moved out beyond the edge. The cameras scanned down the gigantic green cliff. There were very few visible features. However, there were numerous indications of hatches of varying size and shape.

When Corky rounded the corner so he could see down the front of the ship, the whole configuration changed. Several broad, horizontal gashes marked the flat end.

"I think we've found the support aircraft for the Green Hulk. It looks as if there are four hangars on the upper side and four on the lower half. I don't see any doors. Maybe there is some sort of force field. I've seen such things in ScFi movies," chuckled Corky.

"There had to be shuttles around somewhere," said Dandy. "Just get some good photos for Bea and come back. We'll leave a closer inspection until we solve a more immediate problem. Pull the shuttle under Taran. Maybe the Hornitoads won't shoot at it for fear of damaging their escape vehicle."

Corky was able to make a quick trip across the hot deck. After getting out of his suit, he went to tend Tom. Dandy met Candie in the Fish House. Beatrice turned down an invitation to join them, opting to inspect the new photos Corky had provided.

Candie wrinkled her nose at the pilot's beans and franks choice. As she nibbled on her side of broccoli, she was watching Beatrice. "She's getting strung tighter and tighter. She's really worried about Tom and Doughboy. They both are fading away. Tom can't figure any way of plugging Doughboy into any power source that would be of any use to him. Tom's energy level is getting so low it is hard to see any change. At least, he isn't suffering physically."

"If that were me, I'd be suffering mentally," said Dandy.

"Me too. But Tom is holding it in check. We've got to get away from here."

"As soon as you and Corky can get ready, I want you to go forward and see if you can get access to the control room. Also, keep an eye open for the armory. Probably the main armory is elsewhere, but there may be one for the bridge crew. What I'm particularly interested in is the ship's weapons. I think there will be an assault on Taran sooner rather than later, and we don't have any way to defend ourselves."

"How do you think the attack will come?"

"I expect to see that ship again. It's a long hike to get up here. The next time they'll have more personnel and be better prepared. They've seen our A/Gs and they'll probably have something to challenge them."

"What are you going to do?"

"I'd rather go out exploring with you, but I think now one or the other of us should be close to the controls. I'm going to consult with Beatrice and see if we can fill in a few of the missing pieces."

Dandy absently rubbed Doughboy with his foot as he leaned against Beatrice's console. "What can you make out of the new stuff?"

"I gave Candie the layout of the bridge area. There are all sorts of clusters of what I suspect is communication equipment and sensor arrays. There are similar clusters along the sides but not as extensive. There should be access panels all over the place to service that equipment.

"You better be careful accessing this section. Unless there is damage on the bottom that we can't see, this third may be intact. Maybe those creatures in the Green Hulk breathed some other sort of gas that might be harmful to us. It could still be there."

"We were in some tightly closed rooms in the middle section and I didn't notice anything about the air."

"Yes, but you didn't open your suits," countered Beatrice. "We were afraid of poisonous gas. I don't think that gas scenario has proven out. Whatever killed those creatures, killed them all instantaneously. There are some curious marks along the side of the Green Hulk. Corky only got a glimpse of them when he passed beyond the corner on the side where the Hornitoads disappeared. He was scanning the end and got out far enough to get a shot down the length."

Beatrice started bringing up part of a file. "There is a mark running longitudinally that could be a weapons mark. The surface is discolored."

As the picture came on the screen, Beatrice enhanced part of the frame. It showed a smooth green side with what looked like a dirty smear running off into the distance. It was not horizontal, but rose as it moved off. The second section was in the corner of the frame. It was so far away it was difficult to see, but there was something that could have been another smear.

"I think those are some sort of weapon strikes. Probably an energy that killed all those guys where they stood, sat, slept, whatever. That damage we saw on the rear section certainly didn't kill those guys sitting in the elevator control room." Beatrice made her statement with the force of considered conviction.

"That would add another dimension to stellar warfare if a weapon could instantly kill all the crew and leave the ship intact. Do you suppose such a lethal charge would damage the power supply?"

"There's no telling. We don't know what kind of power runs this ship."

Dandy gazed off into the distance for a bit. "I assumed any power we found was probably emergency backup. Maybe we could generate our own juice."

"Why do you need all that power?"

"I want to be able to fire the ship's guns if we are invaded. We have only that one gun we took from the Hornitoad. That won't be enough if there is a full fledged assault on Taran. If we can't find anything useable in a day or two we'll have to forge ahead without protection to find a way off this thing. Tom is running out of time."

Ironmonger's warning began to sound. Dandy jumped back to his station. He tried to raise Candie and Corky on the radio but there was no response. He growled to Beatrice, "They must have entered the hull."

"I don't see any sign of them. I can't be sure from this angle but I think there is an open panel."

"See if you can get a direction on that signal, while I scan for alien aircraft."

It was a nervous two hours for Dandy and Beatrice. Ironmonger's alarm would sound for a few minutes and then go silent. Then it would go off again, which required another scanning of the horizon. Candie and Corky were out of communication in the hull, completely unaware of the repeated alarms.

As the second hour started to wind down, Beatrice started to fret about their air supply. "There may not be any breathable air inside this section of the hull. They'll have to get out of there before their tanks run out. As it is, they'll have to breathe Ironmonger air on the way back."

Dandy grunted. His attention was focused on his console. He was getting a slight electronic indication of movement to the front of Ironmonger, but the cameras didn't show anything to account for the reading.

"Something's happening," shouted Beatrice. She switched her cameras on to Dandy's screens. All along the top of the Green Hulk, long tubes were sprouting skyward.

"Those are the ship's guns," said Dandy with a little yip to punctuate his observation. "They've found the weapons controls."

Beatrice broke into his celebration. "They're overstaying their air. If they are any distance inside, they'll run out of gas before they can get out."

"Hold the fort. I'm going to take them some air tanks."Dandy broke for the elevator before Beatrice realized he was leaving her alone in Taran. Of course, Tom was there, but in no condition to be of any help. Dandy set a record suiting-up. He threw several air tanks on a cart before taking the elevator to the shuttle.

Dandy was not nearly as adept at piloting the shuttle as Corky. In his haste, he almost side slipped into one of Taran's legs. Using the A/Gs and maneuvering thrusters, Dandy made his way toward the access panel. He had to set down some distance from the opening to avoid sucking everything, including his teammates, out of the access hole.

He grabbed two tanks and headed to the entry. The access was similar to the one by the elevator. Apparently Corky and Candie had climbed down the twenty feet to the bottom, where they burned a hole through into an interior passage. Getting back up was going to require climbing, which would use a lot of oxygen. When he got no response from his crew members, he ran back to the shuttle to get a line. When he returned, Corky was at the bottom of the pit.

"You guys should be about out of air."

"I am. I was going to test the air in the shaft."

"Stand by," said Dandy, as he threw a hitch around an air tank and quickly lowered it into the hole.

Corky attached the connector to the new tank before it was untied form the rope. He took several deep breaths before completing the hookup. When his breathing leveled out he said, "Candie doesn't use as much air as I do, but she must almost be out too and she's deep in the ship."

Corky stopped talking for a moment. "Candie says she's got only a few breaths left."

Dandy sent down another tank. "Take this to her and then you come back here. I'm coming down."

As Corky disappeared, Dandy tied the end of his line to part of the access panel mechanism. Before rappelling into the ship, he checked with Taran. "Bea, any signs of alien ships?"

A very taught, scared voice came back. "No."

"Come on. Bea. Keep functioning. When Corky comes out, I'm sending him back to pick up some equipment. Then he'll be back with you."

It was awkward rappelling in a space suit. He landed rather heavily, but he didn't break anything. As soon as he was inside the hull, he could pick up the radio communications.

Corky was saying, "A couple of big breaths and you'll be alright. The boss wants me back at the entry. I think he wants you to stay here."

Dandy jumped into the conversation. "Candie, if you're feeling alright, come out with Corky so you can lead me back in. Corky, I want you to go back to Taran and collect that relay equipment we used before, so we can talk from here to Taran."

Corky climbed out of the hull and Candie led the way back into the gun control center. Dandy found himself in a long, narrow room. There was a faint green glow sufficiently bright to find his way around. It was a strange looking place. He counted six consoles down the length of the room....three per side. There was a center console that looked to be the most elaborate.

Candie had been explaining on the way in that they had found the bridge, but it seemed only to have controls for flying the ships, and nothing they found looked like it pertained to defense. They had found this room just before Corky had to leave because his air was almost out. Candie still had some air so she wanted to see if that room was of any value.

"Humans don't fit in this ship. When I stand on that stool at the center console, I can only reach part of the controls on the layout. I punched some of the buttons until I got a response. Some lights came on the board and I think some generators started. I could feel vibrations. After whatever I started happened, the generators, if that is what they were, shut off. That's as far as I got before I ran out of air."

"You did something," said Dandy. "Suddenly the whole ship is bristling with tubes pointing straight out. I think those are guns of some sort. However, they certainly don't throw cannon balls. Show me what you did. By the way, were there crew members on the bridge?"

"There were bodies all over the place."

"But none here. They must not have been in a fight when whatever got them, did."

The controls were way over Candie's head. She had to hop up to grab one of the handles protruding out of the console. With difficulty she clambered up onto the stool. From the stool she could lean across to the panel. A few buttons were within her reach.

"Is there enough space so you can stand on the console without stepping on the firing button?"

Carefully Candie stepped onto vacant spaces between controls until she was standing on a flat console surface of the array. Dandy climbed onto the stool. "Which control brought out the guns?"

"The purple one on the right."

After a couple minutes of study, Dandy started pushing buttons. "I wish I knew their order if importance....up/down, right/left. Raising the guns is a preliminary step, so other prelims should be in the same area." He touched two buttons without any response, but the third one brought results. All four walls, plus the ceiling, lighted.

"Those are huge viewing screens," said Candie. "Look at the horizon line along the bottom edge. All the other consoles have lighted up. This must be a central control."

"But it looks like each station is manned....or aliened, in this case." said Dandy. Candie groaned. The joker continued, "There are stools in front of each station. This one is probably a master station."

Candie did a complete turn, surveying the entire room. "From the looks of the displays, I think each of the side consoles controls one of the three segments....half of the sides and half of the top. The two at the ends of this room are for the end guns. They must be controlled from this center unit."

"Then there has to be another room the same as this in the bottom half to cover the other portions of the ship. The gravity is reversed on the other half. We won't have to worry about that part anyway because we're sitting on those batteries. Now, we have to figure out how to aim and fire these things....if they still are in working condition." Dandy went back to inspecting the control panel.

"I'm going to play around with one of the other consoles." Candie slipped over the edge and dropped to the floor. She clambered up on one of the other stools. "This layout isn't nearly as complicated as yours. The purple button here is lighted." Candie started moving things around.

"What did you just do?" demanded Dandy with considerable force.

"This?" said Candie as she moved a metal object that looked rather like an upside-down mushroom.

"That's it. Watch the screen in front of you when you move it."

When Candie moved the handle, a circle with a cross through the center moved across the screen in a like manner. It was like a cursor on a computer screen.

"I hear that generator sound again," said Candie. "We've turned something on."

"The handle on this console doesn't seem to work the same way. I'm not getting any image on the screen. If this station is like mine on Taran, there must be a selection procedure to tap into the other stations."

"Could this be your aiming device? Watch this." A line appeared between the edge of the screen and ran to the circle. When Candie moved the circle the line remained attached. Another line came on the screen, followed by more and more.

Then they all disappeared....then reappeared. "The buttons be-low the handle apparently activate the various guns and the handle points them."

"Now we have to find out how to fire them. One after another, three green lights have come on. I wonder if that is telling us we are charged up."

"I've got the same here," reported Candie.

Both Dandy and Candie were almost knocked off their perch-es on the alien stools by a severe jolt. Neither had the external gains turned up in their suits, but the crash could be heard without them.

"You didn't fire a gun did you?" said Candie in an accusatory manner.

"No, I think that was something hitting the ship. Look behind me." The rear screen showed numerous objects moving toward the Green Hulk. Dandy counted eight vessels. They varied con-siderably in size and speed. "We need to know how these guns are fired," said Dandy, his voice dripping with anxiety. "Get on that back console and see if you can blow those guys out of the sky."

"Look behind you. Where did that sucker come from?" A huge object hovered in the front, left battery screen. Little detail was visible because of the low resolution on the screen.

"Its close or its awful big," said Candie as she slid off her stool and climbed up on the one in front of the target.

"There's a bunch more coming up from the rear. I count eight. Any ideas how to fire these things?"

"I don't see any trigger mechanisms and I've pushed all the buttons I can find."

"It should be something that can't be set off accidentally."

There was another jarring impact that nearly toppled the two humans from their precarious perches.

"They must be firing at something," muttered Dandy as he punched at the board.

"Look at the upper left edge of my screen. That blob must be Taran."

"Do you see the shuttle?"

After a pause, Candie answered. "No. It may be under Taran and I might not be able to make it out."She didn't sound too convinced of her own speculation.

"Did you look at the Green Hulk aliens' hands?"

"No, but I saw the shots you sent back to Bea."

"Did they have claws?"

"I don't know if they were claws, but they had long, slender fingers."

"There's a hole in the top of this aiming handle, but it's too small for my glove and probably my bare finger. I don't have anything that can be pushed down the hole. There might be a firing button down there. Wait a minute. The tongue on my utility belt buckle might do the trick." Dandy stood precariously on his stool while he unfastened his belt. "It's not long enough. It just barely touches .Do you have anything longer?"

"No."

Dandy jumped down from the stool and went searching through the cabinets and draws. He found nothing that would help. Dandy was staggered by another impact.

"One of the lines to the bull's eye just went out. They must be firing at the guns. Those ships coming up from the rear apparently can't hover. They are flying in big circles."

There were two more impacts.

"You'd better hurry up with your trigger finger or we won't have any guns left to fire back. They just got two more."

"Hang on," said Dandy as he rushed out the door as fast as a spacesuit would allow. Candie stood watching the guns on her board blink out with each impact.

When Dandy reappeared, he handed her a funny looking dendritic object a foot long. "Don't get squeamish. See if that will fire the gun."

When Candie brought the strange thing up into the dim light, she realized it was an alien hand. It was broken off at the wrist. There were four fingers....two opposing two and a fifth, long articulated finger with multiple joints. The end was hard and pointy.

Candie brought her remaining guns to bear and inserted the long finger into the hole. There was no discernible effect in the Green Hulk outside of the third green light on the console dimming slightly. There was an external reaction. The big blip moved slightly.

"That's it. Do it again," yelled Dandy. He hadn't been able to activate the central control, so he took his fight to the left-center console. Following the format Candie had established, he was able to get the aiming device working. He picked up one of the circling ships. It was much smaller, further away and moving. He missed. He picked up the ship again and missed again. "This is as bad as trying to shoot Teal on a down-wind leg," complained Dandy.

"Butcher," said Candie as she sent another salvo into the big ship. The blip moved backwards and began to descend. Candie fired again before the ship dropped below her range. Each time she hit it there was a perceptible shudder to the craft.

The smaller ships began to take evasive action, making them harder to track. Three came directly toward the top of section number one. Dandy fired at one and missed, but he inadvertently held the button down as he tried to retarget the ship and raked the ship with a continuous beam. The ship disintegrated. A vibration went through the Green Hulk as the ship parts hit the side. The debris also took out a couple of the guns.

The other two ships passed over Dandy's guns and made a landing beyond his fire-control area. Two more of the circling craft made a landing approach. Candie tried her hand at a moving target and missed. When it made a turn to come right at her, Candie stuffed a burst down its nose. Dandy's target broke off and tried to dive over the edge, but Dandy got it.

While the gunners were occupied with the closing targets, the other three craft had swung around to the back end of the ship and, practically grazing the top surface of Ironmonger, came in below the level of the guns.

Candie had changed sides. She was trying to depress the guns enough to get any of the small ships that had landed.

"I can't get low enough."

"There's probably a fail-safe to keep gunners from blowing holes in their own ship. There may be a way to override it on the master control panel."

As Dandy started to climb up on the center control stool, Candie said, "Hold it. I've only got fifteen minutes of air left. How about you?"

"Ten."

"We've got to get out of here. Did you bring more tanks?"

"There's a bunch in the shuttle. Maybe Corky left some at the access panel."

"I think Bea was right about the air in here. When Corky burned through the wall, I was above with my helmet open. I got a whiff of something that set off my cough center and my tear ducts. It may have been this air."

Those Hornitoads are a long ways off. It will take them time to get here, and we can't be of any help if we've suffocated. Let's go."

Both shuffled through the bridge and down the passage to the access hole. Dandy thought he had made a wrong turn because there was no glow of light from the open panel. Candie assured him they were going the right way. Their flashlight picked up the burn on the wall. Looking through the opening into the shaft they could see no light.

"Did Corky close the hatch before leaving?"

"I don't know why he would," said Dandy. He stepped through into the airlock. "There's debris blocking the opening."

"Is it one of the aircraft we shot down?"

There was no immediate reply.

"Well,' said Candie as she tried to shove Dandy out of the opening to get a look.

"No, its not one of the alien aircraft. It's our shuttle. I can read some of the markings from here."

"Corky!" cried Candie.

Dandy tried to call Corky over the radio, without results. He switched on his external communication device and called repeatedly. Candie was trying over her radio. There were only vague echoes.

"Beatrice will be all alone in Taran," said Candie.

Dandy tried to call Taran, without results. They were inside the dampening confines of the Green Hulk. He flashed his light around the interior of the chamber and around the corridor.

"There are no air tanks. We'll never get out that hole up there. There are tons of stuff on top.

Candie didn't say anything. She stood waiting for Dandy to lead off somewhere.

"While you were looking around, did you find any weapons that might blast a hole in this thing?"

"No."

"We've got to get to the hangars or bays, whatever they're called. Did you find anything pointing the way?"

"No, but there are elevators."

"Lead the way. Apparently we have power in this portion of the ship. Let's hope the elevators work. It's too far to walk. We don't have enough air."

When Candie pushed the button, the elevator door opened. Inside there weren't floor buttons, just three stacked one on top of the other. "There are no controls. It must be voice activated," said Candie.

Dandy immediately pushed the lower button. "We've got to go down, so let's go. Count the symbols that show in the button.

Those are probably the floor numbers. I'll bet that the hangars are at least twenty-five floors below us. We'll start checking at twenty."

At twenty he pushed the center button. When the door opened he flashed his light down the corridor. "That doesn't look like it. There are some bodies out here." He pushed the down button. On the thirtieth floor the door opened into a glassed-in corridor looking out into a huge area with various types of small spacecraft lining the sides. On the other side of the elevator was another hangar facility with different type craft tethered into slots. At the front end were two gaping slits, showing the drab horizon of Ironmonger.

"The doors are open. There should be Ironmonger air out there." declared Dandy. "Now all we have to do is get out there."

Periodically there were airlocks to the flight decks, but no matter how they pushed the buttons, the locks wouldn't cycle.

"I'll bet they won't open when the bays are open to space," said Candie. "One would need a space suit to go out and there probably is a suiting room where we can get through."

"That would be on the other side, but that is too far away. We could never make it."

They were hustling along the corridor toward the rear. Dandy was looking for some object to use to break the barrier. Nothing useful presented itself. At the end of the runway the glass walls became metal. Dandy snatched open the first door. They found themselves in a repair facility with alien bodies all over the place. There were plenty of tools about, but no glass. There were solid doors instead.

Dandy was getting less gas to breathe. He tried to look at his gauge without being obvious. It read empty.

"How much?" asked Candie.

"Zero."

Candie started to unhook her tank to share what little she had with Dandy.

"No. Keep it. I want you to drive that mover through the bay doors." In his spotlight, Dandy had a huge machine equipped with forks used to lift disabled craft. It was locked into a stanchion so it could not float around during weightlessness. Dandy started to move toward it but stumbled. He went to his knees. His world was beginning to spin. He felt himself being jerked up. His hands were on the deck and his feet were under him.

He was doing a gorilla walk with Candie's insistent voice pounding in his ear..." Move it, keep it going. Don't crap out on me now."She kept up a continual babble even after she dumped him on the apron of the vehicle. She climbed into the cab and began inspecting the controls. She was having the same problem as in the fire control center. Everything was way above her head. She didn't want to expend the energy and thus the air to climb onto the stool, but she couldn't do anything from the floor. By the time she got on top of the stool, she could feel her air was running out too.

As this was a utility vehicle, the controls were simple. She found the starter and a lever like on a boat to control speed. She revved it up to jam it forward. The holding clamps shattered as the machine surged ahead. She was moving but not in the right direction. She couldn't find any way of turning the infernal thing right to head for the doors. As she leaned forward to reach further on the console, her knee bumped one of the two handles the aliens had for their second pair of hands. The handle moved slightly and the vehicle turned. Candie grabbed the right handle and pulled heavily. The vehicle took an abrupt right turn and headed at an ever-accelerating speed toward the door that separated her from the flight deck.

The crash and rending of metal sounded like a beautiful symphony as the machine plowed through the wall. Candie let it run a ways down the runway before halting. There would be escaping gas from the ship.

Dandy was lying on his back, not moving. Candie snapped up her face shield and breathed in the foul air of Ironmonger. While she was still coughing, she opened Dandy's shield. He didn't respond. Candie yelled at him, but still no response. She couldn't try to resuscitate him in that bulky space suit with its attendant equipment. She buckled her knees and dropped her weight onto his midsection. That brought a little cough, which progressed into more coughing and finally a little movement.

With some prodding and cajoling, Dandy finally sat up and began to function again. As was his nature, he took care of important things with dispatch. "Thanks," he said.

Keeping with her usually competitive style, she replied by saying, "I'm not going to let you leave me with all the heavy lifting to do. Not that I couldn't do it, but that wouldn't be fair."

"Well, you're going to have to do that heavy lifting for a while until this raging headache slows down. This foul air isn't helping."

"Get on the trolley. I think we need to move further from that room. We're getting whiffs of Green Hulk air." Candie move much closer to the open doors of the hangar. The air wasn't as foul.

The two didn't have much recovery time because there was a jolt to the ship that registered clear down to the hangar level.

There was a hitch in her voice as Candie said, "I hate to think of what's going on above. If Corky didn't make it back from that crash, Bea's all alone."

"Yeah, I know. We've got to get back up there to see if we can salvage anything."

"How do you propose we do that? We can't go back inside the hull without air. And then our only chance of getting out would be if we can cycle one of the air locks from the inside."

"First, let's get to the opening to see if our radios will reach Taran."

Candie drove the rig to the edge. Dandy tried to raise the ship without success. "You try. My power supply is getting pretty low." Candie's attempts were not successful either.

"We don't know if our signals aren't getting through or there is no ship to receive them.

"Or Bea is curled up in a corner somewhere," said Candie, who had never been very sympathetic to Beatrice's panic attacks.

"If Corky died in that crash and two other crew members died of asphyxiation, plus Tom at death's door, I'd probably be curled up in a corner somewhere myself."

"Yeah, sure," said Candie with a tone of disbelief. "How do we get out of here?"

"First, I want you to drive this thing through those glass walls where we got off the elevator. The units on this side are space craft and probably no good under gravity and atmosphere conditions. The other side seemed to have craft more akin to atmosphere maneuvering.

"When we go through that wall, we'll be in Green Hulk gas again."

"We'll just have to hold our breaths. If you can't get all the way through on the first try, back out far enough so we can breathe."

Candie maneuvered her machine around. It was huge thing with four widely spaced solid tires. The engine was some sort of energy-pack powered thing that ran silently except for a whine when it was wound up. In front, were two fifteen-foot-long rails which conformed to the under body of the space craft line up on the side of the hangar space.

The first run at the wall of the hallway punched holes through with the rails. Candie found the lift control. She ripped most of the wall out with one big heave. She backed out for a breathing spell and then rammed the wall on the other side. She ripped it out and punched on through into the second hangar space. She didn't stop until she was near the open hangar doors where the air would be cleaner.

The space they were in was enormous. There were two marked lanes situated toward the center of the ship. On the outside edge of the flight deck was a row of aircraft with wing-like configurations. They were all facing out toward the flight lines. It wasn't until they got closer that they realized there was a great long line of similar planes stretching on behind the ones they saw on the front.

Candie pulled their vehicle up to the one on the end of the line.

Dandy dismounted to inspect the aircraft. "These are designed to operate in gravity and atmosphere. Look at the heat shields. They have enough wing space to have somewhat of a glide. There must be some way of landing these things that we don't know about. They don't have wheels, but pads." Dandy walked behind the ship. "These don't use any combustible fuel. There are lenses back here."

"There are some on the underside as well," said Candie, who joined in the inspection. "That probably explains the landing gear."

"Will you bring that oversized go-cart over here? This thing is much too high for me."

By climbing on the vehicle frame, they were able to get onto the wing. It was a scramble to get through the raised cockpit cover into the craft since they didn't have six-foot long legs.

"Oh, no. Those damn stools again," said Candie.

"This is a one seater. It does, however, have a seat belt."

"Lot of good that'll do ya. Strap in and you'll be six feet away from the controls."

Dandy climbed onto the stool so he could inspect the flight instruments. "These things have armament. At least, there is a firing array similar to what we found in the gun room. But, I don't see any display. There must be a sighting mechanism around here somewhere."

"Are we going to need an alien hand to be able to fire that thing? I foolishly left mine upstairs."

"There are a lot of replacements lying around," said Dandy, rather absently. "There is no handle. You probably have to change the attitude of the plane to change the aiming point. It will be good to have some artillery, but more importantly we have to get that thing into the air. Come up here. There seems to be some sort of relationship with the controls on your go-cart."

Dandy crawled onto the side of the console. Candie replaced him on the stool. "That will be the off/on button. The cart has one lever to go forward or back and that also controls the speed. There are two levers here. I'll bet one is for lift and the other is forward."

After checking that the levers were in a neutral position, Dandy punched the start button. A loud purring sound greeted his effort. He tapped one of the levers a bit. There was a slight forward rocking but they didn't go anywhere. He touched the other lever. There was an impression of lift but they remained stationary.

"We're tethered in some manner," said Dandy. "I didn't see any physical clamps where we were looking. There must be some sort of energy device."When the motor had started, many lights came on. One was blinking. Dandy pressed the button and the light went off. There was a faint motion to the craft. Dandy touched a lever again. This time the craft moved forward a bit.

After considerable probing, they found that the steering mechanism was controlled by buttons in the balance handles.

"We've got to get topside. Strap yourself onto the stool. I'll stand on the stool between your legs. I'll handle the lift and speed. You'll have to try anchoring me and also control the direction we're flying."

When they were arranged as best they could be, Dandy lifted the craft slightly off the deck. Then he eased the throttle ahead gradually. The craft responded slowly. "Bring us around to the left. We'd better go the end of the runway so we can get a running start. I'll need all the room I can get before we reach the opening. As the plane started to change direction there was an explosion that blew a ten foot hole in the wall between the two hangars.

"What was that?" demanded Candie, who was sitting well below the window level.

"I think you just found the trigger. You blew a big hole in that metal wall. Try it again."

"Try what again?"

"You triggered something. It must be in those handles. Try it again."

Wham. Another hole opened up in the wall. There was no sound or reaction on firing, but the results were devastating.

"There a sort of trigger mechanism down here. The second set of hands are bulky so the there isn't a little hole as it was for the fire control. Here it is. The button in the handle on the right releases the handle to move either right or left. The left button is the trigger."

"Boy," said Dandy, "am I glad to have some way of fighting back. Let's go see if anything is left up there or are we destined to spend the rest of our lives on his thing."

"Let's not think about that yet."

Chapter 20

Both humans thought they were goners. When the craft left the runway, the bottom dropped out. They fell almost to the surface of Ironmonger before Dandy was able to adjust the lift of the plane. One step was that Candie had to pull back on the steering handle. Another part was the velocity of the ship. Initially, he depended on lift like he would have with the A/Gs. But with the alien craft, lift was created in part by the thrust. Once they got coordinated and leveled off, they both could breathe again. Dandy had his copilot bank to the right and bring them along the side of the Green Hulk. They started gaining elevations as they wobbled along. Candie was over-compensating. She couldn't see where she was going and had to depend on Dandy's spoken word. Her reflexes were such that as soon as she got an order, she executed it too quickly. Dandy kept talking her along until she smoothed out considerably.

By the time they had reached the end of the Green Hulk, they could look over the top. Taran was visible a long ways away.

"She's still there," reported Dandy. "I hope Bea was able to keep the aliens out."

Dandy was skimming along the top of the Green Hulk toward Taran. He had to keep more elevation than he would have liked because Candie was still wobbling somewhat. "I see something out there, but I don't see those four ships that we couldn't shoot down. Taran has moved. It's not in the same spot."

"Taran, Taran come in." intoned Dandy into his mike. "Taran."

No answer.

"Do you see any of the aliens?"

"I don't see any of the alien ships. But there is debris all over the place."

As Dandy reached the front third of the Green Hulk, he said, "I want to land this thing with a lot of runway ahead of me. If I see any hostiles ahead, I'll have you point the ship at them so you can give them a shot."

Dandy slackened speed. He began to lose lift. Abruptly the craft began to drop. By ramming the lift control forward he averted a very bad landing. It still gave them a jolt.

"You're still a lousy driver," groused Candie.

"This thing doesn't need a runway to land," said Dandy as he picked himself off the console where the impact had deposited him. We're still a long way from Taran. I'll try to move us closer."

Candie objected. "We'd better try communicating with the ship. If anyone is functioning, we'll look like another batch of aliens attacking. If there are aliens inside, we don't want to get any closer.

"Good thinking."

To get to the canopy release, Dandy had to climb onto the console. When the top lifted, he dropped over the side on the wing.

"How are your batteries?"

"They're dead. I've been out longer than you"

"Mine aren't in very good shape. Taran, Taran, can you hear me?"

No answer.

"Taran, Taran. Bea, can you hear me?"

No answer.

"That's too far to walk and I don't want to be without the artillery on this ship. Let's move it in closer. We'll leave the canopy up in case they send a radio signal we can hear. Also Bea can probably recognize us when we get closer."

Candie strapped herself down again and Dandy stood in front of her. Slowly Dandy brought the alien craft closer to Taran. Since Candie couldn't see out, he was giving a running commentary on what he could see.

"I can see some large pieces of debris from the ships we shot down, but there isn't too much small stuff. Bea or Corky moved Taran. I can see the old hole. Now Taran is on the other side of the access where our shuttle came down. Off where the alien ships landed, there is a lot of debris too, but no ships as such. It looks as if a big area of Taran got badly scorched. I wonder if the alien ships exploded."

Dandy brought the craft down. "We can walk from here.   If any of TC is still there, they should be able to recognize us at this distance."

The pair climbed out onto the wing and stood there for several minutes, hoping to get some sign from Taran, but nothing came.

"It looks like you'll going to have to go knock on the door," said Dandy.

"I'll do it, but why me?"

"If we both go, we won't be able to get back up here if something goes wrong. At least, I can pull you up far enough so you can swing aboard."

Dandy was getting himself situated to lower Candie to the surface when he was interrupted by the sound of metal on metal.

"Look," cried Candie. "There's Bea."

Beatrice was standing just outside the elevator door beating on the durathane with a metal object. When she had their attention, she dropped the hammer and began jumping around like a little girl in between coughing fits. Candie waved back as Dandy crawled back into the cabin to move their craft closer to Taran.

As they neared, Beatrice broke into an uncoordinated, flailing run to meet them. When Candie dropped to the ground Bea flung her arms around the space suit trying to hug it. Dandy got the same greeting. Tears were streaking the librarian's face. She kept repeating, "I'm so glad to see you."

They headed back for the ship. Bea was in the middle with an arm wrapped around each of her companions. Dandy was trying to find out what happened. He decided he was going to have to ask short answer questions. "Did you move the ship?"

"No."

"Corky?"

"Corky never came back from the crash."

"Who moved the ship?"

"Tom."

"Tom?"

"You won't believe it."

"Tell me later. Have you had any word from Corky?"

"No. He never answered any calls. He was trying to go get you two when the alien ships started coming in. They shot him down."

"Are there any Hornitoads around now?"

"Not since two ships took off."

"Candie, you and Bea take care of Taran. I'm going to see if I can find Corky. I'll leave as soon as I can get new batteries and a fresh air tank."

Dandy delayed long enough to pick up the dolly Corky had made to move equipment to the first access panel. Then he set out at a brisk shuffle toward the crashed shuttle. It was a long way away, but Dandy told his soccer legs to get going.

As he approached the shuttle, he could see the skid marks in the hull. The shuttle had hit the surface and begun a long slide that abruptly ended when it dropped its nose into the access panel opening. The ship was upended, with its tail stuck in the air.

The configuration of the shuttle was somewhat like an old van where the driver's compartment was almost over the front wheels. As Dandy circled around the wreckage, he was calling to Corky, with no response. He could see the windshield had been broken out as the top had been crushed down. Dandy could not see inside. The entry doors were further back on the body of the vehicle. The one on the left was badly crumpled. The other door was misshapen but partially open.

Fortunately, the doors swung inward so he didn't have to try lifting the weight of the door. The added few inches of the dolly gave him made it possible to jump up to catch hold of the jamb. By chinning himself, he could see the back of the pilot's seat. It had been broken on one of the impacts. Corky's hand hung down in sight. Dandy snapped his face shield back so he could call without electronics. There was no reaction.

"Taran, Corky's in the cabin, but he's not responding. I can't get in with my suit on. I'm going to take it off. I'll be out of communication for a while."

"Don't forget, it's below freezing out there," said Candie. "Don't turn into a popsicle."

"Yeah."

After being in a space suit as long as Dandy, removing it was not a nice thing. This time the Ironmonger stink didn't bother him. As soon as the air hit his sweaty body, he was chilled. Quickly Dandy scrambled up the side and squeezed through the small opening. He had to kick to the side so when he dropped into the cockpit he wouldn't fall on the pilot's seat. He hit the back of the co-pilot's seat and fell against the floor, which was almost vertical. The contact with that much cold metal made him shiver violently.

Dandy crawled over Corky's broken seat into the knee hole of the console and squatted down beside Corky. He was held in place with his safety harness. The impact had shoved Corky's knees under the console. From the amount of clearance between the seat and the console wall, Dandy guessed that Corky's legs were broken. He was lying with his chest on the control panel. The seat was pinning him down.

Carefully, Dandy removed the glove disconnecting the electrical contacts. The hand was warm to the touch. But he couldn't tell whether the warmth was just the contrast with his own frigid finger, the artificial heat from the suit, or Corky was still alive. He felt for a pulse. He had never been very proficient in taking a pulse. He had to first control his shivers, but he thought there was a faint pulse. From then on, all his actions were predicated on Corky being alive.

Mounted on the wall next to the crushed door was the medical kit. Dandy ripped open a pain ampoule exposing the long needle. He jabbed it through the space suit into Corky's thigh.

It was obvious that he could not extract Corky without shifting the ship. He tried to key the shuttle com system, but it was dead.

Dandy slithered out of the shuttle and dropped to the Green Hulk. He was shivering so badly it was difficult to get back into his bulky, stiff suit. As soon as he could hook up the helmet, he called Taran.

"Candie. I can't be certain, but I think Corky is alive. He's probably broken up somewhat. He's trapped and I can't get him out until the shuttle is moved. I'm coming back for the alien shuttle. Get suited up. Get a ladder so we can get in and out. Also we need rope."

Dandy turned up the internal heater and started back for Taran.

Before Dandy got back, he could see Candie fussing around the alien craft. When he arrived, she was standing on the wing. She pulled up a ladder after him and stowed it in the cockpit. As they got situated on the stool, Dandy filled Candie and Beatrice in on what he had found.

Quickly, they maneuvered the craft to the crash site. Dandy positioned it to pull directly back along the skid marks. He left

Candie at the controls while he threw a line over a sturdy part of the frame. At the shuttle, he hooked the line onto a ring designed originally to lift the craft into Taran while on Earth.

Not knowing what might happen if one stood behind an alien craft when it engaged it ray propulsion, Dandy moved off to the side to give directions. Since the Candie was going to have to steer the machine, she stood on the stool and engaged the lift and then the thrust a little at a time. The slack came out of the line. Then Candie increased the thrust. With a great scream of distressed metal the shuttle toppled back onto its bottom. Dandy winced at what the jarring impact may have done to Corky.

Candie stopped pulling and Dandy had to use the dolly he had originally brought to bash the door further in so he could get through suited up. The bent seat and the roof of the shuttle were still pinning Corky to the console. Dandy still couldn't see into the helmet. Carefully, with his gloved hand, he broke pieces of the smashed face plate away until he could see part of Corky's face. The face was pale with blood streaks across it, but he didn't have what Dandy envisioned as the color of death. Dandy worked his glove off and touched Corky's face. It was cold, but still supple.

Dandy climbed out of the shuttle so he could talk with Candie. "It is going to be easier on Corky if we can drag the shuttle back to Taran and remove him there where we have some tools available. When I get back in, take up the slack and see if you can tow this thing back to the ship."

Before reentering the shuttle, he threw the dolly in. "Give it a try. Oh, as soon as we get back, go to supply and get a couple tubes of durathane cutting compound."

Candie carefully lifted the craft and then put on the forward thrust. The shuttle put up a terrible screech, but it began to move across the surface of the Green Hulk. It was a noisy journey and not all that smooth.

It wasn't more than a couple of minutes after they halted that Candie stuck her head in the shuttle door handing him a two tube of compound and starters.

"How did you come up with these so quickly," said Dandy.

"Tom."

"There's something going on here I don't know about."

"Later."

"You're the medical expert around here. See if there is any-thing you can do for Corky while I start burning him out of here."

Using the compound, Dandy burned a new, larger door in the side of the shuttle. Then he went to the front to cut away a por-tion of the roof to release the pressure on the back of the seat. He had Candie move out of the way before setting it off so that molten metal wouldn't drip down her back. Returning to the in-terior he drew lines around the mountings for the seat. With a poof, the seat burned lose and Candie and Dandy could pull it back to get at Corky.

Candie pulled his helmet off. "He's alive, but both femurs are broken. He's probably got a concussion. I hope there is no inter-nal damage."

Between the two of them, they were able to drag Corky and his chair through the new door onto the Green Hulk. They tipped him onto the dolly and pulled him to the elevator. They bypassed the changing room and went directly to the command level. Beatrice met them at the door and helped maneuver the dolly into Corky's room. Tom was seated at his console and waved to Dandy as he passed by.

Candie quickly shucked her suit. Dandy collected her gear and headed down to the changing room to properly clean him-self and his suit. By the time he got back up to the upper level, Candie and Beatrice had gotten Corky cut out of his suit and stretched out on his bunk. Both of Corky's legs were swollen and discolored.

"I was right," said Candie. "Both femurs are fractured about four inches above the knees. I've got him sedated now while I try to get the swelling down. Then I'll use those new casts the com-pany provided for us. Right now I'll work on a nasty cut on the forehead. Bring me a cup of tea and then go talk to Tom."

After delivering the tea, Dandy went over Tom's station. Tom didn't get up, but extended his hand. "I'm certainly glad to see you in this condition," said Dandy, as he wrung his friend's hand. "What's been going on?"

"Let's go into the Fish House, so we all can eat and I'll tell you a fabulous story," said Tom. "I'm still pretty slow. Would you get me some beef, potatoes and peas?"

Beatrice came out to join them just as the two men were opening their food bags. She joined them with a cup of coffee."

"Okay, you guys. Tell me what happened."

"You start it out, Bea," said Tom.

"Everything was happening so fast. Alien ships were coming at us. You and Candie were inside the Green Hulk. The big guns were waving around, but nothing was happening. Then the aliens attacked. You guys started firing and knocking down aircraft. You hit the huge ship and it pulled away. Three of the alien craft landed and Hornitoads began to advance. I suddenly realized that you two would be running out of air. Corky took the shuttle to go after you since we couldn't communicate with you inside that thing, but he got shot down. I tried and tried to call him and you two on the radio. Then I realized that the shuttle had blocked your exit. Suddenly I was all alone with Tom who was completely disabled.

"All I could do was watch the clock tick down on you air supply. Aliens were advancing and there wasn't anything I could do about it. I was stranded all alone on this alien ship. I couldn't seem to move."

During the whole recitation, Beatrice had kept her eyes on the table before her. She looked up with misery written all over her face. "I just couldn't move. Finally, I got my foot to move to touch Doughboy, but he wasn't under my seat. Even he had abandoned me. I just sat there and watched the Hornitoads advance.

"I have no idea how long I was there. Then I heard Tom call my name. When I looked around he was standing in the doorway to his room. I was so glad to see him." Beatrice ducked her head and went silent.

"What happened?" said Dandy in frustration.

Tom picked up the story. "I could hear all that was going one, but I was to the point I couldn't move. I could hardly blink my eyes. Then I was aware that Doughboy had crawled up onto the bed beside me. I was afraid something had happened to Bea. Doughboy snuggled down alongside me. I felt a sort of tranquility I had never experienced. I thought I was dying. As minutes passed I began to feel stronger. I had never felt badly, but I had been drained of all energy. I regained enough strength to move my arms and legs. Then I became aware that Doughboy was shrinking in size. He became a limp, fuzzy white blanket. I think he gave me his energy that I might live.

"Anyway, I could see over the monitors that the Hornitoads were getting close. I had trouble getting to my feet. I had the will, but my body was so weak I had trouble moving around. I got to the door and called Bea. She hugged me so tightly I almost went down again," said Tom with a smile toward. Bea.

Beatrice was blushing beautifully.

"Bea helped me to my station and I was able to lift Taran off and scorch all the invaders. By the time I had swept the decks, the other craft took off. I set back down, but I didn't have enough stamina to go searching for either you guys or Corky. I decided it was better that I stay with the ship until I had regained my strength."

"You're saying Doughboy somehow transferred his life's energy to you?"

"Apparently. I'm alive and functioning and he's a door mat. My wounds have scabbed over and they're itching like crazy."

Beatrice was silently crying. Dandy said, "Bea?"

"Don't get me wrong. I'm so happy Tom is better, but I am going to miss Doughboy. I think he did that for me because I was so unhappy and alone."

"That wouldn't surprise me a bit," said Dandy.

Candie stuck her head out of Corky's room. "Dandy, will you help me get these casts on?"

It took an hour to get the inflatable casts onto Corky. With Beatrice's help they put him back on the dolly for a trip down to his work area so Candie could check the bone alignment under the shop x-ray machine. Candie calculated that a brief look under the industrial strength machine was preferable to letting his bones knit improperly.

When they got Corky back on his bunk, Candie was about ready to collapse. Tom said he was fit to stand watch while the others went down to rest.

Chapter   21

TC gathered in the Fish House for a meeting. Corky attended, using the wheelchair he had made for Tom. Tom no longer needed it. Beatrice had quit shaking. Candie was wearing her dangly earrings, denoting that she was in high spirits.

Dandy grinned at the assembled faces as he leaned against a table. "Glad to see you all could make it. I hate to be a spoil-sport but I'm about to call a halt to this vacation and head home."

"Are we going to take the scenic tour or are you going to insist on a direct route?" asked Candie, with her familiar smirk.

"We'll probably have to make a side-trip or two before we can really get underway."

"I presume you have laid out our itinerary," said Tom, getting into the mood.

"We have a couple of things to work out, but we should be underway soon. Now that we have fuel, I can't see hanging out here any longer than is necessary. There are some folks around here that don't seem to like us." Dandy's face lost its broad smile, signaling he was ready to get down to serious matters. "Candie, you've kept track of such things. Is Ironmonger still on its same course?"

"Yes."

"In relationship to our sun, what is its general direction?"

"If you look at our solar system from the edge, we're in the upper ecliptic, currently at about a thirty-degree line from the sun. Ironmonger is moving on a forty-five degree angle to the ecliptic, going back above the sun and off to the side a bit."

"What does all that mean?" said Corky.

"It means Ironmonger is getting a little further away from Earth but at not that fast a rate. It will be hanging around a long time, which is not a good idea. What kind of world do you think it would be if Hacker could get hold of some of Ironmonger's technology? If we have a chance, I'd like to get it moving further out into space."

"Gal X wouldn't pass up on that technology either," said Candie.

"You're probably right, but we don't have to pay attention to the bottom line," said Dandy. "If the opportunity presents itself to turn this junk heap, we might take advantage of it. However, our more immediate goal is to disable that force that reeled us in. It seems to me, we can't counteract the darn thing, so we'll have to eliminate it. To do that we'll have to find its source."

"I think we have two sources," said Beatrice. "One is the source of the warning signal, which I think is different from the attractive force."

"Why?"

"You asked me to locate the source of the warning signal before the last attack. I got a reading from two diametrically opposed directions. Neither corresponds to the location of the force that pulled us down."

"Can you pinpoint the source?"

"No, just the directions."

"That signal couldn't be coming from the core. It could never penetrate all the junk.

"No," said Beatrice. "They seem to be coming from fore and

aft. The directions align with our direction of travel."

"Could we have some sort of satellite system?" said Tom.

"I'm beginning to suspect that," said Dandy. I hadn't been able to figure out how the original Ironmonger could be the source. There's too much junk buildup. Besides, the signal seemed to be of the same strength no matter what our relative position was to Ironmonger."

"If they are satellites, how are we going to do anything about them?" asked Candie.

"You and I are going to shoot them down."

"Yeah, sure."

"Why not? We've got a nifty, armed shuttle sitting outside. The first order of business is for Tom and Corky to design a seat that will put us in a position so we can operate the controls on it. Then we'll fly down to the hangar level and rig up another shuttle. We'll do some practice runs, looking for Hornitoads. If we can find them, we'll disable their aircraft, leaving us free to concentrate on other things.

"Oh, that reminds me. Corky, you've been shirking your duties." said Dandy as he frowned at the handyman propped up in his make-shift wheelchair.

"What? What?" said Corky, who always did more than he was asked or required to do.

"We don't have a name for those aliens in the Green Hulk."

"Oh, the 'Insectos'?" said Corky.

"You mean you had a name all along?"

"Sure, isn't that what they look like? I had a name, but no one asked me," said Corky with a shrug.

Dandy was pleased that the little exchange brought smiles and a general relaxing to TC.

With renewed vigor, the crew set about necessary housekeeping chores such as cleaning and checking equipment, filling air tanks and seeing to personal items...laundry and hygiene.

Beatrice carefully picked up the deflated Doughboy and placed him in a storage drawer under her bunk. She could open the drawer and brush her dangling foot against his moleskin-like surface as she read.

Dandy missed Corky in the shop. Tom had provided a working drawing for the alien shuttle adaptation so a human could work the directional handles with his feet. An extension moved the firing trigger up to where it could be worked by a human hand. It was quite a stretch to get to some of the Insecto controls.

Dandy found the internal gas supply for the shuttle and vented it before it killed someone.

When the seating extension was installed in the alien shuttle and a second one loaded aboard, Dandy and Candie went on training flights back and forth along the length of the Green Hulk. When their competence level rose high enough, they dropped over the side and went on a more extensive flight. They always kept the Green Hulk in sight with one eye while watching for Hornitoads with the other.

As soon as they both had the hang of flying the shuttle, Dandy flew into the gaping hangar opening. He pulled up to the line of parked shuttles. This time they had equipped themselves with a ladder. They moved the seat adaption into another shuttle. They didn't need tools because Tom had designed it to be installed with hand operated clamps.

Before they took off, each closed the canopy and tried to talk to the other. The material used in the alien craft dampened their signals leaving them with only sign language, which was made even more difficult by the perpetual Ironmonger gloom.

Dandy opened his cowling and motioned Candie to do the same. "On the way out, I want to test fire the weapons. They're some sort of ray gun. I have no idea of what they can do. I want to know their range, power, recharge time, and power drain. So keep track of things. Let's see if we can hit the tower-like structure on the horizon line."

Candie had the same initial problem as Dandy when she left the hangar. She didn't have enough lift or speed when she dropped into space. She dropped like a rock until more power was applied. From her lower vantage point, she picked out a distinctive pile of debris and tried to aim at it but from her point of view she couldn't line up the sights. She pointed the craft as best she could and fired. The impact was much further away than she had intended. As she started to rise, she took a shot at the tower and apparently overshot it. There were two eruptions near the tower showing that Dandy was getting better shots.

Both craft landed near Taran. Dandy motioned Candie to turn the shuttle around so it faced toward their target tower.

Later, Dandy was standing on the seat so he could see through the Insectos sights to line up a target. Then he installed a make-shift sight of Tom's design that the humans could use from their vantage point.

During their flights, the Ironmonger warning had started again. Beatrice got as accurate a reading as she could before it stopped.

Tom continued to get stronger by the hour. He insisted he could handle installing antennas and relays so that the pilots could be in communication with each other and Taran. Beatrice went along to assist and make sure Tom didn't overdo it. Corky watched the scanners and screens while Dandy and Candie rested before the assault on the warning devices.

After their experience of running out of air while in the Green Hulk, the two alien shuttles were loaded with extra air tanks, batteries and anything that might be useful in any sort of emergency. Dandy had vented the alien breathing gas from the new shuttle, to be on the safe side. From his wheelchair, Corky had assembled a couple of portable directional finders tuned in on the warning signals.

During the suiting-up process, Dandy speculated, "Those satellites could be some distance out. They can sense very low-level activity. If they are close, they shouldn't be able to pick up activity around the curve of Ironmonger."

"Just follow your directional finder and the satellite should be on the other end." said Candie philosophically.

When the pair took off, Dandy headed forward, while Candie went seeking the trailing one. Candie was expected to reach her objective long before Dandy. He would have to exceed Ironmonger's speed to close the gap to his satellite.

As Dandy put some distance behind himself, a look to the rear blew a bunch of preconceived ideas. He changed direction so he could fly across the front of Ironmonger.

"Bea, can you make out anything through my helmet camera?"

There was a pause. "Virtually nothing. It's just a dark blob against a dark background."

"We'll have to fly around Ironmonger before we make any more plans." Dandy resumed his course toward the satellite.

Candie kept flying toward an invisible point in space in the wake of Ironmonger. She had no way of telling how far away she was from the target. They would be closing at an incredible speed, which was making Candie nervous.

"Dandy, do you have any idea how far out those satellites are?"

"No, we have no way of telling."

"I'm going to swing to the side and try to establish an angle that will give me some idea of the distance. I don't want that thing suddenly appearing in my windshield."

"Good thinking."

Since there were no instrument readings that made any sense to Dandy, he had to rely on his own senses. He knew he was closing on the satellite because Ironmonger was falling to the rear. The direction finder kept him going in the right direction. He could see nothing against the darkness.

Candie, if you haven't come across the satellite by now, it is a long ways out."

"I'm getting closer. The angle is changing, but I can't see anything. It must not be very big."

"Come around and home in on it from the rear. That way it won't run into you."

"I'm close to it. I'm in its backwash. I can just barely make it out. It looks like a black refrigerator. There's a faint glow from the drive lenses. How is this thing fueled?"

"There must be a particle beam powering it. That would explain a couple of anomalies I experienced. Twice my shuttle has jumped forward with no encouragement from me. Must have passed through the stream, which added energy to my output."

"One down," announced Candie.

"Congrats, I'm still chasing mine."

"Oops."

"Oops, what?"

"I'm getting another signal. There must be a redundant system."

"Go after it. If you've got one there, I've probably got one here too."

After Candie destroyed her third box, she was rewarded with silence. Dandy was just closing on number two.

Since it was Candie's turn to play catch-up, the two shuttles arrived back at Taran within a few minutes of each other.

"Before we unsuit, we need to get some pictures of the ends of Ironmonger. What could you see from the rear end?"

"Very little. It is in darkness. I did see a blue glow in what looked like a big navel."

"That's a general description of the front end too, but more detail is visible. I want to photograph it. We will be looking into its mouth."

Dandy called Tom. "Send Bea down with a portable camera we can plug into the antenna. We'll be taking Candie's shuttle because it should have more fuel than mine. I'll be cameraman and take a look down Ironmonger's throat."

When Candie negotiated about a quarter of Ironmonger, they found a mammoth, gaping hole. The emanating light wasn't blue, but orange.

"This hole is many times bigger than on the other side," said Candie.

"This end is eating the garbage heap. The other end is where the propulsion energy is expelled. The debris it collects is what fuels Ironmonger."

"Beatrice thinks this thing could be eons old. That would mean we are eons behind the alien races."

"It looks that way. Make a couple of passes so I can look down its gullet. If you feel the slightest tug, get us out of here. I don't want to be pulled in there. We'd come out the other end as a glimmer of blue light."

As Candie moved closer, Dandy started shooting pictures of the phenomenon.

"I'm beginning to feel a slight draw, but nothing I can't steer through," said Candie.

"Let's make one more pass. If it starts getting any stronger, break off."

They made the second tour without incident. "Let's head back, but make a wide sweep to the right. Maybe we can locate the Hornitoads. I'm hoping to launch shortly and I'd hate to have those guys show up to screw up our party."

Candie did as ordered, but all they saw below them was the jumbled mass of alien space debris. As Candie turned to the port to head back home, she elevated her craft to be able to spot the Green Hulk.

"There it is. They didn't get their big ship much beyond the horizon," said Dandy. "It's squatting on a pile of old ships. I don't see any of the small craft hanging around."

"I don't see any place where they could have landed." said Candie. "I'll bet the big girl couldn't get any further after we put some shots into her."

"Make a pass at her. If we see any activity, try to put a couple more shots into her. That should give them something to think about. Maybe a little more damage will delay anything they may have in mind."

Candie tilted over into a dive and accelerated. When they got closer, they could see what looked like ants scrambling along the top and down the sides. Repair crews were working on damage inflicted by the Green Hulk's big guns.

Without prompting, Candie opened fire. There were two guns on the ship, which alternated their firing sequence. There was no explosion to signify a hit. The impact area seemed to shimmer and then turn into a surface resembling a dry, cracked mud flat. There must have been some impact, because figures were falling off the scaffolding that had been erected over the earlier hits.

Candie swept on by without attracting any return fire. "That should keep them busy a while longer," said the pilot with a grin.

When the pair got back to Taran, they found an upbeat trio. Tom had rigged Corky's couch so he could be properly strapped in for takeoff. Beatrice had even cleaned her room of all dangerous projectiles. Tom had been busy in the lower levels making sure everything was secure.

Candie went up to the control center to prepare for takeoff. Dandy stayed below to help Tom on jobs when his strength wasn't sufficient.

"It really looks vacant below without the shuttles. That puts us at a distinct disadvantage if we run into any trouble."

"We'll just have to try getting back without getting into any difficulties. I wish we could bring along those Insecto shuttles, but their lift capacity wouldn't get them this high. We could probably winch one into the bay, but that would take too much time. And right now we don't have enough able bodies. I want to lift off as soon as everyone has a chance to get a little rest."

Six hours later, Taran was ready and the crew was strapped in. Everyone was all smiles as Dandy brought the A/Gs generators on line. Gently he eased the slide forward and Taran slewed a little to one side. Dandy fired the main engine. He was no longer worried about burning a hole in the hull.

The increased pressure forced the crew into their couches. Taran streaked skyward. Breathing became more difficult, but not one was complaining. Corky was experiencing pain in his broken legs, but he wasn't about to bitch about it. It didn't take long before they had broken away from Ironmonger's weak gravity. Dandy eased off on the main engines, while Candie searched for the nearest Solar Jet going in their direction.

Above and below the plane of the planets, there were fewer jets. Candie set the coordinates. Beatrice scanned for any visitors. Once the systems were functioning properly, Dandy had everyone adjourn to the Fish House for a little celebration.

As Corky happily munched on his nachos, his only complaint was that the CEO, Malvane, hadn't sent up a beer to go along with his snack. Candie put on her dangly earrings for the occasion. Beatrice was talking Tom's ear off over her new theory she had come up with from the pictures Dandy had sent back. She believed that Ironmonger was powered by a tiny singularity. She postulated that due to the suspected age of the garbage scow, no mere mechanical device could generate that much power over such a long time span. The singularity fed upon the debris it sucked in.

Candie was trying to bait Dandy about his over-extended vacation in a less than desirable spot. Dandy apologized saying, "Sorry Ironmonger didn't have a spa. You'll really have to work to get rid of those thunder thighs."

Candie was about to give him a whack but pulled off because Dandy was no longer paying attention to her. He was looking off into space as he sat with his fingers splayed out on the table top.

Dandy erupted out of his chair. "Damn." He dove for his console. He yelled at Candie, "Has Ironmonger changed course?"

Candie slid into her seat and had an immediate reply. "Yes."

"It's reeling us in again."

"What started that up?" ask Candie.

"It's just twenty hours since you guys went after the satellites," said Beatrice. "They turned the system on, but they didn't send the signal to turn it off. You blew them up."

"I'm not going to waste fuel trying to resist the force. All I want to do is change Ironmonger direction of travel so it will leave our solar system without getting any closer to Earth. Candie, find the Green Hulk. I want to set down near where we took off."

Dandy made a big circle until Ironmonger was outbound from Earth. Then he settled down on the Green Hulk. This time the hull was in darkness since it was now on the shadow side.

The main engine flame punched another hole in the hull. Dandy landed Taran a considerable distance from the old site because he didn't want to damage the shuttles. Using the A/Gs he was able to sideslip enough to get them away from the hole and the super-heated metal.

Gloom was spreading fast through TC. The crew had been celebrating their return home when suddenly they had been clamped back in jail. Dandy didn't want any defeatist attitude to take hold.

As soon as Taran was firmly settled on the hull, he flipped on the intercom so that, as he talked to Candie, all could hear.

"Candie, I'm going to see if one of those alien shuttles has enough power to fly against that damn beam. I think it has. There isn't very much surface and those things have a lot of thrust. I'm going to drop a few shots down Ironmonger's throat. If Bea is right and there is a little singularity powering this thing, maybe I can interrupt the signal. If I can knock out the ray, I'll be back and we'll head home. However, be ready to lift off is something unexpected happens. Saving the ship is your first priority."

Candie followed Dandy down to the changing room to help. She clearly was not her normal bubbly self. She had looked down the maw of Ironmonger and knew the potential dangers. With pull of that attractor ray it might be even more hazardous. If that was a singularity in there and he disrupted it too much, there might be one hell of an implosion.

When Dandy was suited up, he pulled another air tank out of the rack. Candie followed him into the elevator for the trip to the ground level. Neither had anything personal to say. Any comments were purely business. When the elevator stopped and before Dandy snapped his face-plate shut, Candie reached inside his helmet to brush her fingers lightly along his cheek.

"Come back," is all she said before triggering the door.

As Dandy stepped out into the darkness, he was well aware that Candie had far exceeded her normal reserve. Oh, they had petted and made love, but that was mutual self-gratification without any thoughts of future entangling emotional alliances. This time it was different.

It was a long hike to the shuttles. Dandy had had the foresight to lash the ladder to the shuttle so it wouldn't be sucked away by Taran's A/Gs. Before long he was strapping himself to his makeshift seat. He hooked into the antennae. All he had to say was, "I'm off."

He had to engage much more lift to the shuttle to raise it off the hull. He added enough thrust to turn toward the front of the Green Hulk. When the shuttle was pointed in the right direction he shoved both levers sharply forward. The shuttle leapt off the deck. With the thrust, the lift coefficient was enhanced so he was skimming along over the hull. He increased the thrust. By the time he reached the edge of the Green Hulk, he had enough speed so the drop beyond was manageable. Dandy continued to increase the power. He was moving fast. In fact, he reached Ironmonger's gaping mouth so quickly he was unprepared. He shot by the opening. At that point the shuttle was going at right angles to Ironmonger, and Dandy was almost run over by the monstrous ball that was now in pursuit mode.

Dandy moved well out in front of Ironmonger. When he came around, he was headed right toward its throat. He fired both canons as fast as they would fire. He could see no results. He had to sheer off.

"I've fired a whole salvo right down the gullet. I can't see any results. How about you?"

"Nothing here, except we've speeded up a bit," said Candie.

"You may be just feeding its energy source," said Tom.

Dandy came around again. This time he fired at the interior walls. He could see no results. He had the impression that he could see images resembling heat waves. But the images veered off and went right down into the core.

Trying to disrupt an unknown timing cycle in an unknown location had been akin to clutching at straws, but he had to try something. That didn't work so he'd try clutching some more straws. He headed back to the Green Hulk.

"Candie, turn on the lights so I can find you and see to land."

Dandy elevated until he could see Taran standing like a light-house. He landed near the access panel. He had brought Corky's key with him.

"I'm going inside. Stand by for an emergency take-off if neces-sary. I'll be out of radio range. Dandy didn't feel like getting into a conversation over his plan. He let himself into the Green Hulk and made his way into the firing center.

He wished he'd lugged the ladder down when he had to clam-ber up onto the various stools in front of the firing boards. Finally he lined up the starboard guns in a pattern to his liking. Four guns from the center section were aimed as straight down as possible. Four guns from the front and rear sections were angled down toward the center. He hoped that at some point deep inside Ironmonger they would converge. When he turned on the control panels, he heard the hum of generators or some sort of power source, engage.

When everything was set up, Dandy pulled his version of a trigger from a pocket. He didn't want to have to use the hand of a dead Insecto, so he had made his own trigger finger. It was a short metal rod with a ball on the end. It looked like a gear shift on one of the old standard transmission cars. Dandy fired the center guns four times. He couldn't hear anything, but he had the impression a slight tremor went through the hull. He moved to the forward gun for four shots and then to the rear for a like number. It wasn't long before he could feel the strain of trying to get up on the stools in a space suit. The next trip he fired eight times from each station. He was not getting any warnings from the panels that he was running out of energy, so he continued his firing sequences. About half an hour went by with no tangible results, but he continued making the rounds. He had no way of knowing if the attraction ray was still working. He decided that after firing for another half an hour, he'd go outside so he could communicate with Taran to see if there were any results.

While he was moving to another station, there was a slight lurch of the Green Hulk. Something was happening. Another series of shots brought a more noticeable movement. He figured he was making the base for Ironmonger unstable, but the important thing was to drill down to the core.

To facilitate climbing up on the stools, Dandy had opened some drawers in side cabinets. With another lurch of the Green Hulk, his manufactured steps slammed shut. While searching through the contents of the drawers to find things to use as wedges, he picked up a metal object, which felt overly heavy. He took Corky's key out of a pocket. It was heavier than he remembered, although he had not noticed it when he opened the hatch this time. Apparently that ray attracted small metal objects as well as space debris. He now had a way of telling if the ray was still functioning.

There was another heavy lurch further to the starboard. Dandy adjusted the guns to keep them firing in approximately the same direction.

Dandy flipped on his external sound system and he was greeted with a calliope of sound. Stressed metal was shrieking. Objects were falling. Dandy fired salvo after salvo.

The Green Hulk shifted again. This time it came to rest at a much more precarious angle. The pitch was enough that Taran might be in jeopardy. He was banking on Candie to keep the ship upright. She might have to lift off and find another place to set down.

An explosion shook the hull, throwing Dandy to the floor. As he collected himself, there was a great roaring sound all around him. He had to turn off his external mike. Taran was airborne. He could feel the pressure of the flame in the hull. He grabbed Corky's key. It was still too heavy.

Candie had launched against Ironmonger's ray. That meant she'd be burning vast amounts of fuel. Dandy staggered to his feet. He went to the central console which controlled the middle section guns. He aimed all that he could bring to bear into the hole he'd been making. He started a rapid firing sequence. The energy meter began dropping to a lower level. He turned on his exterior sensors but he could not hear if the generators were working. The distress sound from the ship drowned out everything else.

The power level rose enough for another salvo. The hull was vibrating constantly from all the various forces upon it. Suddenly, there was a severe tilt toward the rear as if the center of the ship had collapsed into the hole.

The power was down again. Dandy scrambled out of the door and headed back to the access hatch. Because of the new angles, it was easier to clamber onto the hull.

Taran had lifted off. It was sitting on a tremendous tail of fire. She was using too much fuel. Panic clawed at Dandy.

Before diving back down the shaft, a quick glance around the area registered an orange glow punctuated by brilliant flashes from new explosions. It resembled an erupting volcano. Candie's shuttle was gone. His was a pile of wreckage hanging on the edge of one of the holes that Taran had punched into the hull.

Dandy shuffled at his top speed back to the firing center. He was sweating heavily from the physical exertion. But he could also smell the reek of fear. With the new tilt, it was easier getting back on the stool. The gauge was creeping up slowly. Too slowly. It gave Dandy time to think. He didn't want to have to think about anything but eliminating that damn ray. Any other thoughts made him stink.

Candie would never be able to land on what he had seen of the Green Hulk. It was too steep. If she could hold it upright with the A/Gs he could never approach it. He'd be sucked up just like the Hornitoads. Even if she could sit down on another section he'd never be able to get to Taran. Should she land on the regular surface, he still couldn't get to her. Besides his air would not last long enough to make the trip. There was a volcano erupting under the Green Hulk. The bottom half of the Green Hulk would be upside down.

Dandy accepted the proposition that he was trapped on the Green Hulk without food, water, and in a short time, air. He didn't like the thought, but he could accept it much more readily if his friends could escape from Ironmonger.

The gauge seemed to have slowed to a crawl. There was enough energy for a few more shots. He checked the aiming screen. The whole center and rear sections had gone blank. The signals must have been cut off. Dandy repositioned the guns on the front section as best he could and started firing a slow, methodical routine, pumping one shot after another in the same hole.

Explosion after explosion racked the hull. The noise was deafening even through his helmet. Dandy kept firing as the power gauge got lower and lower. The lights on the read-out flickered. The room was plunged into darkness. The entire array was dead.

Dandy tumbled off his stool when a heavy jolt hit. He crawled around until he located his electric lantern. He lurched out of the door making for the access opening. The glow from the fires lit the last part of his journey. He turned out his lantern to conserve its batteries.

As he stuck his head above the hull, he was greeted with a sight that made it all worthwhile. Taran was streaking toward the stars. Dandy made a mental note that Candie had powered down to a fuel-conserving level. He flipped on his radio, but he didn't say anything. Taran might already be out of range of his weakened batteries. If not, any communication now would just add anguish to TC, knowing he had survived the holocaust he had created. Candie would probably try coming back. That would endanger all of them in a useless venture.

Dandy stood for a while watching the eruptions coming from where the center portion of the Green Hulk, had been. Flames leapt skyward lighting his surroundings. He checked his air supply. It was getting low. He moved away from the access hole so he wouldn't get a snoot full of Insecto breathing gas when he opened his face plate to test the Ironmonger air.

A shallow breath brought on a prolonged coughing spasm. He had to go back to his own air supply to get his breathing under control.

He moved toward the disabled shuttle. The extra air tank he had brought along was in it. Maybe he could salvage the air and prolong what now appeared to be the inevitable. Two of the three shuttle legs hung into the hole. The upper leg had collapsed, putting the craft almost flat on the deck.

Dandy scrambled onto the fin-like wing structure. The cowling was shut, but badly cracked. Using Corky's key, he banged away enough of the material to get to the release. It was a struggle to raise it enough to crawl into the cockpit. Dandy retrieved the air tank. As he clambered up the inclined deck to squeeze out, he grabbed the seat adaptor he had made.

He hesitated a moment, in thought, before clawing at the easy-release fasteners. The seat came loose. Dandy delayed long enough to change tanks. He was willing to sacrifice the small amount of air left to eliminate weight. He had a lot of travelling to do.

Earlier, he'd found the elevator and the attendant staircase where it entered the bridge. He held little hope the elevator would work, but he had to make sure. It appeared there was a ship-wide energy failure, so Dandy headed for the stairs. "Okay, guys do your stuff," he said to his legs.

Dandy was grateful he was heading down. The steps were very tall, which would have required excessive exertion. He could hop from one to another without sucking in too much air. It was awkward carrying the shuttle seat until he found he could rest in on top of his helmet without bashing his brains out.

He tried to keep count, but before long he had only a general idea of how many levels he had negotiated. The explosions continued, periodically knocking him into the walls. He guarded his lantern at the expense of his body. It was difficult enough negotiating the slanted steps but periodically he came across an Insecto body he had to circumvent.

By the time he'd cover what he figured was about half the way, his legs were beginning to protest. He'd already given them quite a workout in the gunnery station. He pushed on another twenty levels before he let himself take a break. As he sat in the darkness, his mind toyed with his future, which didn't look too promising. When his legs quit trembling, he shook the gloomy thoughts out of his head and resumed his downward path.

Some of the access doors had been jammed shut. Others could be opened, but with considerable effort. From the earlier trip he remembered that the stairwell door to the flight deck had been open. He hoped that it was not one that had been slammed shut. The flight deck couldn't be too far away. He stuck his head out each open door to check. As it turned out, the right door announced itself to him. A glow lighted the landing. Earlier, Candie had rammed an opening through the hallway into the flight lines. There had also been the glassed in area. Light from the inferno outside was flickering on the walls.

Dandy made his way through Candie's opening onto the flight lines. In the faint light, he could make out a jumble of shuttles along the far side of the airstrip. Dandy's heart skipped a beat. They were no longer in a neat line, ready for takeoff. The tethers must have been released when the power failed. With the tilt of the deck, the small aircraft were in piles.

As Dandy crossed the flight lines, he tried to see the extent of the damage with his lantern but the batteries were dying. He switched it off and navigated under the weak glow of the fires. When he got closer, the situation looked even grimmer. The shuttles were never meant for physical contact. As they had fallen on top of one another, they crumpled. Out of the hundreds of shuttles stored there, surely there would be one that was undamaged. Of course, he had to be able to get it out. There must have been fifty or more craft on the front line and there were several lines fading back into the recesses of the Green Hulk.

Everything he could see along the front line was broken or badly dinged. He wandered into the pile. The search was taking too much time. Periodically, there was a line of support columns. Dandy noticed that to the right of the columns there was a clear space. He selected one opening and made his way to the rear. He was rewarded with a shuttle that had only a small dent in the port fins structure. It might cause some drag in the atmosphere, but in space it would make no difference. Of course, that was predicated on the theory that he could make it into space. While he and Candie had been scooting around Ironmonger, no thought had been applied to space flight. However, Dandy was working on the hypothesis that the shuttles were designed to fly outside the atmosphere, because the mother ship was not designed to enter the atmosphere and the shuttles would have to be able to function in both environments. By climbing crippled ships that were closer to the deck, Dandy made it onto his slightly dinged ship. A check from the topside revealed no further problems. When he turned on the console everything appeared functional. The power gauge was at maximum.

Dandy had to use the last rays of his lantern to get the seat bolted on. He vented the alien breathing gas and gently turned the ship toward the alleyway. At one point, a badly damaged shuttle lay partially in his way. Using the shuttle lifting capacity, he was able to soar over the obstruction. It was a very nervous few minutes before he had navigated himself clear of the wreckage.

As soon as the nose of the shuttle was pointed toward the opening, Dandy gunned it, rising along the tilted deck until he shot out of the Green Hulk. He wanted to get away from the volcano erupting below him. He didn't really think he'd come across any Hornitoads, but he didn't want to take any chance. He tilted the craft enough so that he could look down. There was a deep glowing cavern where the center section of the Green Hulk had been. The back section was about ready to slide into the hole and the section he had just vacated wouldn't be far behind. As he veered further away, he could see the original maw of Ironmonger. It was glowing brightly, too. It appeared that the two openings would eventually join.

There was a pall of smoke hanging over Ironmonger. Not much could be seen through it. He had to get above the pollution. Now he had to figure out how to fire up his craft to get to orbital speed. Dandy rummaged around the board but couldn't find anything. He flipped the shuttle over so the light from Ironmonger gave him some visibility. The only thing that seemed a possibility was the lever for the forward thrust. It had a T-handle. The front side was light and the back dark. Other than the dim board light, that was the only color code he could see. He was looking for a speed control and that lever was the only thing he could find. He slipped his glove off so he could try feeling what he could not see. On the far side of the lever was a button. It was right where a three fingered creature could press it. Dandy had been looking for something he could thumb. When the button was depressed the lever handle swung a hundred and eighty degrees and slipped back to the starting position on the scale. He put his glove back on and shoved the control forward.

When Dandy burst into the open and the universe lay before him, it was a thrill to be shed of Ironmonger. Another thing that he thought he would find out there was Taran, but he could find no sign of her. If Candie had remained under power, he should have been able to see her even after the elapsed time, but the void was bare. If she was coasting he'd probably never be able to see her. He started gently spinning to see if Taran was in a synchronous orbit, but he could find nothing.

He didn't have an antenna hooked up to get his signal out of the cabin, but he tried sending one anyway. No response. Since he was still suited up and on his own air supply, he opened the canopy and tried again. There was still no reply. Dandy had a sinking feeling. He'd bested Ironmonger and he'd gotten away, but his friends hadn't waited around to see if he could do it. His rational mind told him there could be all sorts of reasons for not being able to hook up—they were waiting out there somewhere, but his batteries were dead; they had heard him, but he wasn't receiving. Maybe they had concluded he was dead after all the explosions on the Green Hulk and they had headed home.

Then he realized home was on the other side of Ironmonger, since he had made it change its direction of travel just before landing Taran the last time. He brought the shuttle around and headed at top speed to circumvent Ironmonger. His gas was running out. He had to make his move quickly.

When he got clear enough to see back in the direction of Earth he couldn't detect any fiery tail. Another scenario came to mind. Maybe Candie had tried to go back to Ironmonger to pick him up. If she had tried to set down anywhere on the Green Hulk it wouldn't have worked. The surfaces were all at too much of an angle. She would have had to set down somewhere else. He picked up speed again to complete the circuit.

Dandy severely tested the heat shield on the shuttle by going back into the atmosphere. When he got his speed under control, he circumnavigated Ironmonger. With the eruptions, he had a pretty good view of the surrounding landscape. There was no sign of Taran. Dandy shot skyward again.

He set himself in a synchronous orbit, so he could watch the display on Ironmonger. At least he had beaten Ironmonger. He would rather die in space than on a garbage heap. The thoughts of maybe being eaten by the denizens of that garbage scow didn't appeal to him. At least he had been instrumental in getting the four other members of TC into a situation where they had a chance of getting home. It would be up to them to make it work.

When he got down to the last of his air, Dandy decided to maneuver himself into a position where he could take a shot at Earth. It would be a guess at best, but that really didn't matter. He would point it in the right direction and open the throttle to maximum and maybe someday he might arrive in close enough proximity to Earth that an astro-archeologist would find him and put the story together.

Dandy was having trouble controlling his thoughts. He didn't want to dwell on his mother. He didn't want to call up the memory of Candie touching his cheek. Shellee, the little daughter of his proctor, Walter Hale, kept trying to worm her way in, but he slammed the door on the whole bunch. To let those images in would mean that he had failed. His life would be labeled a defeat. And Andy Dawson couldn't stand going out as a loser.

Vigorously, shaking his head, Dandy struggled to climb out of his self-indulgence. His final act of defiance would be to launch his carcass toward Earth. He had been staring at the pyrotechnics of Ironmonger without seeing them. Suddenly, the shuttle went pinwheeling through space. Dandy became alert and manipulated the controls to regain stability. When the motion stopped, he was seeing Ironmonger through the parabolic arch between Taran's legs.

While he'd been wallowing in self-pity, Taran had sneaked up and given him a puff with a maneuvering thruster. His depression vanished and he was thinking again. His radio was still silent, so he and Candie were going to have to get on the same wavelength through mutual understanding. His only access would be through the shuttle bay. He had wondered if he could bring an alien craft aboard. His original assessment, without the benefits of measurements, had been been that it might be a little over-wide and over-tall.

Gently Dandy moved the shuttle below Taran and then came up between the legs. Candie had turned on the exterior lights. The bay ramp was slowly opening. There was no question that he could get aboard, providing his air lasted. The gauge was creeping close to empty.

Candie was suited up, standing at the head of the ramp. She was tethered to a stanchion. She was holding another line.... the one from the winch that they had rigged while on the Green Hulk.

Dandy wasted no time in bringing the shuttle to the end of the ramp. Gently he lifted the front leg enough to get it onto the ramp. Candie moved forward to secure the winch line to the leg. She backed up enough to look at the height. Her hand signals indicated that there was a clearance of a couple of feet. Dandy moved forward. Another hand motion told him to lift a little more so the back legs could clear the edge. When he had all three legs on the ramp, Dandy cut the power and popped the canopy. He drew his hand across his throat as he pulled himself from the cockpit.

Candie had anticipated the problem. She had a tank on a rope at the edge of the ramp. In the weightless environment, she floated the new tank to him. Dandy was able to make the exchange before the old tank was completely exhausted.

Dandy returned to the cockpit. He and Candie maneuvered about three-quarters of the shuttle in before Candie indicated a problem. When he got out on the fin, he saw that the ship was a couple of inches wider than the opening. From the fin he could step right onto the deck of Taran.

As soon as Dandy touched Taran, he was nearly overwhelmed. He felt as if he were home. He was glad Candie was far below him on the ramp because he wasn't one to let that much emotion out in public.

Before he could do anything, he needed to replace his battery and put on a pair of magnetic shoes. Candie had thought of that, too. They were in a container next to the ramp.

When his radio became operational again, Dandy said, "Thanks for dropping by to give a man a lift."There was a jumble of sounds as everyone tried to answer at the same time.

Returning to the business at hand, Dandy clomped down to ramp to Candie who was making sure the shuttle didn't drift away.

"I think, if we raise the right foot a little, the tilt will let it slip in." It took some work, but finally the alien shuttle was sitting in Taran's bay. Both shipmates had a great sense of accomplishment as they looked at their handiwork.

In the pressurized elevator, both snapped open their face plates. Dandy slipped off his glove and gently moved his fingers across his friend's face. "I'm back."

The symbolism wasn't lost on Candie. Momentarily she held his hand against her face before touching the elevator button.

Chapter 22

It looked like it was going to develop into another celebration but Dandy wanted to move Taran out of possible harm's way, just in case Beatrice's singularity theory might be right. He didn't want to be around if something went wrong.

Actually it hadn't been very many hours since they had celebrated their setting course for home. This time, everyone was physically exhausted and psychologically drained.

Dandy got TC back into their routine. On this trip, they weren't in as big a rush as on the one coming out. They weren't going to drive between jets. It was going to be slower, but they would conserve fuel in case some other emergency arose.

For five days they jumped in and out of small jets. But, as Dandy brought them out of the last jet, he said, "If you can find another one like that, we could eat up another big chunk." They had been in the jet long enough that he could feel a good stubble on his face. Corky, who beard was much heavier than his, was badly in need of a shave.

"Corky, can you tell if these jumps in the jets affect your legs in any way?"

"They're still throbbing all the time. I can't feel any difference, yet."

"Those breaks aren't that old. It just seems like ages ago," said Candie. "You've got to give them some time."

Dandy got together with Beatrice concerning the mountains of information she had compiled while they were on Ironmonger. He assigned each crew member, depending on expertise, certain aspects of the mission on which to write reports. Beatrice was charged with getting together another photo report covering all of their alien encounters. They would air it as soon as they got into range. The Catholic Church would really go into orbit with four new alien species....fully documented....to try to debunk.

It had been a quiet day. Everyone was occupied with assigned chores. Beatrice pulled her earphones off, letting them hang around her neck. She sat straight up and became alert. "He's back."

Tom stiffened too. He had come alert, but not in response to Beatrice. He was reacting to some other stimulus.

"Tea House is here," said Beatrice.

Dandy didn't need Bea's pronouncement. The hair on the back of his hands were standing up straight up. Candy was trying to hold her hair down.

Beatrice got that faraway look, indicating she was conversing with Tea House. It turned into a long conversation. At one point tears were cascading down Beatrice's face. Candie mouthed "Doughboy" to Dandy. The conversation continued on. Dandy went to the machine for coffee for himself and tea for Candie. Tom was in a world of his own, but Corky was being left out of it because he was confined to his seat. Dandy went to Corky's rescue, helping him in the makeshift wheelchair. Dandy moved him into the Fish House and got him a cup of coffee too.

Finally Beatrice turned to the assembled group. I've been telling Tea House what has happened and what Doughboy did for us. He wants to talk to you like he did last time....through me. Here goes...."

"My physical friend, Beatrice, has told me an incredible story of love and concern for others. Beatrice's first question of me was why had Doughboy returned to you. She was concerned he had been mistreated again, causing him to flee a second time. I am certain he was not fleeing. I think he returned because of a love bond he developed with Beatrice. Somehow he found his way back to her. My journey here was more difficult. It took me so much longer because I was following his faint energy patterns. Doughboy was apparently able to home in on Beatrice directly. It is a strange phenomenon that will keep our scholars busy by ages."

Dandy observed that either Tea House had become much more conversant in the English language or he was communicating much better with Beatrice. He was not stumbling over sentence structure nor using the wrong word as he had done on the first time around.

"This love bond," continued Tea House, "was strong enough that when Beatrice was anguishing over Tom's gradual decline, Doughboy was willing to pass his energy on to her friend to reverse a death sentence."

"You mean he sacrificed himself because of his love for Beatrice?" said Candie, in an astonished voice.

"In a sense, but it is not as dire as it sounds. Doughboy didn't die. He just needs his energy replenished. Before he transferred his energy reserve to Tom, he put out a call. I had been searching for him after his second departure....without success. When he called, I was able to trace him here."

Beatrice stood up and slowly walked into her quarters. A moment later, she reappeared with Doughboy. He looked like a completely deflated, white beach ball. Beatrice placed him on the floor in front of her station. She returned to her couch.

Slowly Doughboy began to inflate into what became about an eighteen inch fuzzy ball. When the growth ceased, Doughboy immediately elongated himself and like an inch worm, moved across the floor until he was under Bea's dangling foot, where he settled down.

"I see my nibbling is still taken by his position in this new order. I have a feeling it has something to do with the concept of 'love' as Beatrice used it. This is not quite understood by my kind. We have many similar feelings. We cherish, honor, de-sire....all those things, but love seems to have some added fea-ture we don't comprehend."

Beatrice held her finger up, indicating she was speaking on her own. "I think the element missing in your world is 'touch'."

"Touch?" asked Tea House.

"Well, it may be a combination of love and tactile expres-sions of that love. Lovers seem to want to be in physical contact. Without touch, being together becomes an intellectual exercise without great passion."

All of TC was staring at Beatrice. Noticing their looks, she blushed and said, "Okay, sometimes I read romance novels. Anyway, that's what I think." Beatrice turned away.

To fill the silence, Dandy asked Tea House, "Can you tell us what was wrong with Tom?"

Beatrice resumed her translating duties. "He was infected with an organism which feeds on life energy. In a species that has a finite supply, such an infection is usually fatal. Since my species is all energy, we have virtually an unlimited supply. We collect energy from the universe. When Doughboy passed his energy on to Tom, the organism drowned. It will not be a further problem."

For the first time Tom spoke up. "How did I get infected? It was the Bird-kins wasn't it?"

"Bird-kins?"There was a delay while Tea House and Beatrice confirmed. "Yes, I am not directly familiar with that species, but many species carry an amazing array of weapons. Their claws were apparently contaminated with the organism. That may have been natural or by intent."

"You are taking Doughboy with you?"said Candie.

"Yes, he is a cherished member of my family."

"Do you think he will stay?"

"This time I think he will. He has reached a state of content-ment. He is proud of his small contribution to your mission.

He had always been a recipient of your affection. He wanted to participate. You see, on another level we have been in constant conversation since he was re-energized. Doughboy wishes me to pass along his sincere thanks for helping him through some very hard times. In addition I wish to extend my own gratitude for your services to Doughboy.

"An aside, when we get back home, you five will join our pantheon of heroes. In our society, information is distributed instantly to all. Everyone already knows you, and soon your recent exploits will become fable in our story history."

"Why would we be of any significance to your people?" said Corky.

"We can observe many species because of our nature, but seldom do we interact and on many of those occasions when our presence became known we were viewed with fear. You are a limited, but remarkable species. Before we go, I have been asked to perform one other little service. Doughboy wishes me to repair Corky's legs."

"Wow," cried Corky, "they don't ache any more....just itch like crazy."

"Good-bye friends." Doughboy disappeared and the hair on Dandy's arms lay down again.

"Oh," said Beatrice. "What an experience. I have to record all this before it fades. I've had another glimpse into a whole new, wonderful world. I'm making history, not just recording it. Yes!"

Candie and Dandy smiled at one another. "With Bea, no information will ever fade away, "said Candie as she headed for Corky. Moments later, she and Tom were shoving Corky toward the elevator and the shop x-ray unit.

Dandy checked the vicinity for visitors and the rate of progress toward a promising Solar Jet.

Beatrice had never really trusted the voice-print on her computer, but she plugged in the mike and began dictating. She had too much to say for mechanical input.

Twenty minutes later, Corky came walking out of the elevator with a broad smile on his face. "They can't even find a trace of the break. Boy, I'm glad to be out of those casts."

"You and me both," said Dandy. "You were beginning to stink so much I was about to hang you in the spacesuit deodorizing chamber." Everyone laughed except Beatrice, who wouldn't rejoin the human race until she'd recorded everything about her Tea House encounter.

Dandy nibbled away at the intervening distance to Earth. TC set about recording all the information gained on Taran's second voyage. Dandy started sorting out the files into what information were strictly Gal X secrets, what might be released to the scientific community, and what could be told to the public. He had Beatrice edit a little film showing clips of the Pretzis, Bird-kins, Hornitoads and Insectos. They decided to keep Tea House and Doughboy secret except for the top echelon of Gal X. The public might be able to handle corporeal species they could see, but invisible intelligence with teleportation capabilities would probably be too much.

The images Beatrice had launched while on Ironmonger would not arrive at Earth until a long time after the spaceship sat down on the New Mexico desert. Taran popped out of a Solar Jet so close to home that it surprised everyone, especially Gal X's competitors and all the advanced industrialized governments. From that point on, Taran would slog in under its own power. Dandy didn't want to give any competitors any hints on their methods of travel.

Malvane was promptly advised that Taran was coming in. When the ship got into reasonable transmission range, he moved into the communication center.

"Welcome home, Taran," said the CEO. Timers were set to measure the response time, which would give a good indication of the distances involved. It took twenty minutes to get an answer. Dandy responded, "We are glad to be back. The ship and crew are in good shape."

"Gal X is pleased to hear that report. We'll talk further when there is less delay."

When Taran got into closer proximity to Earth, Malvane instructed Tom to activate a program that was unknown to TC. Malvane's image came on the monitors. With a broad smile he said, "After your last trip, we installed a super secret, narrow band relay so no one can eavesdrop. You may speak freely on this system."

In a conference-style call, TC and the CEO went over the finding of Ironmonger and what it represented. TC reported that they had worked their way out of some circumstances, but all was well, and Ironmonger was on its way out of the solar system. They didn't go into much detail because even though Centurion and Hacker may not be listening directly, there was no telling where its agents might be lurking. Besides, a lot of what the crew had to relate was not for general company consumption.

Dandy got permission to have another little TV show-and-tell broadcast to the world. Malvane would make arrangements and then give Dandy the particulars. Since they had a secure link, Beatrice started downloading her files, just in case something unforeseen happened during landing.

When Taran reached a position near Earth, the crew staged their TV show on a frequency and at a time set up and advertised by Gal X. Because of the renown from their first such show following their initial trip into space, there was no problem getting an audience. Virtually every TV set in the world would be on at the same time. The only difference this time was that the debunkers were already lined up to contradict any new revelation about the existence of life beyond the confines of Earth. Too many vested interests were at stake not to put up a vicious fight.

Dandy made the introduction of the crew. Each had a few chatty words to say about how nice it was to be back. Then he turned the show over to Beatrice, who came on like a college professor. She presented a montage of photos showing each of the new species they had encountered. She showed action clips, followed by selected close-up stills, giving more detail. Then she enhanced the shots to get even a better look. The show lasted only half an hour, but the crew felt they had caused sufficient consternation around the world.

The day following the TV show, Malvane again appeared on TC's monitors. "As before, you guys have created a firestorm. Practically every level of human endeavor is clamoring for attention. Scientist from all over the world demand to share in one phase or another of information. Physical anthropologists and that whole ilk want access to your alien files. The religionists are screaming their heads off again.

"One problem that seems to be developing is that governments and their military are getting much more insistent that we share our propulsion technology. As you get closer, watch out for military aircraft. They will be trying to collect flight information. Our Air Force says it will be protecting our borders from foreign intrusion but I suspect they will be trying to gather intelligence on Taran while keeping others away from what they believe is theirs. They are bringing a lot of pressure to bear on us to give them our secrets. Of course, as soon as that happens, some politician will sell it to our enemies for a campaign contribution.

"There is one other situation that warrants vigilance. We have reports Centurion has bought three more of those devices that punched a hole in Taran the first time you were up. We haven't been able to trace them but I wouldn't be surprised if Hacker wouldn't try to deprive Gal X of Taran's services.

"It sounds like we should consider some sort of Rimlick maneuver," said Dandy.

Malvane smiled, remembering how Dandy outfoxed Hacker, the computer genius who headed Centurion, with his reactions, which defied all common logic. He had called them Rimlick maneuvers.

Malvane was smiling, but Hacker was growling. As the Centurion CEO ate his beef bok choy, he watched his computer screen for the latest information concerning the incoming Taran. Outside of the initial greeting from Malvane to the ship, there had been no further communication.....at least that Centurion could intercept. His computer readouts said that there was a 100% chance that there was some other method of communication that he had not identified as yet. Hacker's temper was barely in check. The TV show that those kids had put together furthered Gal X's claim to their preeminence in the aerospace arena. Centurion had failed to acquire the Taran technology when that damned kid had lifted off, foiling Colonel Tokla's assault. That little fiasco had cost Centurion dearly. They had lost a good percentage of their elite armed force. There was even a worse loss when that damned Dawson had attacked Centurion's World Headquarters with some sort of alien technology that turned all their silicone chips into sand. Recovering data had really been expensive. It had interfered with Hacker's clandestine attempt to buy or steal Taran technology. Now Taran was heading home after another historic voyage.

Hacker had worked himself into a fresh frenzy. He bent over his keyboard and began issuing orders, which were enhanced by veiled threats. He had to be able to eavesdrop. He sent out another command for Colonel Tokla to check his installations once again. Every time they tried a military operation, something went wrong. This time Hacker wanted to make certain that Taran was knocked out of the sky. His reputation had been tarnished. His whole rise through Centurion had been based on his computerized predictions. That damned Dawson's Rimlick program had so far been one step ahead of his programs. That situation had to change.

On his cell, Colonel Tokla read Hacker's first order to recheck his emplacements. Tokla's rebuilt face with all its keloidal scars twisted into a snarl. One of these days that insolent pipsqueak would go too far. When Tokla did anything, it was perfection and it didn't need re-examination. If anything went wrong, it would not be traceable back to his inadequacies. Any failure resulted from faulty information.

Tokla had positioned his four narrow beam generators in the best spots to cover Taran's New Mexico landing site. The only thing that could save Taran now would be for it to land elsewhere. And that alternative could not be his fault.

After receiving Malvane's warning concerning Centurion having three more of those machines that punched holes straight through one of Taran's legs, Dandy calculated that the weapons must be set up in near proximity to their landing site. Dandy considered setting down elsewhere, but that caused such a storm, it would rip up acres. The plume of debris could be seen for miles, making hiding impossible. Then there was the security. The only place that had sufficient company troops to provide protection was New Mexico. If they set down elsewhere, eventually they would have to move the ship to its home because all the service facilities and personnel were there. Another alternative would have to be devised.

TC thought Dandy's new maneuver would work. However, the operation plan brought loud, prolonged arguments. Dandy had devised the plan for himself to execute but Candie pointed out that his place was at the controls of Taran because he was the best driver, and if something went wrong, he should be maneuvering the ship. Candie argued that she was as well qualified as he to carry out the Rimlick maneuver. The crew sided with Candie. To celebrate her victory, and to rub it in just a tad, she put on her flashy, dangly earrings.

For the three days before Dandy brought Taran into the desired orbital range of Earth, there was a flurry of activity. Under normal conditions, he would have aimed his descent to break into the atmosphere and drop down in an orbital path directly to New Mexico. But, with the warning about Centurion's new acquisitions, that didn't seem prudent. Dandy started the standard descent and then sheared off, ending up over southern Mexico and establishing a geosynchronous orbit above Tikal. In the turbulence of brushing the atmosphere, a huge heat image was created for the infrared scanners. Careful inspections of the radar screens might have revealed a speck falling away.

The alien shuttle had been backed down the ramp. It was attached to Taran by a tether to the front leg. As the air friction increased Corky cast the shuttle free. Candie added enough lift to pull it away. The drag of the small amount of air and Candie's careful manipulations held the shuttle behind as the massive ship careened through space. The speck tumbled toward Earth. Whenever the heat became too high, Candie added enough thrust to reduce the free fall to a manageable amount.

Once Taran had left the shuttle behind, Candie nosed over into a descending glide toward the central Mexican plateau. When below radar range, Candie went streaking north, silently skimming the ground.

Moving across the Mexican deserts caused no problem. She picked up some attention along the US border but was gone before reports could be made. Avoiding populated areas as much as possible, she made her way to Denver along the Front Range of the Rockies. Sighting calls were going in, but most people thought they were seeing a UFO. When the military couldn't confirm any radar sighting, response was slow.

Candie came straight in over the Red Rocks and dropped a prolonged burst from her cannon into the long reflecting pond along the northern edge of Centurion World Headquarters. Instantly, the water turned into a cloud of steam. The two story tall masonry towers in the middle of the pond crumbled into charred dust. There was no explosion as when a bomb or artillery shell hit, but it sounded more like a clap of thunder as the molecules came apart.

Hacker was almost knocked off his chair. His office was on the top floor overlooking the reflecting pond, but when he became CEO, he had ordered the windows removed. Now a bricked up wall formed the mounting surface for a huge logo for Centurion. However, his computer console had access to all the external security cameras. From the camera mounted on the roof directly over his office, Hacker could see a dense cloud of steam and dust. A brisk diurnal breeze was blowing the debris down slope. As the air cleared the wreckage of the pond and columns became visible, alarms were going off all over the building. The lines to the in-house phones were all blinking. An intercom from the receptionist came on.

"Sir, tune to the Taran channel 18."

That channel was one that Centurion had compromised a long time ago. When Hacker flipped it on, he had to wait for a moment until the speaker repeated the message. "Hacker, are you listening? I have a message for you." There was a pause before the message was repeated.

Hacker patched into the radio and snarled, "Who wants to know?"

"Good morning, Hacker, this is Andie Carson," said Candie in her sexiest voice. "Swing that camera mounted over your office across that dried up pond to the Red Rocks. I'm sitting on top."

Hacker maneuvered the camera along the top of the Red Rocks. Sitting like a fly on top of the tallest one was a strange looking craft pointed right at him. He adjusted the camera and zoomed in on the craft.

A cute, blonde girl with short hair was smiling directly into the camera. "Here I am," she said, as she wiggled her fingers at him. She was dressed in a space suit, but she had removed the helmet. Her long earrings flashed in the morning sun as she flipped her head.

"Do I have your attention? Good. My message is that Taran is headed for a landing at the Gal X base in New Mexico. With the first flash of light from one of your new toys, I will finger the trigger and reduced that entire building and all that is in it to a pile of parched sand....just like the pond. Have I made myself perfectly clear?"

There was a substantial pause.

"I won't ask again."

Hacker was beside himself with rage, but an even stronger motivating factor was self-preservation. From what he'd seen of the pond, she probably could reduce the building to rubble. "I hear you."

"Order Tokla to stand down."

There was another delay as Hacker set up various scenarios on his computer. He didn't have time to think up all the possible combinations before that blonde jabbed him again.

"Get that order out or I'll reduce this place to a landing site for Taran."

Hacker sent a message to Tokla to desist and he also asked

for notification of compliance.

Tokla was in radio communication with his four units. He ordered them to stand down and then reported back to his CEO.

Hacker reported to Candie that he had complied.

"Now we sit and wait. By the way, don't try evacuating the building. One of those little people running around down there could be you or one could be trying to get off a shot at me. Don't try it. I have a hair trigger."

After Candie had dropped away over Mexico, Dandy entered the coordinates that his navigator had left. Taran moved into an orbit that would set it up for a New Mexico landing. When the signal came in from Candie that Hacker had reportedly called off Tokla, Dandy headed for the landing site.

Hacker's desist order had caught Tokla by surprise. The Colonel had his personal vendetta going with Gal X in general and with Taran's pilot in particular. On several occasions that kid had made Tokla look bad. Few had ever survived such egregious actions. Now there was a 97% probability of a kill. He found it hard to believe that Hacker had called the operation off. Hacker had been thwarted in even more encounters than Tokla. On the corporate level, the stakes were much higher for Centurion. Something wasn't adding up.

When one of his units picked up Taran's arrival, Tokla was advised. The flight path would bring the ship within range of three of his firing positions. It would be like ground-sluicing geese.

With success so close, Tokla started breathing hard. He fired a message off to Hacker saying that the target was in his sights and asking for a confirmation of the disengage order.

"Don't shoot you stupid bastard. Are you trying to get me killed?" was the immediate reply on Tokla's computer screen.

That gave Tokla pause. He didn't know what was happening, but from the sound of things, taking a shot at the ship might get that arrogant bastard off his back. Of course, it may not be in his best interests to get rid of the boss before the Colonel had set up another situation. So he sent out the order for his units to hold their fire.

At Centurion HQ there was a state of panic. There were hundreds of employees who knew that something had just obliterated several hundred feet of reflecting pond. Hundreds of windows overlooked the havoc. A panic evacuation had started, but before it had gathered any volume, the electronic doors were shut and the CEO had ordered everyone to stay in the building.

However, some who could get past the sealed doors made a break for the parking lot. There had been a constant flow of cars and trucks passing back and forth along the two mile access road to the parking lot. When flight became evident, Candie moved the shuttle slightly taking a bead on one of the enormous red rocks looming several hundred feet over the road. Picking her time when there was a break in the traffic, she shot the crown off the rock bringing tons and tons of huge boulders crashing onto the roadway. That effectively sealed off all vehicular traffic to and from the building. Candie reestablished her aim on Hacker's office, saying sweetly, "Mr. Hacker, I thought I told you to not to let people go running around. It might be bad for your health."

Using the surveillance cameras, Hacker looked with dismay at the damage. He realized he had probably been looking at alien technology. Gal X didn't have any energy gun in the works. They had devised the propulsion systems Taran was using, but they had never been particularly interested in weaponry. From the TV cast he knew that they had encountered several alien species. They must have brought back home some of the technology. How much?

In New Mexico, Unit One demanded, "Fire or no fire?"

Tokla didn't immediately reply.

"Fire or no fire?"came a pleading request. His men knew the penalties for screwing up, and the unit was about to panic.

"No fire," said Tokla.

Both of the other units in the flight path asked for "no fire" confirmation, which Tokla grudgingly gave. Not being able to fire was really spoiling his party.

As Dandy approached the landing site, the whole crew was on alert for some sort of attack. Because of a possible threat, he came in much hotter than usual. He waited longer to flip the legs down to retro fire the engine. He was pushing the hull temperature to its upper limits, but now the pilot knew Taran's idiosyncrasies and capabilities better than anyone else.

It wasn't hard spotting the landing site, because Taran had cleared the surrounding desert for hundreds of yards. All vehicles were underground, and any aircraft had left for safer havens. The block house entry building was the only visible structure.

Dandy set Taran almost in its former tracks. As soon as the vortex subsided enough to extend the long range antennas, he called Candie.

"We're down. Didn't see anything suspicious. Come home."

Candie lifted the shuttle a little above the Red Rock to be able to take aim and she blasted the two other passages through the rocks that gave access to Centurion HQ. Of course, that also took care of all the utilities into the complex, which meant that Hacker didn't see Candie leave and that he was locked into his room until the auxiliary power was brought on line.

Tokla had heard and felt the twin sonic booms as Taran reentered the atmosphere. From his vantage point on a mesa many miles to the southeast, he could see the tiny spot grow in size until he could see the flip and glow of the engines breaking the speed. It was quite a sight to see that hulk slowly descend on a tail of flame.

That was the first time Tokla had witnessed Taran in a landing mode. The first time that smart-ass kid returned to Earth, he had killed Tokla's four fighter jets, leaving Tokla and three other pilots dangling from parachute lines miles from anywhere.

This time Tokla had camouflaged his ray guns in freighter trucks with trailers. The pieces themselves were not particularly bulky, but the generating equipment required substantial space. The colonel had positioned his units so that just prior to Taran's reentry, they moved to turnouts in the highways as if the drivers were resting or checking mechanical problems.

Tokla advised Hacker that Taran was down. Hacker acknowledged, but the flow of words across Tokla's screen stopped before the end of the sentence. Tokla's queries went unanswered. Tokla smiled. He'd done exactly as directed. But, now there were no further instructions and he was free to act on his own.

One of the units was not far from Tokla's vantage point. He ordered the driver to bring the gun up onto the mesa. Maybe he couldn't shoot Taran out of the sky, but he figured he could punch a bunch of holes in it. Maybe he'd hit something explosive. He might even be able to pop some crew member.

It took a little doing to be able to depress the radar antenna and the snout of the ray generator low enough to pick up Taran, sitting on the valley floor.

By the time Tokla set up his equipment, the four TC members were in the underground control room talking to Malvane and company officials. They were awaiting the impending arrival of Candie before going to the mess hall for what had all the earmarks of a raucous welcome by the facility workers. Since no outsiders were permitted into the restricted launch area, they could celebrate without interference. It seemed as if the whole world was congregating at Gal X Headquarters. Everyone wanted a piece of the space heroes.

The crew securing Taran felt the first hit, but they couldn't identify the source of the slight vibration and the faint accompanying sound. But, the second shot almost hit a technician working in Corky's domain. Suddenly he was looking through a six-inch hole in multiple layers of material at a mesa to the south.

The tech hit the alarm, which brought the whole facility to the alert. "Something's melting holes in the hull," shouted the Tech into the intercom. "It's coming from the south mesa."

Dandy jumped to the com console and opened a channel to Candie's shuttle.

"Candie. Tokla's punching holes in Taran. He's on the high ground to the south."

"I'm not far out. I'll take a look."

Candie had been skimming under the radar. She swung a little to the starboard so she could circle around instead of coming in over Taran. The truck and trailer weren't hard to spot on the edge of the cliff.

"He just hit us again," said Dandy.

"It won't be long now," said Candie, as she settled down on the rocky ground a hundred feet behind the Centurion vehicles. There was a luxury sedan parked behind the truck and trailer. Equipment extended above the top of the truck through a trap door. Diesel exhaust was puffing out of the trailer as the generator labored to recharge the firing unit.

Candie moved the shuttle enough to bring the fancy car into her improvised sights. The vacant vehicle disappeared into a ball of fire as the gas tank exploded. One of the rear doors of the truck swung open as a man in white coveralls jumped down to see what had happened. He ran around the far side of the trailer without seeing the shuttle. There wasn't much left of the sedan. It had become a cloud of dust being carried skyward by the flaming gasoline.

Two more white-clad techs jumped to the ground and disappeared around the trailer. Then the door swung all the way open so the figure dressed in a dark suit could survey the scene before exposing himself

"Ah, Tokla," murmured Candie, whose mild amusement broke into full fledged glee. She shifted the shuttle to bring her firepower to bear on the truck. Tokla caught the motion. A look of astonishment crept over his face as he realized he was confronted by something completely beyond any previous experience.

Candie popped the canopy, flipped up the colored visor and yelled, "Hey, Tokla, you'd better run." With a gloved hand she flipped her dangling fingers indicating a direction away from the truck.

Recognition of who was calling and the meaning of the warning came simultaneously. Tokla screamed, "Run," and hit the ground running in the indicated direction. When the boss commanded, the techs responded. They ran too.

Candie let them get a few feet away, but not too far, before she disintegrated the truck. Tokla took a suit-destroying dive into a shallow defile. Candie shifted positions and blew the trailer. After the fireworks subsided, Candie yelled, "Ta, Ta, Tokie. Have a nice walk."She flipped her face plate shut, lowered the canopy and almost snapped her head off with a show-off quick-start.

Epilogue

Fall was definitely in the air, but during the midday Dandy could still sunbathe in a protected area. Candie continued swimming laps between the dock and the raft, which made Dandy shiver at the mere thought of it.

They had undergone two weeks of intense debriefing at the New Mexico site. TC had endured one interview before a frenzied press corps.

As a break, the two were back at Malvane's mountain retreat, hiding out until some of the excitement calmed down. After Candie had left Tokla afoot, she had tucked the shuttle in between Taran's legs to minimize spy satellites view. Soon it was draped and taken to one of the service elevators that moved heavy equipment below ground. It wasn't long before word was out that there was probably an alien ship on Earth.

The U.S. Military was threatening legal action if Gal X didn't turn over alien technology. The company lawyers weren't particularly afraid of court action, but there was some concern that under an obscure national security regulation, the government might try forceful confiscation.

Denying the existence of alien species was becoming about as difficult as denying the Earth revolved around the sun, but various religionists were still trying.

The company was delighted over the outcome of Taran's second voyage. The hierarchy hedged on the truth somewhat by reporting to the world that the energy anomaly that Taran had chased was an asteroid on which was mounted alien technology. The Taran crew had averted what, at best, would have been a near miss with Earth by causing enough of a disturbance to alter the asteroid's course enough to take it out into vacant space. The answer didn't satisfy many, but that was all they were to get. Outside of TC, only half-dozen others knew the whole story.

Candie spread a dry towel on the porch beside Dandy. "I don't know how much more of this inactivity I can take."

"It felt great for the first few days," said Dandy, "but time is already beginning to drag. Have you considered what is ahead of us?"

"I think the military calls it 'debriefing'. It's more like interrogation, as far as I am concerned. That could go on for months."

"Or years. Everyone is so tied up in what we brought back, it may be years before they think up another mission."

"At least one thing pleases me," said Candie with a smirk. "Hacker and Tokla are out of Centurion and the company is in such shambles that it shouldn't present too much of a threat for a long time.

Dandy rolled onto his stomach to begin a series of pushups. "Now, neither of those jokers is under any corporate constraints. They may be even more dangerous. We'd better keep in shape."

ISBN-13: 978-0-9847524-2-3